'I would defend you to my dying breath,' he said.

'Our people are enemies, Valdar. Enemies,' she replied.

'Are *we* enemies, Alwynn?'

'We are certainly not friends.'

'We were lovers.'

'That is in the past.'

He went over to her, magnificent in his nakedness.

'It will never be over between us as long as I have breath in my body.'

AUTHOR NOTE

Having looked at the Lindisfarne raid from a Viking perspective, I became interested in looking at what it might have been like from a Northumbrian one. In particular I wanted to tell the story of how a woman might react if she accidentally fell in love with a Viking.

While I was mulling over the possibilities my fellow historical author and friend Annie Burrows asked, 'So, when are you going to tell Valdar's story?' Valdar was the man left at the altar when Kara's husband, Ash Hringson, appeared after a seven-year absence in *Return of the Viking Warrior*. And I knew I had found my hero.

As I did my research I was intrigued to learn about St Cuthbert's storm, which happened in 794. When raiders appeared for a second time, apparently they were suddenly swamped by a terrific storm. The King of Northumbria managed to kill the leader and the rest either drowned or were killed. After that the raids in Northumbria decreased significantly for a time, but remained a concern.

I do hope you enjoy reading Valdar's and Alwynn's story as much I did writing it.

I love getting comments from readers and can be reached at michelle@michellestyles.co.uk, through my publisher, on Facebook or on Twitter @MichelleLStyles

SUMMER
OF THE VIKING

Michelle Styles

Published in Great Britain 2015
by Mills & Boon, an imprint of Harlequin (UK) Limited,
Eton House, 18-24 Paradise Road, Richmond, Surrey, TW9 1SR

© 2015 Michelle Styles

ISBN: 978-0-263-24787-9

Harlequin (UK) Limited's policy is to use papers that are natural,
renewable and recyclable products and made from wood grown in
sustainable forests. The logging and manufacturing processes conform
to the legal environmental regulations of the country of origin.

Printed and bound in Spain
by CPI, Barcelona

Born and raised near San Francisco, California, **Michelle Styles** currently lives near Hadrian's Wall with her husband, a menagerie of pets and occasionally one of her three university-aged children. An avid reader, she became hooked on historical romance after discovering Georgette Heyer, Anya Seton and Victoria Holt.

Her website is michellestyles.co.uk and she's on Twitter and Facebook.

Books by Michelle Styles

Mills & Boon® Historical Romance

Viking Warrior, Unwilling Wife
An Impulsive Debutante
A Question of Impropriety
Impoverished Miss, Convenient Wife
Compromising Miss Milton
The Viking's Captive Princess
Breaking the Governess's Rules
To Marry a Matchmaker
His Unsuitable Viscountess
Hattie Wilkinson Meets Her Match
An Ideal Husband?
Paying the Viking's Price
Return of the Viking Warrior
Saved by the Viking Warrior
Taming his Viking Woman
Summer of the Viking

Mills & Boon® Historical *Undone!* eBook

The Perfect Concubine

**Visit the author profile page
at millsandboon.co.uk for more titles**

For Linda Fildew,
because she always likes a good Viking story

Chapter One

June 795—off the coast of Northumbria

The possibility of returning alive to Raumerike and Sand hung by the slenderest of threads. After weighing the odds, Valdar Nerison figured he was never going to see his nephews again, never going to sit under the rafters of his hall and never going to breathe the sweet air of home again. He knew that in his heart. He'd known it ever since the mutineers had struck five nights ago, killing his friends, including the leader of the *felag*.

Girmir, the leader of the mutiny, would strike before the ship reached Raumerike's shore, most likely when the familiar outlines of the houses came into view. But right now they needed Valdar alive to navigate with the sunstone. Girmir's mistake was that he assumed Valdar believed his bland reassurance about how valuable he was.

The only question in Valdar's mind was the timing of the escape. When should he make his move? They watched him like ravens and had taken all his weapons.

Valdar bent double over his oar as the rain and the waves lashed him, trying to reason out the best moment. Rejecting first one plan then another as unworkable. With each passing day, it became clear that the men believed Girmir when he proclaimed that they would acquire gold and slaves beyond their wildest imaginings if they followed him.

As the gale intensified, Girmir started muttering about making a sacrifice to the storm god, Ran. A human sacrifice. 'Better one should die than the entire boat,' he announced. It chilled Valdar's blood.

Valdar glanced to his left as a flash of lightning lit up the sky. In the distance he spied the shadowy shape of land. For the first time since the mutiny, a glimmer of hope filled him. One long-ago summer, he and his brother had learnt to swim. Even after all this time, he reckoned that he just about remembered the strokes. One chance to get it right.

'The storm increases. Ran and Thor are both in a terrible temper,' he shouted as another blast from Thor's anvil reverberated through the sky.

'If you are serious about a sacrifice, do it before the entire boat is swamped.'

'Do you wish to challenge for the leadership?' Girmir came forward and put a knife against Valdar's neck. 'You know what happened to Horik the Younger when we fought. And to Sirgurd.'

'Your boat now, Girmir, but I'm entitled to an opinion.' Valdar ceased rowing and stared at the usurper, who had attacked at night, killing Horik before he could reach for his sword. Then forced Sirgurd to fight when he was clearly ravaged by fever. 'The storm may be difficult to ride. We should put to shore.'

'The only way which will quiet the gods in this weather is a life. I've seen it before.' Girmir nodded towards where the youngest member cowered beside his oar. 'A noble thing to give one's life for one's friends. Someone should volunteer.'

The boat became silent as all the men paused in their rowing.

'Me?' Valdar enquired as the wind howled about them.

Girmir adopted a pitying expression. 'We have need of you and your navigational skill, Valdar Lack-Sword. I gave my word. You will see Raumerike again.'

'If it is such a noble thing, then we should draw lots,' Valdar said, ignoring the jibe and laying the trap. Girmir would murder him as soon as the cliffs of Raumerike were spotted. Earlier if it suited him. Once an oath-breaker, always one. 'Let the gods decide…unless you fear their judgement.'

Even Girmir's loyal followers muttered their agreement. Girmir's beady eyes darted right and then left, seeking friends and finding none.

'Which will it be?' Valdar pressed, as another lightning bolt ripped through the sky, highlighting the men's drenched and pinched faces. 'Which is Ran most likely to be satisfied with—your choice or his?'

The other man blanched slightly, belatedly realising he had tumbled into a trap. 'I will abide by the gods' decision.'

'You will not mind if I hold the counters,' one of the men said.

Girmir bowed his head. 'Go ahead and Valdar Lack-Sword can prepare them. I wouldn't want to be accused of cheating the gods.'

Valdar retrieved a set of *tafl* counters from his trunk, placed them in a sealed pouch, carefully showing everyone the one black stone, and gave the pouch to the man who'd asked for it.

After days of inaction and humiliation, it felt

good to be doing something. One way or another, he would regain his self-respect before he died. For too long he'd lived with this hungry animal gnawing at his belly, telling him that he should have heeded Horik's request and sat up with him that night.

He should have woken before Horik the Younger was murdered, before his own sword was taken from him. He should have gone against his years of training, followed his instinct and become involved before things spiralled out of control.

If this boat went down, other than the boy, there was not a man he'd try to save. They had Horik's blood on their hands. They had all stabbed Horik's body under Girmir's orders to prove their undying loyalty. When Valdar had made only a token stab at the lifeless body, he had seen Girmir's face contort and had known that his fate was sealed.

'Go first, Girmir, you are the leader!'

Sweat beaded on the man's forehead. 'Ha! A white counter!'

One by one each of the *felag* took their counter. The youngest blanched as he saw he'd drawn a counter darker than the others. Valdar put his hand over the boy's. 'Open your hand and turn the stone over. You only think it is black.'

The boy did as Valdar bade. 'The stone gleams white on this side. But I thought…'

'Funny how that works.'

Valdar regarded the cliffs on the horizon as he weighed the pouch in his hand. He could do it. He knew how to swim. His body tensed with nervous anticipation. Better to die fighting than to be slaughtered like a sheep. Cheating the gods to palm the black stone from the boy? Maybe, but they had deserted him five nights ago.

'The gods want my hide today.' He held the jet-black stone aloft.

He waited as the other warriors glanced between each other and muttered. But the relieved look on the boy's face was worth it.

Girmir shrugged. 'The gods have decided. Your arms will be bound, Nerison, but Ran prefers his victim alive so I shall not slit your throat. I'll let him do it.'

Valdar closed his eyes. He should have expected Girmir's sadistic twist of binding his arms. His legs would have to be strong enough if he couldn't free his wrists. He would be able to make it to the shore. 'As you wish. But know one day there will be a reckoning. The gods will punish those who break their oaths.'

Girmir clasped his forearm after he gave Valdar his share of the takings thus far. 'Your sacrifice will appease the gods. You may have your sword returned. You behaved with honour. May you die with honour.'

After buckling his sword to his waist, Valdar tossed the sunstone to the young boy. 'Have charge of the navigation now. Use it well. Like I showed you.'

Girmir's eyes bulged. 'He can navigate?'

'You wouldn't want to lose another navigator, Girmir. How else would you make it back home?'

The boy's ears coloured pink. 'I've always admired you, Valdar. I know what you did for me.'

'Then tie my ropes.' Valdar grasped the boy's hand. 'Will you do that for me?'

The boy's eyes grew wide. 'Aye, I will.'

'Good lad.'

'When you return home, the sunstone will be waiting for you. Just ask for Eirik, son of Thoren, and they will find my cottage. My mother moves about a great deal,' the boy whispered. 'The Norns are not finished with you. I know this in my heart.'

'I'm to be sacrificed.' Valdar moved his wrists, creating a gap. 'How can they not be ready to snip my thread of life?'

'My mother always says this.' The boy tied the ropes with a bit of slack. 'You have to believe that the Norns decide when your thread is snipped, not you.'

'Get on with it!' Girmir shouted above the rumble of thunder. 'Thor's anger increases.'

Valdar nodded and balanced on the snarling bear post on the prow of the ship. The wind whipped fiercely about him. He tried to think of all that he had done and had left undone, but all he could think about was the low white cliffs he spied on the horizon. There was a slim possibility that he could make it. That the gods wanted him to live. That with his sword arm and the gold in his pouch, he could get justice for the dead.

He listened to the ritual words, then jumped. The water hit him, stinging with its bone-chilling cold. He went down and down with blackness swirling about until his lungs wanted to burst. Then he began to kick his legs. Up and up until his head breached the waves. He wriggled his arms until the knot gave way and they were freed.

The ship had already disappeared from view and all about him was dark grey. Valdar spun around until he spied what appeared to be a white sandy beach and started towards it. With each kick of his legs, more about the technique of swimming came back to him.

Some day there would be a reckoning. And

Girmir would pay dearly, he silently promised. It was as good a reason to live as any.

Alwynn shielded her eyes against the bright sun which now sparkled on the calm blue sea and surveyed the coastline. Last night's storm had brought in more than its fair share of seaweed, wood and sea coal. But there was little sign of bodies or wrecked ships as there had been at this time last year after St Cuthbert's storm had saved them all from invasion.

This time, there was plenty to be had for the scavenging instead of bodies being strewn everywhere.

She gave a small shake of her head. She hated to think what her mother would have said about her daughter, a woman with royal Idling blood in her veins, actually scavenging bits of flotsam and jetsam up from a beach. In her mother's world, high-born women stitched fine tapestries for the home or church and ran well-ordered estates. They most definitely did not dirty their hands with sea coal.

Her mother had never had to survive after her husband died suddenly, leaving a mass of unpaid debts. But Alwynn had—selling off all that she could while still managing to retain the hall and some of the estate.

'I do what I have to do! How can I ask others if I refuse to do it myself?' Alwynn bent down, defiantly picked up a lump of sea coal and held it aloft before placing it in a basket.

If the harvest proved profitable and everyone paid their rents on time, her trouble would be behind her and she could leave the sea coal to others. In due course Merri might even be able to have a decent dowry and the chance of finding a worthy husband. For herself, she simply wanted to be left in peace to cultivate her garden. She wanted the freedom to choose whom she would marry or even whether she would marry. Or if she should enter a convent or not. But for now, she needed every lump.

'You see, I was right!' Merewynn ran up and plopped a double handful of sea coal into the basket. Her blonde curls escaped from the couvre-chef that Alwynn had insisted her stepdaughter wear. Merewynn would be ten in the autumn. It was time she started to act like a young woman, instead of a wild thing who roamed the moors. 'Lots of pickings after a summer storm. We might even find treasure and then you wouldn't have to worry so much about the render you owe the king. It is a wonder we never came down here before. Such fun!'

'Mind you keep close, Merri. And no animals rescued. Our new hall is overcrowded as it is.'

Merewynn pulled a face. 'If we look, I'm sure we can find a little space. A mouse wouldn't take up much room. Or maybe a raven. I've always wanted a pet raven. And there is no Father Freodwald to complain about the mess now.'

Alwynn schooled her features. Their current priest had complained a great deal and it had been a relief when he departed for another longhouse. Someone else would have to provide the large amounts of ale, sweetmeats and blazing fires to warm his bones that the priest demanded as his due. It had been a shock because the old priest had been entirely different. 'The bishop holds him in high esteem.'

'But he dislikes ravens. St Oswald's bird. Can you believe it? He said they nip fingers and make a mess everywhere.'

'Just so we are clear.' Alwynn put her hand on her hip and gave Merri a hard stare. 'We are here to find things to put to practical use, not more animals for your menagerie. I'll not have more land taken from us. You need to have a decent dowry when the time comes. On my wedding day, I promised to look after you as if you were my own.'

Merri gave a deep sigh. 'I liked it better

when you didn't have to be practical, Stepmother. Sometimes it takes a little while before
you realise you need something and then...' She
snapped her fingers. 'A raven could be trained
to send messages. If the Northmen attempt to
attack, we could release it and it'd fly straight
away to King Athelfred and he could pray to St
Cuthbert to send another storm and...'

'You are asking a lot of this unknown raven.'

'Ravens are like that and I want to be prepared
in case the Northmen come to murder us in our
beds.' Merri gave a mock shiver.

'After last year's storm, it will be a while before they try to attack again. They lost a number of ships and their leader. Remember what
the king said.'

'Or maybe we could find a falcon with a hurt
wing,' Merri continued on. 'It could belong to
an atheling who would fall instantly in love with
you and we will all live happily ever after. You
could even become queen.'

'You listen to far too many tales, Merri. The
king is my distant cousin. I wish him a long life.'

'The atheling could come from another kingdom. One without a good king.'

'Merri!'

'Well...' The girl gave an impudent smile. 'It
could happen.'

Alwynn glanced down at her woollen dress. With three patches and a stained lower skirt, it had definitely seen better days. And she wasn't going to think about Edwin's disreputable offer to become his mistress after the king confirmed him as the new overlord in this area. He was from the same sort of mould as her late husband—more interested in his advancement than the welfare of others. She shuddered to think that as a girl she'd begged her father to allow her to marry Theodbald. He'd seemed so kind and handsome with his little daughter cradled in his arms.

'What do I have to offer anyone, let alone a king-in-waiting?'

'You have dark hair and eyes like spring grass. And you are intelligent. You know lots about herbs and healing and your voice sounds like an angel when you sing. Why don't you sing now, Stepmother?'

'A prince needs more than a pretty face for a wife. Athelings need wives who can play politics and bring them the throne. I'd rather be in my garden than at court.' Alwynn pointedly ignored the question about singing. Ever since she had discovered her late husband Theodbald's treachery, she'd taken no pleasure in music. Her voice tightened every time she tried. Of all the things she'd lost, that one hurt the most.

Merri balled her fists. 'Sometimes you have to believe in better days. You told me that. After my father died and all went wrong. And I do believe. One day, everything will come right for the both of us.'

Alwynn forced her lips to turn up. Perhaps Merri was right. Perhaps she had been far too serious for the past few months, but it was hard to be joyful when you had lost nearly everything. It had begun with Theodbald's death from a hunting accident. He'd been drunk and had ended up being gored by a wild boar. There had been nothing she or any monk could do to save him. It was then that the true extent of the debts were revealed and she'd had to take charge. 'Your father's death…altered things.'

The girl gave a solemn nod, her golden curls bobbing in the sunshine. 'I know. But there are times that I wish we still lived in the great hall with a stable full of horses.'

'There is nothing wrong with our new hall. It is where my grandmother grew up and it does have things to recommend it. A large herb garden.'

Merri wrinkled her nose. 'If you like plants…'

'We have no need of princes. I will be able to hold this hall.'

'I know my real mother watches over us from heaven, but my father?' Merri asked in a low voice. 'Where does he watch us from?'

Alwynn stared out at where the early-morning sun played on the sea-weathered rocks. Tiny waves licked at the shore, nothing like the gigantic ones which must have hit the beach last night. 'He watches from somewhere else. We need to pick an entire basket of the sea coal before the sun rises much further. There is a list as long as my arm of things which need to be done today. Gode has gone to see her niece and the farmhands are out helping to shear the sheep. Plus, there is the new wheel at the gristmill that needs to be seen to.'

Alwynn didn't add that she had no idea how to repair the gristmill properly or do a thousand other practical things. And there was no gold for a steward, even if she could find one she could trust. But they would survive. Somehow.

Merri nodded. 'It is easier now that Gode has her own cottage. She always tries to stop me from doing the truly interesting things just because she used to be your nurse and you listen to her.'

'And we will find something to add to your

collection—maybe a shell or a feather. But no raven or falcon. We have too many mouths to feed.'

Merri tugged at her sleeve. 'What is that over there, Stepmother? Is it a man?'

Alwynn stifled a scream. A man's body lay on the high-tide mark. A length of rope dangled from one arm and his hair gleamed gold in the morning sunlight. But it was his physique—broad shoulders tapering down to a narrow waist—which held her attention.

For a heartbeat, she wondered what he'd been like in life. He was the sort of man to make a heart stand still.

She shook her head. Really, she was becoming worse than Merri. After Theodbald, she should know a handsome face was no guarantor of a good heart. She had to be practical and hard-hearted, instead of the dreamy soul she used to be. There could be gold or silver, something useful on his person. Anyone else would have no hesitation in searching for it. The poor soul would have no use for it if he was dead.

'The body will have come in on the storm.'

Merri gulped. 'Is he…?'

'Could anyone have survived that storm? In the sea? You know about the rocks.'

'What shall we do? Get Lord Edwin? You

know what he said—no one should remain alive if they wash up on the shore.'

Alwynn tightened her grip on the basket. The last person she wanted to encounter was Edwin and his sneer. He'd claim any treasure on the body as his own.

She'd vowed to starve before she gave in to that man. And while they were not starving, raising the required gold had taken just about everything she possessed.

'Not yet. There will be time enough for that later. He'd only ask questions…questions about…about the basket of sea coal.'

Merri nodded. 'Good. I don't like him.'

'Few do.'

Alwynn swallowed hard. She hated that she'd come to this—robbing the dead. She took a deep breath and clenched her fists. She could do it. She repeated the promise she had made when she discovered the extent of Theodbald's treachery—she would survive and Merri would marry well. One man's debauchery would not ruin any more lives.

'You remain here, Merri,' she said, tucking an errant strand of black hair behind her ear. Silently she willed her stomach to stop heaving. She had tended the dead before. 'Then you can truthfully say you had nothing to do with the body.'

'Day by day you become more like Gode.'

'Trust me. You want to keep away.' Alwynn knelt down so her eyes were level with Merri's. 'If anyone says anything, you are blameless.'

'I'm involved.' Merri twisted away and kicked a stone, sending it clattering along the beach. 'I know what my father did. If anything, I should be protecting you. He is the one who cheated you and left you with a mountain of debts. Everyone says it when your back is turned.'

Alwynn put a hand on the girl's shoulder. Silently she prayed Merri remained in ignorance of most of it—the bullying, the whoring and the gambling which had racked up the debts. 'The past, Merewynn. I'm concentrating on the present.'

'If the warrior is alive, will you save him? Or will you hit him on the head like Lord Edwin commanded everyone to do?'

'He will be dead,' Alwynn stated flatly.

'Lord Edwin is wrong. Surely you should know if a man is guilty before you kill him. Otherwise you become a murderer. You become like the Northmen.'

Alwynn put her hand on Merri's shoulder. Her

sentiments exactly. 'That's right. If he is alive, we nurse him back to health.'

'Promise?'

'I promise, sweetling.' Alwynn knelt beside Merri and gathered her hands within hers. 'But don't get your hopes up.'

'If he is dead, can I have his sword? I can see it gleaming in the sunlight next to him. I could start learning how to use it. I've no desire to be a nun!'

'Merri!'

With her cheeky smile, the girl appeared unrepentant. Alwynn sighed. Merri knew precisely how to wrap her around her little finger, always had…from the very first time they met. She had been the one bright light in her marriage and she could not have loved her more if she'd been her own.

'If you want me to stay away from the body, you have to promise me something.' Merri tapped her fingers against her mouth. 'I'm not good without a cause.'

'Be good for me and we will have a decent meal tonight.'

Merri's eyes lit up. 'Something other than yesterday's pottage?'

'I promise. I will make some of the singing cakes you love so much.'

Merri screwed up her face. 'But I want the sword as well. You sold all my father's swords. How can we hope to hold the estate without a sword? People want a strong lord or otherwise they might not pay what they owe us.'

'Which people are you talking about?'

'You know…I hear rumours.'

'You shouldn't listen to servants' gossip.'

Alwynn hugged her arms about her waist and turned her mind away from the problems which had plagued her for the past few months. They could wait until she'd investigated the body.

No man could have survive that storm. And she hated the thought of robbing the dead but she was certain she could see the dull gleam of gold on one of his fingers. Anyone else would have no hesitation. And once she had searched the body, she'd arrange for a decent burial. It was more than most would do. But it didn't make her any easier. A distinct feeling of being unclean crept over her.

'If he has a sword, we sell it. Swords are not for young ladies from a good family. Ladies become peace-weavers and woo with gentleness.'

Merri squatted down, resting her chin on her knees. 'Then you'd best hope he is alive as I'm never going to be a peace-weaver. I'm going to learn how to fight and regain the fortune my father lost.'

Rather than answering, Alwynn made her way to the body. Up close, he was even more magnificent. The seawater had moulded his tunic to his torso and she could see the muscles of his back. A man to take your breath away. Or break your heart.

'Right, I'm going to turn you over.'

She reached down and touched his sun-warmed shoulder.

His hand shot out and grabbed her ankle. Alwynn stifled a scream as she broke free and retreated a step.

The man was no corpse. He was alive!

Everything altered. She might be willing to rob a dead man, but not someone who lived and breathed. And she knew she could not do as Lord Edwin commanded. She was a healer at heart, not a murderer.

'Easy now, I mean you no harm.' She placed a firm hand on his shoulder. The muscles rippled under her palm, but they eased.

He gave a slight groan as she pushed him until he lay on his back.

'Do you understand? I want to help you.'

She looked directly into his face. The face of a rugged warrior, one which had been tempered by time, but remained attractive. She hated to think what he'd been through out on the rough sea last night. His face sported several bruises and his arms were scraped raw where he had been dashed against the rocks. There were no obvious signs of internal injuries, but his blue-tinged lips revealed that he must be close to death.

His startling brown eyes held a mute appeal. Her heart twisted. She wanted to save him and not just because she'd promised Merri. She could spend days staring into those eyes. She shook her head to clear it. It made little sense. This man was a complete stranger.

'I want to help,' she said softly. 'I want to get you somewhere where you'll be safe. If you stay here, you will die and I think you want to live.'

Chapter Two

Alwynn sat back on her heels. A light breeze blew across her face and the clouds skittered across the blue sky. The warrior was alive and in need of urgent help, but not here. Not on this beach, not ever.

She and Merri were alone on the stretch of sand, but other beachcombers would arrive soon. And they would follow Edwin's orders, rather than help her save the life of an unknown warrior. She knew that instinctively.

A cold shiver went down Alwynn's spine. They would be here at any moment. And once he was discovered, someone would act…unless she acted first.

'Merri, I need your help. You must be very brave, sweetling, and obey me without question.'

Merri reached her side in a heartbeat. 'He is alive? Is he a prince?'

'Barely.' Alwynn automatically straightened Merri's couvre-chef. 'And I think he is a warrior of some sort, probably foreign. But well-to-do. The sword is silver encrusted and he wears arm rings.'

Merri's eyes grew wide. 'A Northman? You aren't going to tell me to leave so you can run him through with his sword, are you? You promised to save his life. You can't be like all the other adults.'

Alwynn slowly shook her head. Perhaps she should be, but something deep within her revolted at the thought of killing an innocent man. 'There isn't any sign of a boat. Or other people. Northmen travel in packs. We learnt that from Lindisfarne and the raid last year.'

'Or any other corpses!' There was no mistaking the ghoulish delight in Merri's voice. 'If it was a boat, there would be more bodies on the beach. They said dozens were washed up last year and those who had not drowned had their heads cut off.'

'Merri! Who have you been talking to? Neither of us were on the beach then! I sent the steward!'

'Oswald, Oswy the Gristmiller's son. He knows these things.' Merri tapped a finger against her lips. 'Why did this warrior fall off his ship?'

Alwynn swallowed hard and tried to control the knot in her stomach. Her parents would have told her to tell the authorities. Lord Edwin was the new authority in this part of Northumbria and she knew what his answer would be. But when had following the rules ever brought her any happiness? The last thing she wanted was this man's death on her conscience.

'Since when do Northmen travel alone? Or fall from ships?' Alwynn dusted her hands on her apron. She knew all about Northmen and their ways. One of her cousins had survived the Lindisfarne raid. She had heard all about how the Northmen attacked without warning or provocation. And the butchery. How they had no pity for anyone else, let alone God's servants. If this man was a Northman, innocent or not, she'd have no hesitation, but...

'No, he'll be from somewhere else. Until we know for certain, we give him the benefit of the doubt.'

Merri nodded, accepting her word. 'I'm not frightened of him. He has a kind chin.'

'Kindness comes from deeds not looks.' The instant the words left her throat, Alwynn heard her mother's voice. She'd always vowed she'd be different and here she was spouting meaning-less phrases. Her mother had been a master of that—say something witty and seemingly pro-found while expecting everyone else to do the hard work.

Merri's face adopted her stubborn look. 'I still think he is one of the most beautiful warriors I have ever seen.'

Alwynn gave Merri a no-nonsense look. 'Right now, we save his life. And we keep quiet about it. We take him to Gode's cottage. With any luck, he'll be gone before she returns.'

'Who do you think he is? Could he be a prince?'

'I've no idea, but he is a person of conse-quence. A simple seafarer would not be wear-ing gold rings.'

'If you save his life, he'll reward you and then we won't have to worry any more about the debts my father built up. He'll fall instantly in love with you, too.'

'I've little time for your stories today, Merri.' Alwynn glanced over her shoulder. The sun had risen higher in the sky, warming her back and neck. Soon the beach would be flooded with treasure seekers and other scavengers. 'The sooner we're off this beach, the better.'

'What about our basket of sea coal? We can't carry both.'

'People are more important than things. Always.'

Alwynn put one arm about the warrior's shoulders and pulled him to standing. His body buckled and a deal of seawater spewed out.

'Better out than in,' she muttered as her knees threatened to give way from the sheer weight of him. 'Get on the other side. Help me to balance. Dropping him would not do either of us any good.'

Merri ran quickly to the other side and wrapped an arm about his waist. 'I'm stronger than I look.'

Giving a nod, Alwynn started forward. The man's feet dragged a bit, but the movement seemed to rouse him. His deep brown gaze held her again.

'Walk,' she commanded. 'Walk or die.'

Valdar jolted from the comfort of swirling blackness into piercing light. The sunlight on the yellow sand hurt his eyes, nearly blinding him.

The woman's insistent tone had called him from the cocoon of darkness which had held him in its embrace since he had heaved his body on to the sand.

He knew a few things.

First, he was alive and intended to stay that way. The lad's mother had been right about the Norns deciding when men died.

Second, his lungs were on fire and his belly was heaving from the amount of salt water he'd drunk in that desperate swim. As it was, a few more feet of water and he'd never have made it out of the surf alive. But he knew the perils of half-drowning. His elder brother had died of it. Dragged from the harbour after his boat overturned, seemingly fine, only to collapse a few hours later. He needed fresh water to replace the seawater which he'd inhaled.

Third, and potentially most troubling, he knew that he was in Northumbria. The accent was incredibly distinctive. He'd heard it several times in various markets over the years. And Northumbria was the last place he wanted to be. The Northumbrian king had declared that all Northmen were to be killed. No Northumbrian was supposed to trade with a Northman.

The Lindisfarne raid might have garnered gold for the detested Viken, but it had made trading more difficult for everyone else.

In fact, it had been partly responsible for the mutiny. Frozen out of their usual markets, Girmir had demanded they raid Northumbria and get gold like the Viken. Horik had objected as he had no quarrel with the Northumbrians and he'd heard of what had happened to another Viken raiding party last year—butchered.

Horik had wanted to find new markets to the south, something Valdar agreed with, but Girmir feared travelling off the end of the earth.

He needed to be north of here. His friend and fellow countryman Ash Hringson had planned to attend the market in Orkney this autumn with his young son. He would be able to get passage home from there. Then he could expose Girmir as an oath-breaker.

But before that, he had to recover and recuperate away from danger. The Picts, or possibly the Gaels, might be more amenable than the Northumbrians…if he could make it there.

He glanced at the older of the women who now held him upright. She was not in the first blush of youth but there was something about the way her green eyes flashed and her chin was set which took his breath away. She was the personification of a Valkyrie.

The floral scent of her hair filled his nostrils, replacing the fishy tang of the shore. He knew that her shaking him earlier had wakened him from the shadowlands. But beauty could turn treacherous and he had no reason to think she'd

protect him, particularly once she knew his true
identity. No, she was off limits. He'd learnt his
lesson about women along ago and Kara had
proved herself no different.

He had loved her too much and she had used
him. He was never going to be used again. And
he was never going to be the one to love more
than the woman again.

'Water?' he asked, but the word came out as
a guttural groan. He tried again. 'Water. I need
water. Please.'

His stomach heaved again and he knew that
the sands of time were slipping away from him.
The memory of his brother's drowned face
haunted him.

'You understand? Water?'

The woman cocked her head to one side, re-
sembling an inquisitive bird. Her brow knitted.
He tried to mimic drinking.

She gave a slow nod. 'When we get somewhere safe, I'll get you something to drink. But
now we walk.'

He tried to form the words to explain and the
effort caused the skin about his mouth to crack.
The dried salt caused it to sting as if it had been
attacked by a thousand needles.

Valdar's body ached as if a thousand frost
giants had stomped on it. His mouth tasted of

the sea. He tentatively risked a breath. Another splutter of air mixed with seawater. Valdar attempted to ignore it, but his chest continued to heave.

'I need water now or I die.'

She shook her head. 'I can't understand what you are saying.'

'Water or death,' he yelled. 'Your choice.'

She cringed. 'There is no need to shout.'

He put up his hands in a gesture of supplication. 'My throat. Too much seawater. Fresh water or I die.'

She nodded and said something to the young girl, who quickly went and fetched a large jug of water from beside a basket. The woman held it out. 'Here you go. Drink. Then walk.'

'Thank you.'

Valdar downed it, revelling in the sweet taste. Not water, but cooled mint tea. 'More.'

She shook her head. 'You'll be sick. Soon.'

He swallowed. Some of the sea taste had gone, but he still felt parched. 'Need more. You will get me more.'

'Soon, first you walk.'

He shrugged off her arm. 'I will try.'

She gave him a questioning look, but he stood straighter. She moved away from him. Cool air rushed in where her warm body had been. 'Merri, let him stand.'

He attempted to move forward, but his knees threatened to buckle. He was weaker than a new-born colt. He took a step and the world swayed and the enveloping darkness beckoned once again. 'Please.'

She came and put her arm about his waist. Her dark head barely reached his shoulder. And she had green eyes shot with silver. 'Next time, maybe you listen.'

He shrugged her off, put his hands on his knees and tried to draw in deep breaths. Each time he tried, he found himself gasping for air. 'Leave me. Let me breathe. Bring water.'

'Time is running out. We need to get off this beach.' She used her fingers to mimic walking.

Valdar shook his head. Her accent was pleasant and he found if he concentrated, he could understand her well enough. However, the effort made his head spin. 'Where there is more to drink.'

'You do speak my language.'

'I have travelled far. Across many seas.' He grabbed his throat. 'After the drink, my mind clears. I can speak best…better.'

Her brow furrowed. 'And you are from…?'

'A place so tiny and far from here you will not have heard of it. Trust me.'

He waited to see if she'd accept his word. If he said from a North country, she might get the wrong idea. Northumbrians didn't distinguish between the North countries. He hated that he was dependant on her. But the gods had spared him for a purpose.

'Where?'

'Sand, Raumerike.'

'You are right.' A smile hovered on her mouth. 'I've no idea where that is.'

'How far do you need me to walk?'

Her neat teeth worried her bottom lip, turning it deep red. 'Off the beach and into the long grass. We can shelter there until all danger is passed.'

The long grass was a lifetime away. 'What are you afraid of? What is on this beach?'

She glanced over her shoulder, watching shadows. 'I have my reasons. Trust me.'

Their gazes locked. What choice did he have but to trust her? He hated relying on anyone.

'After that water and shelter,' he said. Instantly her brow darkened so he added, 'Not for long. I…I wish to go home in peace. Peace, you understand?'

She tapped her fingers together.

'Please.'

Her brow cleared. 'I know of a vacant cottage where you can rest…before you continue your journey.'

Relief washed over him. His luck had changed. The gods had spared him for a reason. 'You won't regret it.'

'I had better not.'

The sun had dried his sea-soaked tunic to complete stiffness. It rubbed salt into his raw back with every move he made, but that was nothing to the way his legs ached. About the best he could say was that they remained attached to his body. He did not know how long he had swum for and how far the tide had carried him. Then there were the rocks where the waves had dashed him. He could hear them pounding, pounding, pounding and knew he had barely got out alive.

A great shaking racked his body.

He put out an arm, trying to balance, trying to keep the life-giving liquid down.

'Help me…please.'

She sighed and grabbed him about the waist. The simple touch did much to steady him. 'People are coming to scavenge for sea coal. Neither of us wants to meet them.'

'Slow, yes.' Even though some of the words

were unfamiliar, he understood the urgency in her voice.

He nodded and started to shuffle forward, forcing his feet to lift and his body to stay upright. The third step sent him tumbling to his knees. A cry escaped his lips.

Silently he cursed for showing weakness to a woman.

The girl made a face and grabbed his arm, steadying him. 'Stumbling will make things worse.'

'Your daughter?' he asked.

'Stepdaughter. Merewynn. I'm Alwynn of Yoden.' She paused and frowned with intense concentration. 'A place so tiny that you will not have heard of it either.'

He stared at the grass-covered dunes. What sort of man sent a woman out on the beach, where he knew danger was? Where these scavengers lurked?

'Your husband?'

'Dead,' she answered, keeping her gaze away from him.

Her answer explained everything and nothing. Widows must find it as difficult to keep property in Northumbria as they did in Raumerike. Someone had turned her out of the hall. And now they were forced to search for washed-up items on the beach. The Northumbrians bleated that the Northmen were barbarians for attacking Lindisfarne, but they were barbarians not to look after their women better.

'But you must live somewhere,' he persisted. Women this lovely were not without a protector for long.

'Keep going. Don't stop. We're nearly to a spot where we can shelter. I mean to keep you alive.'

He stopped and looked down at her face. A faint sheen of sweat shone on her forehead. She appeared as if a strong wind might blow her over, but he could sense the steel underneath.

'Why?'

'Because I don't kill creatures who wash up on these shores. I wait to see if they are innocent or not first.'

Alwynn concentrated on putting her feet down, rather than looking up at the dune. Every time she looked, it seemed they had barely gone a few steps, but her gown was now plastered to her back from the exertion. The warrior had closed his eyes and once again appeared insensible to their surroundings. With each step they took, he leant more on Merri and her. Typically male. She'd learnt the hard way.

'He's very heavy,' Merri complained, stopping for the third time in as many steps. 'Can't we rest?'

'He requires more liquid. Small beer might be best,' she said instead. 'He has had too much salt water. You saw how the fisherman's youngest recovered once he had small beer last March. It will be easier to fetch some when we are at Gode's.'

'Where do you think he is from? I'd never heard of the place he said. Raume, was that what he said? Is it north or south of here?'

'Does it truly matter? Right now he is alive.'

'What if he were an exiled prince?' The girl gave a little shiver. 'Or a Northman? Do Northmen come from every country to the north or from just one country? What if they were not all like the monsters who attacked Lindisfarne?'

There were times when Merri's questions made Alwynn's head spin. What did she know about the politics? Or where countries were? Or how people behaved? All she knew was that Northmen were monsters who had no respect for anything or anyone.

'He is a stranger, that's all I know. His accent is unlike any I've heard before but he can speak our language. Goodness knows where Raumerike is. Somewhere.' Alwynn adjusted her hold on the man's waist. 'Once we know who he is in truth, then we can decide what to do. But first we save his life.'

She gazed back at the beach where she'd found him. The morning sun sparkled on the waves. Nothing to show the power of last night's storm beyond the debris which littered the high-tide mark.

She couldn't abandon the man, but she wished she knew where Raumerike was. She'd have to wait until the priest in the next parish returned. He knew things like that. And the question would have to be asked carefully. The last thing she wanted was for Lord Edwin to start wondering why she wanted to know.

His accent was very strange and she had never seen the markings on his clothes before. True, the garments were fine, far finer than any around here, but the gold embroidery was different.

There were many countries besides Northumbria. She used to ask about going on pilgrimage and seeing other places, but Theodbald had always refused. He had visited the Franks before his first marriage and after that had seen no reason to go anywhere. So she'd remained by his side, managing the garden and being blissfully ignorant about his mismanagement of the estate.

There was something about the storm-tossed man's gaze which reassured her that he had no intention of harming them. But whatever the risk, she had to take it. Leaving someone to die on this beach made every fibre in her body revolt, no matter what Lord Edwin had ordered.

Time to stop obeying people blindly and take charge of her life.

She'd made that vow on the day she discovered her late husband's debts and she intended to keep it. This was the first test of her resolve. She no longer blindly followed the rules.

'Here you were saying how strong you were,' she said briskly. 'You wanted to take over the feeding of Purebright. Are you saying you aren't strong enough to manage the pony now?'

'If I don't complain, does that mean…?' Merri's eyes gleamed.

Alwynn shook her head slightly. Only Merri could think looking after that cantankerous pony was a privilege, rather than a chore. Merri was ready for added responsibility. She'd shown that over the past few turbulent months. 'I was going to tell you when we arrived home after collecting the sea coal. But, yes, provided you help me now, you may look after Purebright.'

The man mumbled something incoherent,

plucking at her sleeve. Alwynn cocked her head to one side, listening.

The sound of rough voices travelled on the wind.

'Shall we move forward? One step at a time? We are nearly in the tussocks of grass. We can stop there and rest out of sight. Wait until everyone has gone.'

Merri squared her too-thin shoulders. 'I believe I can make that. Purebright would want me to.'

They reached the cover of the grass-topped dunes just as several people arrived at the beach. They were armed with a variety of cudgels, sticks and a pitchfork as well as baskets for gathering sea coal.

Alwynn's heart knocked against her chest. It pained her that this place had come to this. Before the Northmen attacked Lindisfarne, they had welcomed seafarers and looked after anyone who might be stranded. Not now. They had lost too much.

The men started laughing and joking about the dead and what treasure they might find on the beach. Silently Alwynn wished them to hell along with the Northmen who had caused this change. Her Northumbria was hospitable rather than murderous.

'Alwynn?' Merri whispered. 'This feels wrong. We are going to get in trouble. Big trouble. Can we go?'

'Keep down, Merri. Keep quiet.' Alwynn forced Merri's head down lower and put her hand over the girl's mouth.

'Should we get help?' Merri whispered against the barrier. 'Maybe I could get Oswy. He has a strong back from lifting grain sacks.'

Alwynn put her fingers to her lips and shook her head. Merri's off-and-on friendship with the miller's son was going to have to end soon. 'We shall manage, you and I. In a little while. Right now, he must rest. Understand?'

Merri gave a slight nod and Alwynn removed her hand.

'And once we start again?' Merri asked in an urgent whisper. 'Carrying him all the way to the hall will be impossible.'

'As I said, we're going to Gode's. That isn't far. Think about Purebright and how much he loves your grooming. That fat pony has a lot to answer for. I should have kept a carthorse.'

'But...' Merri's forehead wrinkled. 'Father always said...'

'The area around here was very different when your father was in charge.'

'I suppose so.'

'We're doing nothing wrong.' Alwynn made a fist. 'Finders of flotsam on the beach have the first say as to the disposal. Custom from a time beyond our minds. And he did wash up on the beach, our beach. You remember what your father used to say. The beach has always belonged to your family.'

Merri nodded, accepting her word.

'And the mint tea?' Merri's brow knitted. 'Does he need more? Can we get it without…?'

'When we can…' Alwynn gauged the distance from where they lay to the small stream. The lack of cover was too great to risk any movement. 'It will not take them long to strip the beach of anything valuable. Once they have what they want, they will go. Your warrior will survive until then.'

Merri's eyes widened. 'My warrior?'

'You were the one who saw him first.'

Alwynn refused to think about the warrior's eyes and how they had held her. That connection to him she'd felt deep within her gut was nothing. She could not afford to be attracted to any man. And yet… She shook her head. Truly she was becoming worse than Merri for woolgathering.

'But…but…but…'

'He can hardly be mine. Your father has not

been dead that long. We shouldn't have come in any case. Collecting sea coal was a poor idea.'

Merri curled her fingers about Alwynn's. 'I don't blame you. I thought it exciting.'

She snuggled up next to Alwynn and lay very still.

Alwynn lay listening to the man's steady breathing and the banter between the reeve's men who seemed to stay at the other end of the beach. Apparently they'd found nothing of interest.

'Almost gone,' she muttered.

'Oh, no,' Merri cried and darted forward.

'Merri, where are you going?'

Merri grabbed the basket with sea coal and returned, dropping to the ground. 'I couldn't allow them to take that! It belongs to us. We collected it. We need it for our fire.'

'Next time leave it.' Alwynn patted the sand next to her. 'Over here and stay by my side until I tell you otherwise. Do you want everyone to know where we are?'

Merri hung her head. 'I'm sorry, I didn't think... We need the sea coal, though. No one saw me.'

'Tempting fate is never a good idea. How many times, Merri?'

'But I'm quick,' Merri muttered. 'Quicker than you.'

'Hush now. Lord Edwin's steward is headed towards us.'

Alwynn glanced at the warrior. Thankfully he appeared to understand the situation and had gone completely still. She moved closer to him to give Merri some space. Her breast hit his chest as Merri wriggled in.

The steward stooped down and picked something up from the beach. He looked directly at them. Alwynn sank further down in the hollow, half-covering the man with her cloak.

As the steward's gaze intensified, she lowered her head and breathed in the warrior's salty scent.

Footsteps seemed to come closer. The sound of heavy breathing hung in the air.

In another few steps, he'd be on them and she'd have to explain the unexplainable. If she was lucky, he'd take her to Lord Edwin. And if unlucky... A small shiver ran down her back. It didn't bear thinking about.

Her heart thudded. She'd rescued a stranger for no good reason except that she refused to allow him to die. The woman who kept all the rules was truly gone.

Giving up was not an option. She tried to

think about what she'd say when they were discovered and how she'd have to emulate her mother at her imperious best.

She lay there with the sun warming her back, until she thought the steward must surely see them. She prepared herself to stand and started to rise. The warrior's hand tugged her down.

'Stay!' he commanded against her ear. 'I will protect you with my sword arm, but he may yet pass us by.'

For someone who had just survived drowning, his grip was like iron. Alwynn had no choice but to lie still, beside him. With each breath she took, she found she was aware of him and the way his muscles were hard.

Just when she thought they were sure to be discovered, she heard a shout from one of the man's companions and the man headed off in another direction at a quick trot.

'They are going, Alwynn. They're going.' Merri squeezed her hand. 'We will be fine. Our warrior is safe. Everything will be fine. You will see this warrior will bring good luck. He isn't a Northman. He doesn't have pointy teeth like Father Freodwald said they had.'

Alwynn shifted her position and wished she retained the easy assurance of a nine-year-old. Long ago, she'd learnt that most things were far from easily solved. 'Of course, sweetling.'

* * *

Valdar lay utterly still as the woman Alwynn huddled next to him with her stepdaughter on the other side of her.

He concentrated on breathing and trying not to think about the woman and her problems. She'd rescued him, but for how long? How long did he have before she betrayed him?

For some reason the men on the beach frightened her. Normally such creatures wouldn't worry his sword arm, but every muscle in his body ached and he knew he couldn't protect her beyond a few token swipes with his sword. The storm had battered him against rocks before spewing him up on the shore.

He heard the men depart the beach, cursing their lack of spoils and joking about what they would do to any Northman they discovered.

His hand fell back to his side, releasing Alwynn. A thousand questions buzzed about his head. He hated not knowing why she'd rescued him. Why had she taken the chance? Asking was out of the question. He needed her help to escape so he could fulfil the gods' plan for him and bring vengeance against Girmir and all who followed him.

'More drink,' he groaned through parched lips.

She instantly rolled off him. Her cheeks glowed pink, highlighting her eyes and the way a few tendrils of black hair escaped from her head covering.

'You are awake.'

'Can we move yet?' He tried to stretch, ignoring the screaming pain in his shoulder. 'Do you deem it safe?'

'Lord Edwin's men have left the beach.' She absently tucked a stray strand of hair behind her ear. 'Now is an excellent time to move.'

'You know who they were.'

'Yes, I know.' Her mouth held a bitter twist. 'If I'd had any doubt about this particular order to kill strangers being fulfilled, today—the first time I've been out gathering sea coal on the shore—has quashed it.'

'But you disapprove of the order.'

'We are a Christian country. Hospitality should be given to those who don't abuse it.' She shrugged. 'And there are some who take far too much pleasure in changing the custom for the worse.'

He nodded. Her words confirmed what he suspected. She had suffered a recent setback and was unhappy with the new regime in the area.

He fought back the urge to protect her. Alwynn's problems were none of his business. He needed to concentrate on returning home and bringing Girmir to justice. But he found it impossible to completely silence it.

'Do you think you can walk without assistance?' she asked, tilting her head to one side and revealing the sweep of her neck.

'What man ever refuses a beautiful lady when she is offering him her arm?'

Her green eyes darted everywhere but at his face and her cheeks became a delightful pink. 'You speak with a silver tongue.'

'I speak the truth.' He tried to rise and stumbled to his knees. 'My time in the sea took more out of me than I thought possible. It feels like I have fought several battles and yet I've not lifted my sword today.'

'You fought the sea and won. It is enough for one day.'

'That is one way to put it, but until a battle is won, I don't give up.'

She put her arm about his shoulders. Their breath interlaced and their gazes locked. Valdar forgot everything but the curve of her upper lip. His mouth ached to drink from hers.

He leant forward and slowly traced the curve with his forefinger. Her flesh trembled, but she didn't move away from him.

'And that was for?' Her husky voice broke the spell.

'Luck.'

Chapter Three

By the time they reached the small cottage where her old nurse lived, Alwynn's back was screaming from her exertions and her nerves were in tatters. Alwynn was pleased that Gode was off visiting her niece helping with the latest child in that brood. She'd encouraged it because Gode rarely had anything to do with her niece. Proof that her nurse was mellowing in her old age.

Right now the fewer people who knew about this half-drowned warrior, the better. Any whisper and Lord Edwin could be down on them, demanding to know why this man wasn't dead.

She knew what his wrath could be like. She had faced it when she refused his unseemly offer of becoming his mistress.

A small sigh escaped her throat. She had to

face facts. She'd very nearly kissed a stranger. What sort of woman did that make her?

Thankfully the half-drowned man had behaved impeccably about it.

But her body felt alive in a way that it never had when Theodbald had touched her. Then she'd recoiled from his damp touch and had wanted everything over as quickly as possible. The marriage bed had been a duty rather than a pleasure.

One single touch to her lips from this man, from this stranger, and she was ready to melt in his arms.

Alwynn wrenched her thoughts away.

She had to give Merri credit. The girl had stuck with her side of the bargain and helped, rather than finding an excuse to scamper off. Now Merri stood, shifting from one foot to the other. 'Is Purebright mine now?'

'Purebright will be happy to have you combing him.'

'It means you can't sell him if we need more gold. Like you did with the other horses.'

Alwynn shrugged. There was little point in saying how much it had pained her to sell off the good horses and Purebright was far too old and cantankerous to be sold. 'We need at least one pony.'

'Can I go now and tell him the good news?'

'Go. And you can tell any who asks that I'm helping Gode out with the garden.'

Merri gave a nod. 'Don't worry, I can keep a secret…even from you.'

'And that is supposed to inspire me with confidence?'

Merri gave a cheeky smile. 'Shall I get you some more water? Gode lets me do it when I visit her. When I return in the morning, he will be all better, you'll see.'

The man seemed to go in and out of consciousness, sometimes helping to walk and sometimes needing to be dragged. She had serious doubts if he would last the night, but one glance at Merri's earnest face told her that she could not confide that piece of information.

'Get the water before you go.'

'I could stay…if you needed help.'

'I'm the one who takes the risk, Merri, not you. Remember, you weren't with me this morning. And I wanted to tend Gode's garden. No one will find that unusual.'

In the months before Theodbald's death, Alwynn had often taken herself away to Gode's cottage. She had created a garden there which no one could destroy in a fit of temper as Theodbald had done when she had lost the baby she'd been carrying.

'But he is *my* warrior.'

'Now he is *my* responsibility.' Alwynn gestured with her free hand. 'Off with you. Sooner I have the water, the sooner you can tell Purebright the good news. And later you may return and see for yourself how he fares.'

'As long as he doesn't leave before I can say goodbye…' Merri called as she ran to get a bucket from the well.

Alwynn unceremoniously placed the man on the narrow bench outside. Leave before Merri could say goodbye? Alwynn shook her head. She had no idea if he would last the night. But she knew she wanted him to.

Sweat poured down her face and her gown stuck to her back as she tried to get the feeling back into her arm. The sun hadn't even reached noon and she was exhausted.

Her mind reeled from thinking about him dying. She had to do everything she could to save his life. And it didn't have to do with him; she'd do it for anyone. A small piece of her heart called her a liar—there had been something in his eyes which touched her heart. And when his finger pressed against her lips, she had felt as if she was made of precious glass.

Merri rushed back with the water and a jug
of small beer and then ran off again, chattering
about how beautiful Purebright was.

Alwynn smiled. Only Merri could think that
stubborn grass-munching fiend on four hooves
beautiful. She poured a wooden beaker of small
beer and handed it to the warrior, who immediately opened his eyes. The creases about his
mouth were less pronounced. And his skin now
no longer had a blue tinge to it. Alwynn tried
to look at him with a dispassionate healer's eye,
but somehow she couldn't.

She had no problems growing the herbs, but
when it came to people, she found it impossible
to keep her emotions out.

'Drink. You are safe now. You can rest and
regain your strength. No one comes here.'

'Thank you.' His brows drew together. 'I don't
want to put other people in danger, particularly
not you or your stepdaughter. I appreciate the
risk you took for me back there on the beach.'

Something eased in her neck. Unlike many of
the warriors she'd encountered, this one noticed
people beyond the end of his nose. She had originally thought warriors held special place and
that was why they were arrogant. It was good
to meet one who wasn't.

'It is only strangers from the sea who are

feared,' she explained. 'Not strangers from other lands. The men from the North…they come from the sea.'

His eyes became more shadowed and she wondered if the Northmen plagued his country as well. Silently she repeated everything she knew about Northmen and their ways. This man wasn't one of them. She was sure of it.

'I know how the Northmen travel.'

'Then you understand why it is necessary to be careful.'

As he took the wooden beaker, their hands briefly brushed. Another distinct tremor of attraction went through her. She withdrew her hand too quickly and spilled the beer down his front.

All those years with Theodbald's damp hands and crude manner and she'd felt nothing. She'd been convinced that there was something wrong with her. She couldn't even do as Gode had suggested—to think of some handsome saint and pretend. Instead she had felt like a lump of wood and lain completely still, hoping against hope that it would soon be over. Now it was like that lump of wood was covered in little flames.

It should frighten her, but somehow it was also exciting.

After years of being the good daughter and

the good wife, she was finally doing something forbidden.

'I will get you some more.' She hurriedly re-filled the wooden beaker. 'And something to mop up the spill. Clumsy of me.'

This time she kept her fingers well away from his.

His deep brown gaze held hers. He made a slight bow. 'Thank you. And you are right. I need to wash the salt off.'

Unbidden, her mind supplied a picture of his muscular torso. She turned away, aware that her cheeks blazed like an unwed maiden, rather than the woman who had endured more than five years of marriage and who knew what passed between a man and a woman, even if she couldn't understand why anyone would get excited about it. 'It can wait…until you have recovered. I will go and prepare a place for you to sleep.'

'Your cottage?'

'My old nurse's. No one except me or Merri comes here these days.' She knew she spoke far too fast, a bad habit from when she was small. She paused and took a deep breath. 'You will be able to heal in peace.'

He nodded. 'If anyone does come here, I didn't come from the sea.'

'Yes, you understand my meaning.' She

pressed her hands together. 'There is something about lying which sticks in my throat.'

'You found me on the shore, not bobbing in the sea. Therefore you have no real idea how I arrived there.'

'It doesn't take much imagination to guess.'

'You are not breaking any law if you don't actually know,' he said quietly.

'Is it better not to know?'

'Sometimes.'

She caught a faint twinkle in his eye. His eyes were not just brown, but full of many colours. And they had come alive after his drink. She heaved a sigh of relief. He wasn't going to die after all. 'Is your country Raumerike at war with mine?'

'I have never made war on your country.' He pressed his hand to his chest. 'I, Valdar, son of Neri, swear this. My solemn oath I give you.'

'That isn't what I asked…Valdar.' The name sounded strange to her ears, but not unpleasant.

He pursed his lips. 'My country has no quarrel with yours. Why would it? We have a sea separating us.'

The back of her neck prickled. He had come across the sea like the raiders, but he had come in peace. 'And the attack on Lindisfarne by the heathen Northmen?'

His face instantly sobered. 'I have heard of it. The whole world has heard about it. They took the gold and gave nothing but destruction in return. I have always believed it is wrong to make war on people who are not your enemies and have not harmed you. A simple creed, but I believe the right one.'

Something eased in her heart. She was doing the right thing—keeping his existence hidden and giving him a chance to heal.

He might be a foreigner, but he hadn't come to make war against her people or to raid. Merri was right—he wasn't a Northman. He was something else entirely. She released a breath. She wasn't going to save him just to have Lord Edwin kill him. He was innocent and therefore he deserved a chance to return to his country.

'Thank you for that creed.'

'I need the beer-sodden shirt and the salt off me. It itches like you wouldn't believe.'

'Are you capable of doing it?'

'I want to do it. I will find the strength to do it.'

She retreated two steps. 'Surely it can wait. You were near death. You haven't recovered enough.'

His face took on a look of grim determination. 'I remain alive.'

Moving very slowly as if every muscle screamed in pain, he took the tunic off and discarded it along with his sword and belt. Alwynn discovered her feet were rooted to the spot. The sunlight hit his golden chest. It was muscular but not overly so. There were several scars crisscrossing his torso, but it was a warrior's body and used to hard work, not soft and pudgy as her husband's had become.

A dimple flashed in his cheek when he saw she remained there. 'I will keep my trousers on, I think.'

She feigned an air of indifference. 'You must do as you like. It makes no difference to me.'

He picked up the bucket and poured the remaining water over him. The droplets trickled down over his long hair, making him gleam. 'You see, the salt goes when washed away.'

Her cheeks burnt, but she forced her chin high. 'You took a battering in the sea. I wanted to see if I need to get you a poultice for the bruising.'

All colour fled from his face. 'Are you a healer?'

'I can do a bit, not as much as Gode or the monks, but I'm learning. I've an interest in herbs.' She stared at the rough plaster wall of the cottage. Her troubles were none of his business, but she had found solace in gardening. Of all the things, the garden at Theodbald's hall had been the hardest to leave. Her new garden was smaller, but she had brought a number of plants with her. When she was out there, amongst the perfumed flowers and gentle humming of the bees, all her cares slipped away. 'I love my garden. I like to put it to good use and I like coming to Gode's as well.'

He nodded, but pain flashed through his eyes. 'I once knew a woman who healed.'

'What happened to her, the healer?'

'She married someone else and grows big with his child.'

'And where does she live, this healer of yours?'

'In the estate next to mine.' His brown gaze held hers.

He reached down and withdrew his sword from the scabbard. It gleamed dangerously in the sunlight, reminding her that, injured or not, he was still a warrior.

'Here, take it,' he said with his strange accent which caused his voice to sound more like a purr than a command. 'Keep it safe while you get whatever herbs you need. When I go from here, I will take it with me. Until then...a gesture of my peaceful intent.'

She gingerly took the sword. It was Frankish made with gold-and-silver inlay. She could imagine how her husband would have drooled over such a sword. Surely a Northman would not have such an expensive weapon?

'How did you get this sword?'

'I bought it in a market.' A dimple showed at the corner of his mouth. 'How else would I have acquired it?'

'Off the battlefield? Taken from an opponent?'

The colours in his eyes shifted as she amused him. 'I had it made for me. I wanted the right balance for my arm. Not exciting at all. Are all Northumbrians as bloodthirsty as you?'

Alwynn breathed a little easier. The barbarians who attacked the holy island of Lindisfarne surely could not have dealings with the Franks. The Franks were part of the Holy Roman Empire and forbidden from dealing with pagans. She could remember Theodbald explaining this fact with great disdain after the raid happened. One more reason why this stranger deserved to stay alive.

'What do you expect me to do with it?'

'Keep it safe until I leave. A token of my goodwill while I heal. You will be well rewarded.'

'You wish me to keep silent about you being here.'

'The authorities in any country ask too many questions.' He put a hand to his head. 'Right now, I need no questions and much sleep. You understand?'

Alwynn hesitated. 'Do you pledge to protect this household while you shelter within its walls?'

He placed his hand to his chest, displaying his arm rings. 'I swear.'

She stood with the sword in her hands. Her mother would have said that she should go straight away and report this man. Her mother would never have even saved him. Alwynn straightened her back. She wasn't her mother and she made her own way in the world now.

'I will put it beyond use until then. And I accept your pledge, Valdar.' She inclined her head. 'Not that it will be needed. Nothing ever happens here.'

'Then it is lucky you found me.' A smile transformed his face from handsome to stunning. 'A good omen in a sea of bad luck. Perhaps my life changes now. Perhaps I am reborn.'

A good omen for him. Alwynn took a deep breath. She wished she knew whether it would be the same for her—the woman who had obeyed all the rules had lost everything. Maybe it was time she started breaking a few. Maybe it was time for her to be reborn.

Valdar circled his shoulders, trying to focus on working the aches and pains out of his body, rather than think about the way the sunlight had shone on Alwynn's hair or the shadows in her eyes when she evaded his questions about why she'd saved him.

But he knew what he faced here if his true origins were discovered. To the Northumbrians, one Northman would be very like another. It made no difference that he was from Raumerike and the raiders were Viken. Or the fact that he had always considered the raid to be a grave error. Something which had far more consequences than simply taking gold and a few slaves captive.

He hated the slight deception, but having survived the sea, he wanted to live. He wanted to live more than he thought possible.

Silently he pledged that while he was here, he'd do all in his power to protect Alwynn and to return the favour of giving him his life back.

There were many reasons why Alwynn was out of bounds. He wasn't staying, but more than that she reminded him far too much of Kara and that wound in his soul was far from healed.

No one since Kara had intrigued him. It had

hurt to discover that Kara had only wanted to
marry him for the protection he could give her
and her young son. He'd let her into his heart,
the first woman he'd truly cared about, and she
had only wanted him for a friend and bulwark
to keep the estate intact.

He had spent the time since then feeling as if
he was encased in ice and ignoring his sister-in-
law's pointed remarks about how he needed to
marry. Valdar shook his head. His near-drown-
ing had addled his wits.

'I've lit a fire and made a simple poultice for
your ribs. They need to be bound before you
sleep,' Alwynn said, appearing in the doorway.
She'd shed her head covering and shawl and acquired an all-enveloping apron. But it was the
way her dark hair escaped its braid that held his
attention. 'By rights I should call a monk.'

'No!' Valdar struggled to breathe. 'You promised to keep my presence quiet.'

She lowered her brows. 'I retain the right to
call in a monk if you require it.'

'I've been injured worse and haven't required
a monk.' There were no monks in Raumerike,
precious few healers for that matter. Kara was
the only one who possessed some skill. Most
seemed to prefer making sacrifices to various
gods. There was little point in explaining how

he had cheated the gods by palming the black counter and no god would be interested in intervening on his behalf. Things worked differently with Northumbrians.

'And you know best?'

'In this case—yes.' He deliberately closed his eyes. 'The sun's heat is wonderful. Warms my bones. There were moments in the water when I feared I'd never see the sun again.'

'Do you need help getting into the cottage?'

Confirmation if he needed it that he must look like death.

He began to rise and immediately wished he hadn't. In the brief time he'd been sitting, his muscles had seized and refused to obey him. He concentrated and tried again, forcing his muscles to move. Every single one protested as he stood.

'If you have a stick I can lean on, I will go in.'

She hurried to him and grabbed his arm. Her scent acted as a balm, banishing the ache. 'Are you always this stubborn? Is that why you ended up in the sea?'

'I jumped,' he said.

'Why? Was the boat going down? Will more bodies wash up?'

'The rest stayed on the boat.'

'You jumped of your own accord?' Her voice rose an octave. 'During a storm?'

Alwynn would not understand about his gods and their demands. The Northumbrians, like the Franks, followed a different religion. He shook his head. His gods had turned their backs on him. Who was he to judge which god was right? From now on he concentrated on living, rather than thinking about things beyond his comprehension.

He glared at her. 'When the time came, I welcomed it. I wanted to be doing something, rather than waiting for death.'

'Jumping into the ocean during a storm seems extreme.'

'There are many ways to die. I took the way which offered me the most hope of surviving.' He made an impatient gesture. 'I've no idea what happened to my shipmates but they will not be near here. They will have continued on their journey back home, assuming I died. There will be much shedding of false tears when they arrive back in Raumerike.'

'What had you done?'

'Nothing except to attempt to keep an oath I gave.' He ran his hand through his hair. On that dreadful morning when he had stood over Horik's body and Girmir had demanded he show his loyalty to the new leader, Valdar had vowed to avenge his friend's death.

She lifted a brow. 'You keep oaths by jumping into the stormy sea?'

'I don't expect you to understand the ways of my people. Simply trust me that it had to be done and that I broke no laws. I follow a code. The same as my father did and his father before him.'

She rolled her eyes upwards. 'God preserve me from warriors and their honour. But rather than using a stick, take my arm.'

He opened his mouth to ask how a slight person like her could assist him, but then swallowed the words as he remembered how her soft breasts had felt against his side during the journey from the beach. The only reason he had escaped the scavengers was down to her. And he always paid his life debts.

'I will only trouble you a day or two.' He ignored the screaming pain in his ribs. 'Once I am rested, I will move on. I understand what risks you have taken. You will be rewarded. I promise.'

'No reward is necessary. My code demanded it.' Her full lips gave a bitter twist. 'Or don't you think a woman can have a code?'

'I know a great number of honourable women.'

'You want to return to your home and your loved ones. Your honourable women.'

Home. The word left a bitter taste in his

mouth. A place of dashed dreams and unful-
filled promises. He had no idea how people
would react when he told his tale of Girmir's
betrayal and what had happened afterwards.
Would they believe him or Girmir? Girmir was
his jaarl's distant cousin and there had been bad
blood between Horik and the jaarl. Valdar shook
his head. That was a problem for another day.
Right now was about survival.

'Everyone wants a home, a place where they
can feel safe.'

'For now, consider this your place of safety.'

'A refuge, rather than a home.'

She draped his arm over her shoulders and
glanced up at him. A gentle breeze blew hair
across her face. Her eyes were sea green under-
lain with silver and her lips softly parted. Desire
stirred deep within him.

It had been far too long since he'd lain with
a woman. Since before Kara. Perhaps it was as
his sister-in-law counselled him before he left—
a question of time. She hadn't liked it when he
asked her about why she remained unmarried,
though. His brother had been gone a long time
and she needed protection.

Maybe the queer hold Kara had over him
was lessening and he could get on with his life.

After he wreaked his revenge on Girmir, then he would inform his sister-in-law that she could start the search for his bride.

Quickly he removed his arm. Alwynn gave him a questioning glance.

'I am able to walk on my own. I don't want to crush you with my weight.'

'You are without a doubt the most stubborn man I've met.' She put her hand on her hip. 'How do you think you arrived at this cottage in the first place?'

'Calling someone stubborn is a compliment where I come from.'

He deliberately walked into the cottage, setting his feet down hard and not glancing at her again even though he sensed she hovered at his elbow, ready to catch him if he fell.

On the threshold, he stood and allowed his eyes to adjust to the gloom. The cottage was larger than many in Raumerike and boasted three tapestries on the walls as well as a decent hearth in the centre of the room. A long table dominated one end of the room while a simple pallet of straw lay close to the newly started fire.

'When will the owner return?'

'My old nurse uses it. She retired here a few years ago.' Alwynn turned her back and began to fiddle with the pots on the table. 'She and my late husband were less than good friends.'

'Was this nurse a good judge of character?'

She turned her back on him and began smoothing the coverlet. 'A long time ago she gave me permission to use the cottage whenever I wish.'

'You are high-born. I know enough about the customs of these lands.'

Her hand stilled. 'Does it matter?'

'Why did you try to hide it from me? I've no wish to harm you.'

He captured her hand and raised her palm to his lips. She trembled slightly. She quickly withdrew her hand as her cheeks flamed.

She tilted her chin upwards and her eyes blazed green fire. Every inch the imperious lady.

'There was no hiding. I may have been the lady of a great estate, but no longer. Now I'm simply a woman who tends her garden. My mother would be appalled, but I paid my late husband's debts without losing my honour or turning away any of our old servants from their homes, including my nurse. So, yes, my nurse is a good judge of character.'

'Honour is important to you.'

Her eyes flashed fire. 'Without my honour, I am nothing.'

He kept his face impassive. A deep primitive urge to protect her filled him. Angrily he dampened it down. He had no business here. His business was elsewhere. The people of this land meant nothing to him.

'I, too, have honour,' he said instead, seeking to put his debt to her on more formal terms. 'I owe you a life debt…Lady Alwynn. I always pay my debts. Know this and keep it in your heart.'

Her brows drew together. 'What does that mean? A life debt?'

'You saved me. I owe you something for that, regardless of what your code demands.' He allowed a smile to touch his lips. His debt to this woman was no different from the ones he'd owed to various warriors who had saved his back. 'My life is very precious to me.'

'Not jumping off any more boats would do for a start.' She moved away from him. 'I've not done anything special. I am simply the person who happened upon you. Any other decent person would have done no less.'

'And yet I believe you are not supposed to save strangers on a beach.' He made a correct bow. The muscles in his back screamed. 'Ask what you will and if it is in my power, I will do it. You do not need to decide right away.'

'And if I decide after you have gone?'

He twisted his mother's ring off his little finger. 'Send this and I will come.'

Her fingers closed around it. 'And how will I find you?'

'When I go, we will speak of it.'

Her tongue absently traced the outline of her lower lip. 'There is no need. As I said, I am merely a woman who tends her garden.'

'You saved my life.'

They stood looking at each other until a wood pigeon called in the woods. The spell was broken.

'I've made up a bed and you need to drink this,' she said, suddenly all businesslike. She picked a wooden beaker up from the table. 'I made it earlier when…when you were resting outside.'

He took a taste of the strangely sweet liquid. 'And it is?'

'Valerian mixed with mead. To make you sleep.'

'I will rest and then depart.' A great sneeze racked his body, making his ribs hurt anew. 'I don't want to put you in danger.'

'You may go when you are fit to travel.' She placed her hands on her hips. 'And you will catch your death if you continue to stand there partially unclothed.' She gestured towards the bed. 'There is a nightshirt. Put it on. I would have your clothes to lay before the fire.'

'Only half-drowned.'

'When you are finished, call me.'

'You are not going to stay to watch me disrobe completely?'

She quirked a brow upwards. 'I doubt there will be anything interesting to see.'

She turned on her heel and went out of the room.

Valdar gave a half-smile. It felt good to bait her. Something to do which did not involve fighting for his survival or nursing the black place in his soul.

'I will find a way to repay her before I leave,' Valdar vowed under his breath as a wave of tiredness hit him. He breathed in the dusty pleasant smell. For the first time in a long while, despite being on enemy territory, he knew he was safe.

The faint embers of the fire flickered, throwing strange lights on the plaster walls. Alwynn sat in Gode's only chair and listened to the sound of Valdar's uneven breathing.

The warrior hadn't woken since he fell into the valerian-induced sleep, but he had had nightmares. Merri had returned after exercising Purebright. She was uncharacteristically quiet, but Alwynn put it down to the morning's excitement. She also readily agreed to help keep Valdar's presence a secret before she left.

Alwynn had occupied herself by washing the salt out of his clothes and generally tidying the cottage. When her old nurse returned, she would have to have the talk about Gode living alone that she'd been postponing for a few months. Perhaps now that Theodbald was dead and they lived in a different hall, Gode would be more willing. Alwynn made a face. Gode was a law unto herself.

Valdar began thrashing about on the makeshift pallet, moaning in his sleep, calling on all manner of people for assistance.

Alwynn went over and laid a hand on his shoulder. 'Hush, you are safe. But continue to yell this loudly and they will hear you in the next kingdom.'

His eyes flew open and he raised his fist. The embers from the fire were reflected in the depths of his eyes. She couldn't say if he saw her or someone else, but his hand slowly lowered.

He mumbled something indistinct and his fingers picked at the bed covering.

'Pardon?'

'Kiss me. Kiss me like you mean it.' His face became tortured. 'Please.'

She stared at him. Did he mean her? Or some other woman?

'You must lie still. Rest.' She paused. 'Later, I will kiss you.'

'Please! Now! Once before I die.'

The ragged plea tore at her heart. One kiss would not change anything. But it might mean something to him. What if he didn't last the night? What if she never knew what his mouth felt like against hers?

She knelt down beside him and took his face in her hands. His skin was hot to the touch and his eyes fever-bright.

What harm could it do? He'd never remember it.

She lowered her mouth and tasted. His lips parted and she was drawn into a kiss which was unlike any she had experienced before—gently persuading, but intense at the same time. His hand came around her head and held her in place while he coaxed and nibbled. Her entire being became flame and she wanted it to continue.

Then suddenly it was over. His hand, which

had held her head in place, fell back. His eyes fluttered shut.

'Kara never kissed me like that. Ever.'

Alwynn sat back on her heels and touched her aching lips. What had she done? Who was Kara? His wife? His mistress? The woman he loved? It shouldn't matter, but it did. She hugged her arms about her waist, trying to prevent a great hollow from opening and swallowing her up. He wouldn't remember it in the morning, but she knew she'd remember it for the rest of her life.

It had been the moment when she'd proved that she was made of more than ice, that it had been her husband at fault. Another ghost laid to rest. She sighed. But there were plenty more ghosts where that one came from. She might not be made of ice, but she had never borne a live child. Ever.

The familiar but bittersweet longing to hold her own child swept over her. She pushed it away. She had Merri. She was contented in her life. She knew what she wanted.

Valdar thrashed his head about on the pallet and muttered several words. Alwynn froze. She knew deep in her heart what he was and where he was from. Across the sea. From the North. But he wasn't a raider. He'd come in peace.

She smoothed Valdar's damp hair from his forehead and knew she would make the same choice. This man deserved to live. 'What have I done?'

Chapter Four

Alwynn paused in the weeding of Gode's garden the next morning. Sitting still and watching Valdar only kept the thoughts about the kiss they'd shared circling about her brain. She had ventured outside at first light, determined to do something productive.

Thankfully Gode wouldn't mind. More than anything Gode would welcome the weeds being pulled and the action always made Alwynn think more clearly.

The day's hot sun had dried all the damp from the flowers and the hum of bees made the garden alive with noise. Everyday noises which should reassure her that everything was normal and nothing was going to happen as a result of her impulsive behaviour last night. All she had to do was to forget it had ever happened.

Trusting a stranger, particularly a warrior like

Valdar, was madness. She could have put everyone in danger. And she had kissed him. Properly kissed him. The only other man she'd ever kissed was Theodbald. She needed to go back into the cottage and inform him that it was time to leave.

Alwynn stayed where she was. Sending an injured man away wasn't in her nature. The words he had spoken in another language last night had been caused by his injuries. They were fevered nonsense, meaning nothing. It was simply the language of his homeland, and the lateness of the hour and the darkness of the night had made her own foolish mind read far too much into them. Valdar was not a Northman. Not like the kind that had attacked Lindisfarne and butchered the monks anyway. In the bright light of day she was sure of it. He'd given his word and she believed him.

She dug her trowel into the warm earth. After Valdar had departed, then she'd inform Edwin. Maybe give him a day's head start. Northumbria and Raumerike were not at war. How can you be at war with a country you have never heard of?

The last thing she wanted was trouble. As reeve, Edwin needed to know about a stranger in their midst, but exactly when he discovered it was another matter.

She shook her head. Finally she was becoming pragmatic. There was something to be said for her recently widowed state after all.

'My lady.' Oswy the Blount raised his hand in greeting. 'Here I discover you.'

Alwynn nodded towards the grizzled miller, but her heart pounded. The tension in her neck eased slightly when she saw the empty doorway. Silently she prayed Valdar had enough sense to stay hidden.

'Oswy the Blount,' she said in an overloud voice, hoping Valdar would understand the impending danger and hide. 'What brings you to this desolate place? You surely can't be looking for Gode and one of her potions, not after your wife proclaimed that the monks' potions were far superior.'

She gave a studied laugh. Oswy and her old nurse's enmity was the standing joke of the village.

'No, my lady, I came to see you, not that old crone.' Oswy gave a shiver and then a hearty laugh. Once his hair had indeed been blond like his nickname, but now it was streaked with white.

Although he had loyally served under her father and was considered the best gristmiller in this part of Northumbria, lately he always had an excuse to explain why his sacks of flour were light or delayed. The excuses were plausible, but Alwynn wondered—was he really that loyal to her?

The current delay had been part of the reason why she'd been forced to scavenge sea coal.

Alwynn carefully kept her head turned away from the cottage where Valdar lay.

'What brings you here, then?' She forced a light laugh. 'Does your wife require another tablet-weaving pattern?'

He shook his head. 'She is well supplied at the moment, thank you kindly. I wanted to let you know that I've delivered the flour you require. Only the best for my lady. I know how you like the fine flour for your honey cakes.'

She schooled her features 'Fine flour? But only two days ago you told me that there was no possibility of it before the autumn harvest.'

She had thought then that she needed a steward, someone to enforce her will with the point of a sword. But if she provoked Oswy, there was always a possibility that the others would follow his lead. The last thing she wanted was a rebellion. It would play straight into Edwin's hands. The fine lady who could not adequately protect her tenants did not deserve any estate.

Oswy and others saw her as a soft touch, Gode often proclaimed. Theodbald had been

far too interested in his own pleasure to pursue
the rents and Alwynn wasn't altogether sure if
Oswy respected her.

The older man rubbed the back of his neck.
'My son had put the wheat in the wrong place,
which is why I thought I had none, you see. Once
I discovered the mistake, I thought it best to let
you know straight away. We wish to stay on at
the mill, if all can be resolved, my lady. I have
paid my next quarter's rent before time as well.'

Alwynn stood up. There was far more to this
than simply mislaying flour sacks and rediscov-
ering them a few days later. But a non-direct
approach was best. She'd learnt that Oswy dug
in his heels and became stubborn if directly accused of not being entirely honest.

'It is good to know. I am grateful you discovered the missing wheat. And that you paid your
rent so early.' She paused and then invited him
to tell her the true reason for the sudden discovery. 'Is there any other news?'

Oswy wrung his cap between his hands. 'Lord
Edwin departs this afternoon. Tomorrow morning at the very latest.'

She fought against the urge to clap her hands
together in jubilation. The answer to her problem. If Lord Edwin was gone, she could hardly
report Valdar's presence and the manner in

which he was discovered. It had to be done in person. She could not risk the message becoming jumbled and she knew that Lord Edwin could neither read nor write.

And Valdar would be long gone before Lord Edwin returned.

Her jubilation rapidly faded. Lord Edwin's departure also opened other more intractable problems. Without warriors, the people in this area would be prime prey for any outlaw who happened past, even if no Northmen came raiding.

Silently she cursed her husband's feckless ways and her own inability to see it until it was far too late. If she had taken charge, she might have been able to prevent all the wealth being spent.

'He was supposed to stay here all summer because of the Northmen threat,' she said when she trusted her voice. 'He promised protection, particularly after last year's attempted raid on the River Don. We mustn't be left vulnerable!'

She hated how her voice rose and risked a hurried glance at the cottage. She wasn't going to ask Valdar for help. It would be wrong of her.

'During last night's visit he said that people should stop seeing shadows. The Northmen will not return. They fear *us* now. St Cuthbert's storm last year shattered their ships and killed their leader. His interests are better served near the king and he is going right away.'

Alwynn tilted her head to one side. Edwin had visited Oswy? Interesting. It explained much about why the flour had gone missing. Edwin had been annoyed that she retained the title to the few remaining hides of land around her hall, including the gristmill. 'And his prohibition against rescuing any who are washed up from a shipwreck? Lord Edwin blows in the wind.'

'That still stands. It is for our safety. Them Northmen would murder us in our beds, they would.'

'If he truly feels we aren't safe, he should stay and do his duty. A strong sword arm deters much.'

Oswy flushed. 'He has his reasons for seeking the king. There are many who remember that Athelfred once had his kingship taken from him.'

Alwynn made a face. Edwin put his own interests first, not the interests of his people. And it only spoke of one thing—a return to the civil war which had plagued Northumbria on and off for the past few generations. But she couldn't worry about matters of state, she had enough to worry about here.

'He stopped the Northmen last year, killing their leader in a sword fight,' she reminded him.

'He had St Cuthbert's help then. Without the storm, their boats would not have been wrecked. What if he goes back to his wicked ways and God turns his back on all of us?'

'Athelfred is still the king.' She held up her hand. 'I never held with the making and unmaking of kings. Far too many warriors have spent time in banishment. Half the well born had to leave when Athelfred regained the throne. Is it any wonder that the Northmen or the Picts and Gaels or indeed Mercia attack us?'

Oswy screwed up his face. 'My Oswald told me a story this morning when he returned from your hall. You are to marry again. A true warrior. There is no need to worry about outlaws or Northmen attacking any more. You are going to keep us safe. Abbe said that I should have trusted you to begin with.'

Marriage? How did that rumour get started? The back of Alwynn's neck prickled and she had the horrible suspicion that Merri had been unable to resist telling stories. Again. The child was going to be the death of her.

'Where did he get this idea from?' She forced the words from her throat while she did combat with the panic that threatened to engulf her.

'Lady Merewynn and the entire hall buzzes about the possibility. My son could not stop grinning from ear to ear when he returned.' Oswy thumped his fists together. 'It will be like the old days when your father was alive. There will be a warrior to protect us and our crops.'

Alwynn's heart pounded so hard in her chest that she was certain Oswy would hear it. She should have known Merri would find it impossible to keep a secret. No wonder the girl had looked sheepish when she'd asked her to keep the secret.

'He heard this from Lady Merewynn?'

'Yes. She wanted to show off Purebright.' Oswy twisted his cap. 'Please, my lady. If you know a warrior who might protect us, have pity and marry him. I can't afford to lose any more grain. The bandits have attacked me three times this spring. They even threw the grinding stone into the mill race the last time.'

Alwynn firmed her mouth. She knew all about the millstone and had taken steps to deal with it. In her opinion, it had been mischief by Oswald and his friends rather than outlaws, but she had lacked proof.

'Lady Merewynn should not be telling tales,' she said crisply. 'And you should not be believing them. You know what she is like.'

'Rumour is that you refused Lord Edwin's offer because there was someone else and that is why he married that Frankish woman. Is this the man Lady Merewynn was speaking of?'

'The two are entirely unconnected.' She pinched the bridge of her nose. There was little point in explaining about Edwin and his disreputable offer. He hadn't wanted her as a wife, but as a mistress. The marriage to the Frankish noblewoman had been arranged long before he had weaselled his way into the king's affections.

She clamped her lips together. Long experience had taught her that the gossips around here believed what they wanted, even in the face of overwhelming evidence to the contrary.

'I've no plans to wed again. Ever.'

Oswy's face went red. 'You mean to go into a convent and leave us, then? Have I wasted a betrothal gift?'

'No, not that!' The words rang out over the garden as Alwynn spied Gode returning via the lower path. In another few heartbeats she'd be at the cottage and scream. The last thing Gode expected to see was a man in her house. She checked her impulse to run over and greet Gode. Oswy would think it strange if she abandoned him.

She wanted the earth to open up and swallow her. Unless she was very careful, the whole sorry tale would come out and she would risk being branded a traitor for defying Edwin's order. Even though she had accepted Valdar's word that he'd had nothing to do with the Lindisfarne raid, would Edwin? Or would he covet the sword and declare that Valdar should be killed?

'What is a stranger doing here?' Oswy pointed behind her. 'Who is that man? I thought you were alone here, my lady.'

Alwynn knew without turning that her luck had truly run out. She had no explanation for why Valdar might be here. She could only hope he was dressed decently. Her mind searched for an answer, but nothing came. Silently she prayed for a miracle.

'I am the new steward.' Valdar's voice carried across the garden. 'The Lady Merewynn has it wrong. There is no marriage intended between Lady Alwynn and me, simply a business arrangement...for the summer.'

Alwynn stared open-mouthed. All speech seemed to have deserted her. 'That's right,' she gasped out.

Oswy gulped twice. 'The new steward? What is he doing here, then? Why is he in the old crone's cottage?'

Gode stopped, her face appearing as dumbstruck as Oswy's. She tilted her head to one side, looking very like a bird waiting for a worm.

'I was investigating the roof,' Valdar called back. 'There are several holes which need to be patched.'

'The estate requires one. I have been on the lookout ever since my husband died.' Alwynn wrapped her arms about her waist. That at least was not a lie. And would it be wrong to ask Valdar to honour his life debt in this fashion? That he become her steward in truth while he took time to recover?

She turned and saw him standing in the sunlight. He'd retrieved his washed tunic, but he hadn't bothered with the cloak nor had he bothered with his sword, which she'd left on top of the clean clothes.

'I'm honoured to serve such a lady.' Valdar made a low bow. 'I look forward to ensuring that my lady receives her full measure at the appropriate time.'

Oswy's gaze narrowed. 'You're not from around here. Why did my lady hire you?'

Alwynn concentrated hard on the ground and taking slow breaths. Everything was about to come tumbling down around her ears unless she got it right.

'Where I come from, men who withhold the

full measure from widows are considered the lowest of the low. Whether it is in the matter of flour or wool.' There was no mistaking the icy calm determination in Valdar's voice.

She risked a glance upwards. Valdar was staring at Oswy with deadly determination while Gode watched the scene with unabashed interest.

Oswy twisted his cap as his face became flushed beetroot-red. 'There were reasons. I…I lost it, but it has been found again. My lady understands, don't you, my lady? The new flour was to be a betrothal gift, but you must keep it as a token of my…my goodwill.'

'Where I come from, sacks of flour do not move about like living things. They are hard to lose. However, perhaps the flour from your land is different?'

Oswy flushed an even deeper red. 'It is good that my lady understands.'

'Indeed.' Valdar stepped forward. 'I trust those reasons no longer exist. And make up any shortfall.'

'Yes, yes, whatever you say, my lord steward.' The colour finally drained from Oswy's face and then, making his excuses, he hurried away.

Gode came forward. She looked Valdar up and down with a keen eye. 'Are you living here or at the hall?'

'That is up to my Lady Alwynn,' he replied smoothly.

Alwynn winced, waiting for Gode to explode or ask an awkward question about the roof of her cottage. Instead her old nurse did nothing of the sort.

'I could use a man about the house,' Gode remarked. 'Think about it, Alwynn, and the only way you will get me out of here is feet first. Sharing with a handsome warrior is just the thing to warm my bones.'

She bustled into the cottage. Alwynn was torn between the desire to laugh or cry. Of all Gode's possible responses, she had most emphatically not expected that one.

Exerting all of her hard-won self-control, Alwynn waited until she heard Gode rummaging about in the cottage. One problem at a time. The last thing she wanted was to get her old nurse involved more than she already was. She had no doubt Gode would have more than a word to say if she knew what Alwynn had truly done.

'Your nurse approves of me being your steward?' Valdar remarked into the silence.

'She'd approve of a Northman if he put Oswy in his place.'

'Any particular reason why?'

'A feud which goes back years. Something

about a failed promise to her sister, I believe. It just has always been there. It is a bit of a joke in these parts.' Alwynn stared after Gode. 'I was inclined to think she made too much of it because, before this spring, I had always considered him to be loyal to my family.'

'I'll remember that.' A faint breeze whipped the hair back from his face, revealing its hardened planes. 'In my new capacity as steward, this sort of intelligence can help.'

'Are you really going to be my steward?'

'You declared me to be one to your tenant, quite an important tenant. I would hardly wish to contradict you or cause you to find a reason why I suddenly departed.' Valdar's face wore a maddening smile.

'I will think of something plausible.' Alwynn hated that her mind was stubbornly blank except for noting the breadth of his shoulders.

'I am happy to reside here for the duration of my stay,' Valdar remarked, making no move to go from the doorway. 'It will suit my purposes.'

The muscles tightened in Alwynn's jaw. Exploding at him was only going to make matters worse. 'Gode has her own ideas. I had made no decision about where you will be living.'

He raised a brow. 'Indeed.'

She crossed her arms and concentrated on

breathing deeply. When she felt her temper was under control, she continued, 'Your presence will be common knowledge by nightfall.'

'That miller was cheating you, but I suspect you will get the correct amount of flour by the evening.'

'What are you doing? Didn't you hear what I said? Everyone will know. I had it under control. Merri is known for her flights of fancy. But, no, you came out.'

'I overheard your earlier conversation and spied the old lady coming down the track. I thought it best to volunteer.' He raised a brow. 'Before disaster struck. Before your nurse entered the cottage and discovered me lurking. I'm not one to cower and shake waiting for discovery. Think about what could have happened.'

And disaster hadn't struck? Alwynn struggled for a breath. Things had happened far too fast. She hated feeling as if she wasn't in control or that everyone was playing by a different set of rules. 'But it didn't happen. And now everyone will think I have a new steward. They will start to ask questions. Where I hired you from? For how long?'

'I take it that the position is vacant.'

His quiet words cut through her panic. She

drew an unsteady breath and concentrated on a spot above his left shoulder.

'Yes, it has become clear over the last few months—either I can work in my garden or I can ensure rents and renders are collected. It was something I'd hoped to address after the harvest.'

'Why didn't you have one before?'

'Because he cheated me and my late husband. The entries in the ledger did not add up. When I discovered it, I sent him packing.' She shook her head. 'I lost my temper and may have brandished a sword. Thankfully he didn't know I could barely lift the thing.' She gave a careful shrug. It had felt good shouting and brandishing the sword. Finally to be doing something, rather than wringing her hands and waiting to be rescued.

At Valdar's perplexed expression, she added. 'Anger made me strong.'

'Trust me with the true explanation.'

'Because…I didn't wish to get cheated again. I wanted to wait and find someone I trusted.'

He raised his brow. 'By not hiring a steward, you allowed people like that man licence to do as they wished. You risked losing everything.'

Her insides twisted. She hated that he was right and that she should have known better. She should have questioned Oswy's excuses more closely, and seen if he really had no fine flour or not. 'He was always very loyal to my father and even to my husband. Before now, he always delivered the flour early. It was only when I wanted to make a treat for Merri's birthday that I discovered he had not bothered to hold any back for me. I was supposed to make do with the ordinary sort.'

'Then it is well you have me.'

A tiny piece of her died. For one wild heartbeat, she'd hoped that he was indeed the answer to her problems. But it was far too good to be true.

Her luck didn't run to handsome warriors appearing suddenly and rescuing her. She wasn't even certain she wanted rescuing. And there was that nagging doubt in the back of her mind. What had Valdar called out in his fever? Perhaps in his language they had different names for the saints, and he had been praying? That must be what it was. He didn't behave like an uncouth barbarian. But where precisely was Raumerike?

'You must know that I don't have the gold to pay you.'

All the warmth drained from his eyes. 'Did I ask for any payment? My life is payment enough. I will stay until the harvest. My new role will give me ample time to return to health and get my full strength back. The sea nearly claimed me. I can never repay the debt I owe you.'

'Merri talked about you. Oswy gave me a garbled version.' Alwynn put a hand to her head. Valdar would stay without asking for gold. A large part of her wanted to shout for joy. Miracles could happen. But she'd learnt to distrust miracles.

'It matters for nought.'

'I've no idea how far the tale has gone. Or even the precise nature of the tale. I can't believe she did this to me.'

He waved a hand. 'She is young and had an adventure. It is to be expected. This way is better than hiding and jumping at every little noise, yes? There is a reason for me to be here.'

She narrowed her gaze. Was he speaking about her? She didn't hide. She simply found reasons to be in the garden, where things were peaceful. 'What way?'

'Me being your steward until the autumn. It solves your problem and mine.' He held out his hand. 'Is it a bargain? I will get you your due without fear or favour. You can trust me.'

Alwynn regarded his long fingers. There were so many reasons why she should refuse. She had gone against Edwin's direct orders. She had no idea who Valdar truly was, but she had little choice but to trust him. And it wasn't as if she was inviting him into her life for ever.

Her heart gave a little protest, but she silenced it. She was being practical. She could keep him at arm's length. There would be no repeat of last night's kiss, as much as her body might desire it.

Her hand reached towards his. 'Until the autumn, then.'

Valdar held Alwynn's hand in his for a few heartbeats longer than he needed to. Silently he apologised for the slight deception about his origins, but it was necessary. He couldn't risk being branded a raider when he had no intentions of raiding. He hated that her hand felt right in his. There was no good hoping for a future when there was none for him here in this place. And he could make the meeting with Ash Hringson, particularly if he travelled by sea rather than going overland.

She withdrew her hand and her cheeks glowed pink. He wondered about his strange dream of kissing her in the sea. He dismissed it as being fanciful. She was his employer now and even more off limits.

'There, it didn't hurt too much, did it?'

She gave a half-smile. 'It didn't hurt at all.'

'I will stay at the cottage with your nurse,' he said before she had the chance to dictate terms.

When not at work, he had to be prudent and guard his privacy. 'When I take up my duties, I will come to your hall. For now the rumour of me should send the goods flowing in. A way to find out who has been honest and who has not.'

A faint crease appeared between her brows. 'I fear you might be right.'

'Fear?'

'I used to think the best of everyone, but I learnt that was impossible. That innocence has gone.' She gestured with her hand. 'Long gone. Today is one more lesson in a long line of lessons. When will I start to learn? I want to trust, but every time I'm betrayed.'

His fingers itched to reach out and smooth the worry lines from her forehead. He kept them resolutely at his side. He was not going to become involved with her. He had given Kara his heart and she had only wanted to use him. He had no idea what Alwynn wanted from him. All he knew was that he wanted to protect her and pay back his debt. Then he would leave. This time, his heart would play no part. He was behaving no differently than if she was a man.

A tiny voice in the back of his brain called him a liar, but he chose to ignore it.

'A healthy scepticism can be a good thing.'

'I wanted to believe that everyone was honest

and no one would seek to take advantage of a widow.' She screwed up her nose. 'I feel naive.'

'Not everyone is a cheat.'

'Oswy swore to me only last week that he had no fine flour left. And when he thinks I will marry a warrior, suddenly there is fine flour.'

'And he will do the right thing.' He gave in to temptation and touched her shoulder. Her flesh trembled under the thin cloth. He let her go. 'More than the right thing.'

'I wish I felt that way.'

'Remember, in the end he didn't cheat. He decided his interests were better served in standing with you than standing with someone else. Do you know who might have enticed him? It is not easy for a miller to travel.'

Her jaw jutted forward. 'I have a good idea who might have induced him. Lord Edwin.'

'Then your quarrel is with him rather than Oswy.' He stared over her shoulder. 'My father used to say that if you were going to fight, make sure you fight the right person.'

He gave an inward smile. Even now, years later, he could hear the exact intonation of his father's voice as his mother patched up his knuckles from a fight. Valdar had questioned why his father had attacked a farmer rather than the sell-sword who had taunted him. Oswy was like the sell-sword. Alwynn's problem was with his master.

She blinked up at him. The dark lashes were the perfect foil to her green-grey storm-tossed eyes. 'You think I shouldn't punish Oswy?'

'What good will it do? He has paid you what he owes with only a slight delay and I know not to be taken by his excuses in the future. The fine flour might have been genuinely mislaid. And rumours of betrothals always swirl when there is a beautiful widow involved.'

The faintest pink coloured her cheeks. 'I suppose you are right…about giving him the benefit of the doubt, I mean. I must assure you, though, that I am no beauty.'

'How might this Lord Edwin seek to destroy you?' he asked instead, trying to focus on why he was here and not on the shape of her mouth. 'What will he do next?'

With Kara, it had been relatively straightforward about who the rival for her estate was. Was it so simple with Alwynn? Could he do this one thing for her before he left? He hated to think that she might be alone without any male support. He had seen what could happen.

She shook her head. 'Your fight is not with him. You are merely here to make sure all my rent is collected on time. If that is done, he won't be able to touch me.'

'And next year? Or the year after that?'

'Let me worry about that. One harvest at a time.'

The sunlight caught her hair. It wasn't just black but many different shades of brown and black intermingled. He itched to reach out and capture it. He wanted to pull her into his arms and whisper that she should trust him to do the right thing. And yet if she knew the truth about his origins, she would flee.

'And if it comes to a fight?' he asked instead.

'You will need your sword back if you are to be my steward.'

'I have no plans to put anyone to the sword.' He clenched a fist and thought of how his father had acted—the men he'd put to death for less. He and his brother both had vowed not to be like that. And they had both succeeded. Their farms prospered. His sister-in-law proved more than equal to the task of looking after the farms when he was away. But everyone knew when he returned that he would insist on a full accounting. 'The threat of violence is often more powerful than actual violence.'

'But it is a symbol.' Without waiting for an answer, she hurried away. 'Wait here.'

Before he could protest, she had gone.

When she returned, she carried his sword. She held it out to him, balanced on outstretched arms. He tilted his head to one side. Horik had been with him when he purchased the sword. They had laughed about the many battles they would fight together. Someone needed to avenge his shade. Valdar could not start afresh until he'd laid his past to rest. The gods had spared him for a reason. If he forgot that, he would be in trouble. He had a second chance to make things right. He would not be granted a third one.

'What is this for?' he asked.

'A steward needs to command respect. You should wear your own sword.'

Its hilt gleamed in the bright sunshine. Something deep within him twisted. She trusted him with a weapon and it meant more than he thought it would.

He took it and fastened it around his middle. Its familiar weight gave him comfort, but it also reminded him of his duty towards Horik and the others. He would avenge their deaths.

'Thank you.'

Her lips turned up into a heart-stopping smile. Alwynn was the loveliest woman he had ever seen. Had he truly kissed them? Had she kissed him back or was it a drug-induced fantasy like his dream about Horik rising from the grave had been?

He fought against the urge to pull her into his arms and sample them, just to see if it had been a dream or not. He wanted it to have been real. And he did not want to think about how she'd look when she discovered his true identity. It made no difference now. Girmir and the rest were long gone. They would not have time to return and raid. Alwynn was safe.

'I trust you will only use it when necessary. The people around here are simple folk and they have good hearts.'

'For defensive purposes only,' he promised.

Her mouth parted as if she wanted to say more. 'How long before you are fit enough to take up your duties?'

'A day or two.' He tested his sides. His ribs pained him, but he'd suffered worse. He tried a practised swipe with his sword and nearly dropped it. Hopefully he wouldn't encounter this Lord Edwin any time soon. 'Now, shall we go and introduce me properly to your old nurse? Or do you wish her to think ill of me?'

'Gode is a law unto herself.'

'She reminds me of her previous charge.'

Her green eyes met his. It would be possible to drown in them. 'She has a far sharper tongue than me. And her outlook on life is unconventional. It becomes worse the older she gets.'

He nodded. 'I will bear that in mind.'

Alwynn held out her hands and her eyes became huge pools. 'Valdar…she doesn't need to know how I found you. Keep it from her.'

'And my bruises? I suspect the only reason Oswy didn't comment was because I remained in the shadows.'

'She won't ask. She is like that. Gode is precious to me. I won't have anyone else lying for me…and risking their lives for me.'

'Why don't you believe you are worth it?'

'What I believe is that Lord Edwin is a dangerous enemy.'

Giving in to an impulse, Valdar reached out and straightened her head covering. She didn't flinch or recoil from his touch. And he knew he wanted to do more than his duty to his dead comrades. He wanted to make everything right for the woman who had saved him. 'That is your responsibility, but I've no intention of lying. If she asks a direct question, I will answer, but if she doesn't, there is no need to trouble her. Do you understand?'

Chapter Five

When Alwynn arrived back at the hall, everywhere she went, the servants forgot their tasks, fell silent and stared at her. Then they started to work harder than she had seen them work for many a month.

Her stomach knotted. How far had the rumour about her impending marriage reached? Merri had played her last trick. A man's life was at stake.

She looked neither left nor right, but continued on until she reached the stables, where she discovered Merri grooming Purebright.

'Why did you tell Oswald such a wicked lie?' Alwynn asked Merri before the young girl had the chance to open her mouth.

'About what?' Her cheeks coloured as Alwynn continued to stare at her. 'What have I done this time? I swear, Al, I've only been here with Purebright.' She laid a hand on Purebright's now-gleaming white flank. 'He takes for ever to get clean.'

'About Valdar. Why have you spread such gossip? We had agreed to keep his presence a secret until…until I decided what to do with him.' Alwynn winced. 'Anyway, it is not a subject for idle chit-chat and telling your friends.'

'Is that my warrior's name?' Merri's eyes gleamed. 'It sounds lovely. Is he about to leave? Is there any way we can get him to stay? This estate needs a warrior. Everyone says so.'

'Merri! You promised to keep silent!'

'I never said anything to anyone,' Merri protested. Her cheeks turned bright pink, the way they always did when Alwynn caught her doing something that she wasn't supposed to. 'Not about how we found him or anything!'

'Then why did Oswy think I was about to marry a warrior? How did he know where to find me? Why did all the servants stare at me when I arrived back? I swear…'

Merri went white and then red. 'Don't take Purebright away from me.'

'I want the truth, Merri, and then I will decide. Any young lady who is able to look after a pony should be able to keep her word.'

'Oswald was teasing me three days ago. He

said that we were going to have to leave this hall by the autumn because you would never be able to pay the render on time. Lord Edwin had seen to it. So I said you were going to marry an atheling!' Merri put a hand on her hip. 'And to think I swore him to secrecy on the bones of St Oswald. Do you think he knows what can happen to oath-breakers?'

'Three days ago, you told a tall tale.' Alwynn pinched the bridge of her nose. Sometimes getting to the bottom of Merri's tales made her feel as if she had stepped into a bard's tale. 'But did you also tell him about Valdar? How did Oswy know where to find me?'

'Oswald called me a liar about the marriage. And I said he'd know the truth when you gave me Purebright.' Merri patted the pony. 'Only I never expected you to give me Purebright. So some of it is your fault, really.'

Alwynn put her hand to her head, trying to puzzle things out. Sometimes, with Merri, she could never understand the true course of events. 'I wish you had warned me.'

'But then you might not have given me Purebright. And I bet Oswy had gone to check with Gode. Gode always knows what is happening at the hall, particularly with you.'

Alwynn pinched the bridge of her nose. Merri

consistently figured out ways to twist everything to her advantage. But it did make sense why Oswy had appeared when he did. Gode often seemed to know what was happening up at the hall before it became public knowledge.

'Will you be marrying him, then?'

'Who?'

Merri rolled her eyes. 'My warrior, of course. Who else? I think I shall call him Valdar the Valiant.'

'I'm not marrying anyone,' Alwynn said, attempting to regain control of the conversation. 'But Valdar will be acting as my steward for the summer.'

'Hooray! That means he isn't leaving right away and I can show him all sorts of things.' Merri sobered. 'Oswald says that there are Northmen here. A ship with a broken mast.'

All the air seemed to leave Alwynn's lungs. Northmen here? They could have already started burning and looting. She struggled to keep her composure as her heart began to beat far too fast. 'Another of Oswald's tales?'

Merri shrugged. 'I asked him to show me, but he wouldn't. He said it was not a sight for little girls.' She stuck her nose in the air. 'So I followed him.'

'Merri!' Alwynn's stomach clenched. She

wanted to draw the precious girl to her as her mind raced with the possibility of what could have happened to her. Merri had been the only bright part of her marriage. And once they were married Theodbald had basically abandoned the girl, leaving Alwynn to bring her up.

Drawing on all her will-power, she forced her arms to stay at her sides. Merri hated being fussed over. But in her mind's eye she could see the girl's broken body. She had heard the tales. She knew the ferocity all Northmen were capable of. 'Anything could have happened to you!'

Inwardly she winced. The words sounded so weak.

Merri's eyes blazed with a fire that Alwynn had seldom witnessed. 'That braggart Oswald was lying. There wasn't anything at that old inlet. Not one single solitary soul. He just wanted to frighten me. You remember how he cried wolf when he was guarding his father's sheep. No one ever saw a wolf.'

Alwynn absently rubbed her temple to get rid of the beginnings of a painful head. She should have guessed. Oswald was notorious for seeing Northmen and the like. Three times last summer he had sent Lord Edwin out on wild goose chases. He preferred things lively, was his father's indulgent explanation.

'Thank heavens for that! The last thing we need is the Northmen destroying everything we hold dear. I have enough problems getting in the harvest without the added threat.'

'But if they were here, do you think Valdar would defend us?' Merri persisted.

'Why do you think he would do a good job?'

'His has the best sword I have ever seen. Even better than Lord Edwin's. Even better than my grandfather's before my father broke it.' Merri paused and her eyes took on an excited gleam. 'Purebright and I could go on a mission with him. We could be highly useful. I know we could. You'll see. He could draw the sword of Dyrnwyn and it would burst into flames like it is supposed to when the right person draws it...'

'There is no such thing as any of those treasures. Not the sword or the red cloak which makes you a king.'

'But what if there were? I bet he would find the sword. My angel mama will have sent him to save us.'

Alwynn straightened Merri's couvre-chef so it covered up all the blonde curls. Some day soon she was going to have to do something about Merri and her beliefs. She needed to understand before it was too late that heroes did not magically appear from the sea…however much one might wish it were otherwise.

'He will be working and getting his hands dirty, not going off on adventures. And you should be doing your spinning. A new pony is no excuse to neglect your other duties,' Alwynn said, attempting to regain some control over the situation. 'Hard work, not believing in stories, is what has saved this estate so far and it will save it again.'

Merri made a face. 'Purebright's tail needs to be brushed first. Before anything. I promised him.'

'Merri!' Alwynn put a hand on her hip. She had to admire Merri's spirit. When Alwynn was a girl, she'd been anxious to please, doing whatever her mother asked. Her only rebellion had been when she had begged to marry Theodbald. And look how that had turned out.

'What did I say about showing me you could handle the responsibility? That means doing the tasks I have set. Some day you will have to run a great estate. You will need to direct the women or otherwise how will everyone be clothed and fed?'

Merri wrinkled her nose. 'I don't want to be a great lady. Why can't I be a warrior?'

'You were born a great lady who will weave

families together in peace. Be content with that.'
Alwynn put a hand to her head. 'I sound like my
mother. And you are confusing the issue. Bragging to Oswald, no matter why it was done, has
caused problems.'

'I bet we wouldn't have had the rents arrive
today if you hadn't given me Purebright.' Merri
patted Purebright's neck. 'It isn't just Oswy. Others have sent things. They want to be on the right
side of a warrior. You should have put the rumour out that you were getting married weeks
ago. It would have saved a lot of heartache and
worry. People are paying their rents early now
that they know a warrior is here.'

Alwynn went cold. Oswy and how many others had been holding out, waiting to see what
was going to happen while she struggled to raise
the required amount for the king? She firmed her
lips. No, she didn't want to think that about the
people she'd grown up with. It was just that they
wanted to celebrate her supposed good fortune.
Since Theodbald's death, she'd been touched in
so many ways at the generosity of the people
who worked this land.

'It all goes back, Merri. Keeping betrothal
presents when there is no betrothal is wrong.
And they have little enough as it is. We will
make the render if we have all the correct rents.

I will hold on to this land, but in the right way, not through lies or deception. There was enough of that when your father was alive.'

'What will Lord Edwin say? He did offer to help you find a suitable steward.'

Alwynn firmed her mouth. Suitable for him, rather than for her! 'You should not listen at doors.'

'But how else will I find out anything interesting?'

'Lord Edwin has no say over whom I hire. He never has and he never will.'

Merri slipped her hand into Alwynn's. 'Good.'

'Ah, here I find you, Lady Alwynn,' Edwin's nasal whine resounded throughout the stables.

Merri gulped hard and pulled away as Alwynn schooled her features. He was the last person she wanted to encounter, but obviously the rumour had spread far and wide.

'Lord Edwin, to what do I owe the pleasure?' Alwynn placed her hand on Merri's shoulder, preventing her from leaving. 'Lady Merewynn and I were busy discussing her new pony.'

Lord Edwin's narrow features settled into their usual sneer. 'An overly fat pony. If he were my pony, he would be fed less. Should young ladies have ponies like that? You are spoiling her, Lady Alwynn.'

'Purebright is mine!' Merri cried. She slammed down the brush and ran off.

'Forgive Lady Merewynn's display of temper, my lord.'

'You should control that child better.' He made a tsking noise in the back of his throat. 'I would never allow any child I had responsibility for to behave in such manner. Perhaps my wife should be approached to see if she is willing to take her in hand. I make no promises, mind.'

'Lady Merewynn is my responsibility, Lord Edwin. I'm not minded to foster her with anyone.'

'The child needs company and a firm hand. I have said this before on many an occasion. And now that I have a wife, I am in a position where I can help. New husbands don't usually wish to be reminded of old ones...'

A position where he could control any inheritance was more like it. Alwynn knew precisely where this conversation was headed. She'd fought against the suggestion before and would continue to fight. She'd seen what happened to wards and how they were married off to men who furthered the aims of the foster parents or died young. Merri deserved better.

'I've no plans to remarry. Nor do I have any plans to enter the church. I made this quite clear after my husband's death and it remains my avowed intent.'

Edwin's cheeks became stained scarlet. 'I thought… That is…'

'Believing everything you hear, particularly when the source is dubious, is the surest way to lose your path.' Alwynn crossed her arms and clung on to her temper. Silently she thanked God that Merri had fled. If she had remained, there was no telling what the girl might have been tempted to say.

'Of course, of course. Have you given any thought to my suggestion of a steward? My own has a brother who would be willing to oversee…'

'Funnily enough, I have. But, alas, your steward's brother will have to find another position. There is no longer a vacancy on this estate.'

'Anyone I am acquainted with?'

'Doubtful, but he comes with the highest recommendations.' She allowed her lips to curve upwards. 'I used my connections to discover a suitable candidate.'

'Your family connections?'

Her nose itched, as it always did when she was in trouble. Right now much depended on keeping Valdar's origins a mystery. But it felt good to wipe the smug expression off Edwin's face. 'I understand you are departing soon. And here I

thought for certain you were staying for the entire summer to ensure Northmen did not attempt
to take the harvest. It was one of the reasons, I
believe, that the king gave for gifting you the
bulk of my late husband's estate.'

'Alas, the king requires me by his side. He
needs my help before the other nobles arrive for
the law-giving.' He tapped the side of his nose
in a particularly irritating manner.

Alwynn kept a straight face. Her father and
Theodbald's father had both used to complain
bitterly about having to be there early. It was
a burden rather than a privilege and only the
unlucky or the overly ambitious were lumbered
with it.

'Indeed.'

'I have little reason to suppose we will have
trouble with the Northmen this summer.' He adopted a smug stance. 'They were all destroyed
last year, in part thanks to my quick thinking.
None will dare venture out again. They will have
seen how strong we are.'

'If they were all destroyed, how will any other
know our strength?'

'Just like a woman to ask such a question.
Don't you worry your pretty little head. You will
be safe.'

Alwynn clenched her fist and wished she had

the strength to wipe the smile off his face. 'My new steward will be more than equal to the task, my lord.'

'Oswy the Blount informed me that your steward appears to have a good sword arm.' Edwin had the grace to blush slightly. 'He will no longer be considering one of my mills.'

'Oswy is one of *my* tenants. The king takes a dim view of people poaching tenants.'

'He is a good miller. One of the best in the area. My wife prefers his flour. It was merely a friendly chat as I was passing. Something which was mentioned casually.' Lord Edwin gave a false laugh. 'She thought we might be able to tempt him away, but, no, he wishes to stay, particularly now that you have such a formidable steward. Better for him. He has hopes that his son will make a warrior and even dared suggest that I might help him. Can you imagine a miller's son becoming a warrior? Whatever is the world coming to?'

Alwynn crossed her arms as her blood boiled. Oswy had been holding back on the flour, but he had done it for his only son. He obviously hadn't believed her when she'd informed him of the same fact. 'He is always welcome to change gristmills. I am not holding him back, but first he must fulfil all his tenancy agreement. A fair exchange.'

'You can hardly blame the man for looking around. Common knowledge that you barely scraped last year's render together. Men have to look to their families first.'

Alwynn pressed her lips together. This was the closest Edwin had come to admitting that he had tried to steal her tenants. 'Is that so? None have come to me with problems.'

'I like to know what is happening in this neighbourhood. The king did make me the overlord of the area.'

'Because of what you did with the Northmen? How funny that most seem to think it was St Cuthbert's storm.'

His eyes narrowed. 'About this new steward of yours—is he the sort of man you can trust? You should have allowed me to vet him.'

She held out her hands. 'I am grateful for the concern, Lord Edwin, but I feel it is up to me to run my estate how I see fit. My lineage allows me that privilege. The king agreed with me, if you will recall.'

Lord Edwin resembled a fish as he rapidly opened and closed his mouth several times. 'But…but…'

'Enjoy your sojourn with King Athelfred.' She

gave him a hard look. 'I feel confident that everything will remain quiet while you are gone and if not, my steward will be able to handle it. Be sure to give the king my assurances on the matter.'

His snake-like gaze swept over her, making her feel dirty. 'The trouble with you, proud Lady Alwynn, is that you have led far too easy a life. Some day you will see sense. Some day you will regret this.'

Alwynn drew on all of her reserves not to berate him like a common fishwife. 'We shall have to agree to disagree on that one, like so many other things.'

'As you wish, my lady.' Lord Edwin made an elaborate bow. 'You will learn—I am a patient man and I generally get my way in the end.'

He stomped away, his cloak twitching like an infuriated cat.

Alwynn stumbled over to where Purebright stood munching a pail of oats. 'I have to be doing the right thing. Lord Edwin is as much my enemy as any Northman who might be lurking about.'

The back of her neck prickled. She didn't know exactly where Raumerike was but she trusted Valdar. She had no other choice. She had to hope that this time, her instinct was correct.

She wasn't starting to believe in tales again. She was a grown woman now.

Valdar concentrated on circling his arms and getting the movement back into his torso as he stood in the doorway of the cottage. The garden sloped away to his right and the sunlight appeared dappled through the leaves of an apple tree. A pair of white doves played on the light breeze, before disappearing with a soft coo.

He could understand why Gode wanted to live in this spot, rather than sleeping in a crowded hall. There was something about the place that exuded peace and tranquillity. Last night the nurse had been quite vocal on her desire to stay there and her fear that Alwynn would force her to move. After spending time with the nurse, he understood Alwynn's concern: Gode clearly had moments of dwelling with the gods.

'My lady will be here when she is ready,' Gode declared from where she was sweeping the floor. Since she had arrived back at the cottage, she had set to work cleaning and tidying, but otherwise she had left Valdar alone. 'There is no need to keep watching the door like a dog waiting for his mistress.'

'I wasn't wondering and I wasn't watching the door.' He tilted his head to one side. The old woman's skin was a bit yellow and her mouth seemed pinched. She was thin all over except for her stomach. He'd seen similar signs before with his grandmother. 'What pains you, old lady? Does Lady Alwynn know about this?'

'When you are not watching the door, you are standing beside it.'

Valdar rapidly moved away from it. 'Satisfied? Does Lady Alwynn know about your illness? Why does she allow you to stay in this hut on your own?'

The woman grunted and swept a large pile of dirt out the door. She gave one last push of the broom, but then doubled over in pain.

Valdar took the broom from her. The old woman reminded him of his grandmother who had died from a growth in her stomach the year he turned ten. It was the same year his life had changed for ever when his mother had left his father. 'I can do that. You sit.'

'Women's work.'

'I dislike inactivity. The worst part of healing.' Valdar was pleased his Northumbrian words had come back so quickly, but then he'd always been good at languages. His father had been similarly skilled and had insisted both his sons learn as many languages as possible so it would be less easy to cheat them at market.

He rubbed the back of his neck. His father and brother, if they were still alive, would have said that he was crazy. Staying here was courting death, but what choice did he have? Either that or have Lady Alwynn exposed. This way he'd have established his credentials as Lady Alwynn's steward. It would make it easier to travel north when the time came.

A little voice called him a liar. He wanted to see if his dream about the way her lips tasted was true. He pushed it aside. Lady Alwynn was out of bounds.

'You will see plenty of activity in due course…Northman.'

Valdar blinked as his blood ran cold. The old woman had guessed his secret. Or was she simply trying to unsettle him again? He concentrated on sweeping the dust into a neat pile. 'Why do you call me that?'

'You don't deny it?' Gode asked from where she perched, rubbing her belly. 'I know the Frankish accent.' She gave a small preen of her wispy hair. 'In my youth, I was quite a beauty, not this old crone you see before you. A Frankish warrior loved me once. I've never forgotten his voice or the way he rolled his r's. Yours is not like that.'

'The Franks have many accents.'

'Please. I am old, but my wits are keen.'

'I've no wish to patronise you, but an accent is a fragile link.'

'I saw the hammer and ravens you have embossed on the arm ring, the one in your pouch.'

'You looked through my things?' Valdar silently cursed. Of course she had. He should have expected it and thrown the arm ring down a well as soon as he could crawl. He would dispose of it tonight.

'No Christian man would carry such a thing.'

'I come from the North, but I had nothing to do with the raids on your churches and monasteries.' He spread his hands. 'There's no challenge in killing defenceless people, no glory. It is the surest way to start a war. I come in peace.'

'You are but one man. The wolves from the North hunt in packs, destroying churches. There was no ship spied near here or the entire village would be up in arms.' She cackled. 'And people think I am soft in the head.'

Valdar frowned. 'And what will you do with your knowledge?'

Gode shrugged and stood up. 'All the pain is gone now. Occasionally my food disagrees with me. Nothing more than that.'

'You didn't answer the question.'

'My lady is far too honest. She would feel the

need to betray you, but I am old and have learnt to judge a man by his actions.'

'And your verdict?'

'Lord Edwin thinks me a fool and tells me to get off the road when his great horse lumbers past. You take a broom from an old lady and sweep the dust into a neat pile.' The old woman took the kettle off the hearth and poured the hot water into the mortar to make an evil-smelling paste. 'You exposed Oswy, who for far too long has been cheating my lady. That counts for something as well.'

'Why did she trust the man?'

'She liked to believe him because he once bore arms with her father. But I never trusted him, not even when he claimed to have routed Mercians. These old eyes have seen much.'

'Why didn't you tell Lady Alwynn your suspicions?'

Gode rolled her eyes. 'Without solid proof? The feud between Oswy and me is well known. What he did to my sister means that he will never be an honest man in my eyes and my lady knew that.'

The need to protect Lady Alwynn filled him. He pushed it down. He would do what he could, but he had to leave at the summer's end. Even staying that long was a risk.

'And you think she will heed my advice?'

'You keep up the good work and I will make sure your secret goes with me to the grave.'

'My gods have turned their backs on me.'

She tilted her head to one side. 'Because you went into the sea?'

'No, when I failed to save my friend from being slain in his sleep. I broke an oath,' Valdar admitted. 'The gods do not easily forgive such men.'

'It seems to me that the men who slayed him were the ones who broke their oaths, but then what do I know?' Gode gave a near-toothless smile. 'I am but a simple old woman.'

'You are anything but simple.'

She gave a cackling laugh. 'There is more to you than a pretty set of shoulders, Warrior. That is good.'

'I will take that for a compliment.'

'Now, my lady has decreed that you be made fit for work in the shortest possible time. Off with your tunic.'

Valdar eyed the evil-smelling poultice. 'Do you think it will work?'

'It has never failed me before.'

He winced slightly as Gode applied the medicine. But the pain was rapidly replaced by a cool burning sensation. Whatever it was, it felt as though it was actually doing something. He did feel better.

Gode put her finger to her lips. 'My lady comes. I will have your promise, Northman. Nothing about my little bother. No need to worry her. She has enough to keep her occupied.'

He blinked in surprise. Gode had sharper hearing than he'd credited. But he, too, could hear the slight cracking of twigs and the delicate hum of Alwynn's voice. His heart ached to see her.

He ruthlessly ignored it. Starting something between him and Alwynn was a poor idea. It was simply because she had saved him. If it suited her purpose, she'd betray him and he could never trust her to give him her heart.

His father's words echoed in his ears: a witch had cursed his grandfather that neither he nor any of his descendants would ever find love. Any woman they loved would never love them back.

He and his brother had refused to believe the pronouncement. His brother had been happy until his untimely death. And Valdar's sister-in-law had grieved, but had confessed after her husband's death that she wasn't sure she had loved his brother in the way she should have done.

Valdar had taken a chance that the curse had lost its power and had fallen hard for Kara. But

Kara had only sought friendship and a way to keep her home for her son. She'd never given him her heart. He'd been too blind to see her holding back, always giving an excuse why it could go no further than a few kisses and chaste hugs until their wedding night.

Kara's leaving him on their wedding day had ached worse than any physical blow he'd received. And it was then he knew the curse retained its power.

He grasped Gode's arm. 'Will you tell her? Give me the truth, instead of riddles.'

The old lady's gaze held his. 'When the time is right, but such things come best from the source. No woman likes to think her lover has kept secrets. But of course they do keep secrets. Always.'

'We're not lovers, the Lady Alwynn and I,' he replied. 'And are never likely to be.'

'Not yet.' The old woman laughed. 'But I saw how you watched her and she watched you. My lady is entitled to a bit of happiness, but I don't want you breaking her heart. Promise me that as well.'

Valdar silently cursed under his breath. Gode was far too perceptive. But desiring Alwynn was different from doing something about it. Alwynn was a lady, not some common hedgerow wife. 'I don't understand…'

'Will you tell my lady about me? About my illness?'

Valdar regarded the old lady's sallow complexion, understanding finally. 'I have no intention of doing so.'

'Underestimate me at your peril, Warrior. You treat her right and you will have no trouble from me.'

'A threat?'

'Fair warning.'

Alwynn entered. Today she wore a dark green gown which set off her dark hair and made her eyes seem the exact shade of the sea on Midsummer's day. His heart did a slight leap at the sight of her. He ruthlessly stamped it down.

Once the harvest came in, he would make his way northwards. Alwynn wouldn't grieve when he was gone.

Something ached deep within his gut. No one would grieve. No one ever would. His sister-in-law and nephews might be sad if he never returned, but for a few weeks only. They had their lives and he had been away a long time.

There was no one waiting for him like Kara, who had carried Ash in her heart until his return seven years later. Most women didn't give their heart like that.

His mouth twisted as he thought of his mother, how she'd waited until his father was on a voyage and then she'd divorced him, leaving him for a warrior his father had considered a close friend.

All women were alike and he would allow no woman close, least of all a woman who could betray him so completely and so utterly.

'My lady, an unexpected pleasure.'

Chapter Six

Alwynn stopped on the threshold when she saw Valdar was up and moving about. She'd half-hoped that he would have remained in bed and that Gode would need some assistance.

'Is something wrong, Valdar? Gode? You both are wearing guilty expressions.'

'My lady?' Gode asked, giving Valdar a significant look. 'When have I ever hidden anything from you?'

'That is no answer. Valdar?'

Valdar instantly pasted a smile on, but she saw the troubled glance he gave Gode.

The pair were definitely up to something. Maybe it was good after all that she'd come here, instead of supervising the weaving.

'I feel better than I have since I arrived here. All appears to be healing.' He inclined his head. 'Thank you for asking.'

'Your warrior is an admirable patient.'

She nodded as the pair continued to stand stiffly without saying anything.

She cleared her throat as the silence began to stretch. 'Gode seems to have everything under control, even down to making the knit-bone poultice.'

Gode beamed, the first genuine smile she'd seen from her in a long time. 'I still know my way around a sickroom, my lady. I was the one who first taught you the potions.'

'How could I forget my old teacher?'

'The poultice smells rancid,' Valdar commented. 'Surely something could be done about that?'

'It appears to work better that way,' she retorted. All the ease between them from the other day appeared to have vanished. She concentrated on the table with its multitude of wooden bowls and cups. Maybe she had simply imagined it and built it up in her mind. He had no memory of the kiss they had shared. He'd been fevered and probably thought he'd been kissing the woman whose name he'd cried out…Kara.

A dagger twisted in her stomach. She knew what Theodbald had thought about her, how she had nothing to offer a man beyond her lands, and the memory of his words rose unbidden in her mind. Valdar probably thought she'd trapped him into this.

Gode curtsied. 'It does the job. If you were dead, you would not be able to smell it.'

'Beyond the smell, I've no complaints,' Valdar said rapidly.

'Gode will take it under consideration…for the next time. Perhaps some lavender or rose petals?'

'I'm not planning on getting hurt again.'

'No one ever plans for it. Sometimes it just happens.' She tilted her head to one side. 'Why were you standing in the doorway earlier?'

'If I told you that I wanted to make sure no one was coming for me, would you believe me?'

Something died a little within her. A tiny part of her had hoped that he might be watching for her. She was behaving like a young maiden, not a widow with a stepdaughter and many responsibilities. 'Now that I see everything is under control, I should go. The weaving…'

'Stay!' Gode said, moving between her and the door. 'The weaving can always wait. I need you here to keep an eye on our patient. I fear if he is not watched, he will do too much and cause more injury to himself. You know he threatened to repair the thatch on the roof.'

'When the time is right…' Valdar's laugh sounded like liquid gold.

Alwynn narrowed her gaze. Gode surely couldn't be matchmaking. She wouldn't put it past her nurse. And she hated that Gode was obvious about it as well. As if she needed someone to matchmake for her! She was happy as she was, far happier than when she'd been married to Theodbald. Love and desire were things which happened to other women, or in bard's songs.

'Why? What do you have to do?'

'My doves. My darling doves. If you will excuse me, I need to see to my doves. I have been away from them too long. It will take but a moment.'

'Doves?' Valdar asked.

'Gode keeps doves instead of chickens.'

The old woman laughed. 'They are far more reliable, my lady, and they look good on the wing. But I haven't paid them enough attention since I returned. I had our patient to think of. Now that you are here, I will take the opportunity.'

Gode practically ran out of the room, slamming the door behind her.

'I hardly need a nursemaid,' he said, turning his back on Alwynn. 'You may go. When I am well enough, I will make my way to the hall to get my orders.'

Her cheeks flamed and she turned towards the table, pretending to rearrange the bowls. So much for Gode's matchmaking. Valdar wasn't interested. Inwardly she cringed. Why had she hoped that he would be different from Theodbald? She knew how plain she was—far too inclined to speak her mind and her neck and hands were all out of proportion. Then there was her failure to do the one thing required of a woman of her class—bear a living son.

'Gode has decided you are her chick and need looking after. I'd hardly like to be on the wrong side of her.' She stacked the bowls for a third time. 'I stay for her sake, rather than yours.'

'Just as long as you know I don't need it.' His voice flowed over her like honey. 'I'm healing rapidly. When I'm well, there will be time enough to discuss your estate and what needs doing to it. If the rest of the buildings are like this one, there will be plenty to keep me busy.'

'Are you always this stubborn? Whatever must your wife think of you?'

'I have no wife. No children.'

She dropped a bowl and it rolled across the floor to Valdar's feet. 'Oh.'

He handed her the bowl back. Their fingers

brushed and a tremor went up her hand. 'Some day. My sister-in-law is always after me to settle down.'

'Sisters-in-law can be like that.' She cleared her throat. 'That is to say, I hope you do find a wife one day.'

'When the time is right...' He tilted his head to one side. 'Are you tired of being asked about your plans to remarry?'

She inclined her head. 'We will speak of something else, then.'

'Choose a subject.'

'Oswy obviously has spread the word about my new steward. I had a visit from Lord Edwin. He explained his misgivings.' She tossed the pestle from side to side as she rapidly explained about her meeting with the man.

She placed the pestle down awkwardly. Valdar rescued it and put it back on the table, being careful not to touch her this time. Inwardly she cringed. She had been far too obvious. He was being kind.

'What was the true reason he came?'

'He offered again to take Merri for fostering. Apparently I don't provide her with the right opportunities, but I know what will happen if I do. Merri would hate it and she'd...'

'Did this happen to you?'

'The only part of my marriage which was good was finding that little girl.' She shook her head. 'I won't lose these lands. They were part of my dowry.'

'Why do you blame yourself?' Valdar asked. 'Gode told me about how you saved the estate.'

'Gode is biased.'

'You give yourself too little credit.'

Her anguished gaze met his. Valdar's insides twisted. Here was a woman who was trying to do the right thing.

Without thinking, he pulled her into his arms. For a brief heartbeat she rested her head against his chest. He hated how right she felt and he knew in his heart that his dream about kissing her had been real.

She wasn't looking for anyone. She had made that very clear. And it would be wrong to start anything. Alwynn was not the sort of woman you took for one night. She was the sort of woman who needed more than he could offer.

'Why would Lord Edwin want to foster Merri or take your lands?' he asked against her hair, which smelt of sunlight, wild flowers and her.

She lifted her head and he forced his arms to fall away. He had no right to hold her, no right to ask anything of her. Once she knew who he truly was, any desire would fall away. She stepped away. 'I refused an earlier offer of his. A less-than-honourable offer.'

It was easy to guess what sort of offer it had been. An unaccustomed surge of anger and jealousy swept through Valdar. He wanted to run his sword through the man. Instead he concentrated on breathing steadily.

'I see,' he said when he felt he could control his emotions. When he was a boy, his father had taught him that a good warrior does not give in to his emotions. It was only through detaching himself that he could fight effectively. Uncontrolled emotions had no place in his life. He had to put duty above everything, including any woman. The gods had given him a second chance when they had washed him up on these shores. But their purpose had been so that he could right a wrong done to his friends, not to end his family's curse.

'I hope you do.' Her direct gaze met his. 'I am not in the market for becoming some man's plaything. I have worked too hard to give up my independence…for any man. The one good thing about my husband dying is that I have gained a sort of freedom. I am not about to give it up. I've no intention to remarry or to be forced into a convent.'

'In my experience, it is best to wait to be

asked.' He made a bow. 'In case the other party takes offence.'

'Our relationship must be chaste.' She tugged at the neck of her gown. 'What happened just now…me in your arms. It can't happen again. Ever.'

'What did happen? I held a woman in my arms who was upset because she'd been betrayed and needed comforting.' Valdar tightened his jaw. Alwynn was rejecting him as surely as Kara had done. At least she was being honest about it, but there had been something about the way her eyes darkened when she was in his arms. 'I would do the same for any woman. My sister-in-law, for example.'

'Or the healer?'

'She doesn't need my help, not any more,' he said far too quickly as he waited for the ache which always came when he spoke of Kara these days. He silently cursed. The ache was a tiny niggle, almost unimportant, but certainly not the great empty ache he was accustomed to. He had carried the weight of it around for so long that it had become a part of him and now it had gone.

'Are you sure about that?'

'Her husband became a friend after he saved my life in battle,' he explained. 'She followed her heart and chose the right man for her. It took me a little while to see it, but she comes alive when her husband is nearby in a way she never did around me.'

'I see. I apologise for speaking bluntly, then.' She made a mock curtsy. 'I doubt I will need any comforting. Our customs are different from yours. In my country it is unusual for a woman... for a woman to behave as I did. I didn't want you to get ideas. At court they whisper that I am as cold as stone. But I have only done what I had to do to protect my stepdaughter and her inheritance. That is my sole focus now.'

He caught her arm. A tremor went through him, rocking him with its intensity. He concentrated on breathing steadily. Cold as stone? Hardly. Heat as intense as a blacksmith's fire rushed through him.

The family curse was real—he always fell for women who could not return his affection.

But he had learnt his lesson; he would slay the curse by never giving his heart, by doing what the gods had given him a second chance for. Avenging Horik's murder and bringing Girmir to justice.

'No need to apologise. Know that I would do nothing to dishonour you. I've pledged my sword to you and your family. My duty comes first.'

His insides twisted. His duty should have

come first several weeks ago. He should have anticipated the potential for treachery. But there was no need to tell Alwynn of his failings as a warrior.

'For this summer…' Her lips quirked up in a smile. 'It promises to be a quiet one. I doubt your sword arm will get much use.'

'For this summer,' he agreed. He knew then he would seek to defend her as best he could, even to the point of dying. And the knowledge frightened him. He had learnt from his past mistakes. If she discovered his heritage, she'd betray him to her king. The gods had given him a second chance to put things right. And he never mocked the gods.

Alwynn walked quickly away. She had been a thousand times an idiot to go and check on Valdar while she was still upset about Lord Edwin and she should never have rested her cheek against his chest or listened to the steady thump of his heart. She struggled to remember the last time she had felt that safe.

He'd been the one to take his arms away. It was obvious that he had no desire for her. Her mouth twisted, remembering all the cruel things her husband had called her.

'My lady!' Gode came hurrying after her.

'You left too quickly. Before I finished with the doves. You didn't ask about my niece and her new daughter.'

Alwynn halted her steps beside a large oak. The summer sun filtered down through the green leaves as Gode gave a long account about her niece and the latest addition to the family. It shouldn't hurt hearing about other people's babies, but it did. The familiar knot of longing in her stomach started.

'Valdar is doing well thanks to your nursing,' she said to distract her thoughts away from the babies she'd never hold in her arms.

Long ago before her marriage, she'd envisioned having the nursery full. But the cradle had stayed stubbornly empty. Theodbald proclaimed it was her fault; after all, he already had one child. She had to wonder if she had been cursed.

To her, Theodbald had appeared the perfect hero on their wedding day. Someone to keep her safe from the storms and protect her lands. Nothing had turned out as she'd hoped. And she'd learnt a hard lesson about the futility of believing in dreams and heroes.

'The warrior is an easier patient than most.' Gode glanced over her shoulder and lowered her voice. 'Did you discover where he is from?'

'He told me the name of the place when we arrived at the cottage. He made no secret of it.' Alwynn shrugged. Gode did not even know where Mercia was. She would not have heard of Raumerike either. Valdar was no demon in human form. He was far too kind and considerate. 'Anyway, the threat from the Northmen has been exaggerated according to Lord Edwin.'

'And you are spouting that jumped-up nogood's opinions now?'

'Who am I to judge? Valdar swears that though he comes from another land he comes in peace. Thus far good fortune seems to follow in his wake and I could use some of it.'

The tension went out of Gode's body. She suddenly seemed like a frail old woman. Her hands went about her stomach. Alwynn thought again about insisting Gode consult one of the monks. But every time she mentioned it, Gode found an excuse.

'There I am inclined to believe him. He did smoke out Oswy, the old fraud. And not before time. For that alone, I would be happy to kiss his feet.'

'You and Oswy the Blount have been at loggerheads for years.'

'I am honest and he is less so.' Gode rolled

her eyes. 'He promised my sister much and left her with little.'

Alwynn pressed her lips together. She had heard the story of Gode's younger sister being left at the altar since she was a girl. And Oswy told another tale. 'Away with you. You should allow the past to stay there.'

'As you do, my lady? I haven't heard you singing in a long time, but I could almost swear I heard a hum emerge from your lips earlier today.'

'Now your hearing is going.'

Her old nurse's eyes narrowed. 'Your cheeks are flushed and your eyes are brighter. Who made them that way?'

'Honestly, you are worse than Merri. I've no time for such things. I have an estate to run. Save your tales for the children and the kitchen maids.'

'How is a tale going to come true if you won't believe in it?'

Alwynn bent down and picked up a handful of dirt. 'This is what I believe in—the land and my responsibility towards Merri and my people. Nothing else matters.'

'The trouble with you, my lady, is that you are only going through the motions of living. What your husband did to you was awful, but allowing him to kill your spirit is worse. Stop being afraid to live, really live.'

'I've no idea what you are talking about, Gode.' Alwynn picked up her pace. Theodbald's death had opened her eyes to real life. This was real life. 'Once the estate is saved, there will be time for other things.'

Alwynn's mouth tasted of lush promise—sun-lit hills and blue skies. Her body was soft and yielding beneath his. Her skin was smooth and tender. It was as close to paradise as he had ever come or was ever likely to come. He knew and he also knew he wanted more.

He cupped her face beneath his hands.

'Who are you, Valdar?' she whispered. 'Before we go further, I need to know.'

He knew he had to tell the truth before anything happened between them.

'I'm from the North,' he whispered against her lips. 'And I want to love you. I want to do right by you. Let me.'

Instantly the dream changed. Her cry echoed in his ears and she dissolved into nothingness. He looked at his hands and they were covered in blood.

A circle of people grew around him. He recognised the faces of dead comrades. They drew back and Horik appeared, hollow-eyed with torn flesh, accusing him of neglecting his duty, of not honouring him. Of allowing Girmir to go unpunished while he was forbidden from entering Valhal. People must know his story and the truth about Girmir and how he behaved.

Valdar woke with sweat pouring from every part of his body. The message from the dream was very clear. He had to avenge Horik. He had to return to Raumerike and confront Girmir.

And yet, he found it impossible to erase the sensation of Alwynn's lips and her body against his. Every time he closed his eyes, he saw her face and remembered how her body had melted into his for an instant.

One summer was all he asked of the gods so he could honour the life debt he owed her.

The only hope was to work hard until he fell into a dreamless and exhausted sleep.

Chapter Seven

'**A**re you ready to show me the estate or is now not a good time? You seem to have made all sorts of excuses.' Valdar's low voice startled Alwynn as she tried to sort out the various wool sacks several days later. Ever since her confrontation with Gode, Alwynn had been reluctant to return to see how Valdar was doing. Instead she had sent orders via Merri and other farm workers about the rethatching of the hut and the clearing of the barn nearest Gode's cottage.

'Excuses? I've been busy sorting out the return of the betrothal presents. Merri has kept me informed of your progress.'

Besides learning about his progress on the estate, it was clear from the reports that Merri was suffering from an advanced case of hero worship. No one could look that good or accomplish that much in a short space of time. There had to be a flaw in Valdar. Heroes only existed in tales told around the fire on a winter's eve. And if she started to believe otherwise, she would go back to being the same naive woman who had blindly married Theodbald.

She risked a glance at Valdar, who was dressed in clothes which had belonged to her late husband. Although they were about the same height, Theodbald had never filled them out in the same way. The tunic drew attention to Valdar's broad shoulders and the narrowness of his waist. His Frankish sword hung at his side. One glance told her that he was a warrior, but she also remembered the man who begged her to kiss him in the middle of the night.

'I hadn't expected to see you today. Merri said that you were going to inspect the manor farm's cattle.' She made a nervous gesture and sent a stack of spindle whorls tumbling to the ground. She pressed her lips together. 'Clumsiness is not becoming in a lady...' she stuttered out.

She stooped to pick them up, but he was there before her, returning them to the wooden box. 'Maybe you are a person who things happen to.'

Their fingers touched. Her entire being tingled with an awareness of him. She instantly withdrew her hand.

As she did so, she caught a look in his deep

brown eyes which stole her breath away. She wondered that she ever thought them just brown. There were flecks of gold, green and deep brown, all swirling together. And then there was the shape of his mouth. It begged to be tasted.

Her heart pounded in her ears and her lips parted softly. She wanted to lean forward. She wanted to feel his skin against her fingertips.

The sound of a dog barking and Merri's laughter jolted her back to reality. She retreated two steps.

Silently Alwynn cursed her dreams from the past two nights and Gode's outrageous suggestion that somehow she hadn't been to blame for the utter failure of her marriage. If she wasn't careful, soon she'd start believing in impossible things like the thirteen treasures of Britain again.

She made a show of straightening her kerchief and tucking all the escaping tendrils away.

'Shall I put these here?'

'They belong over there. I like things to be tidy and organised.' Alwynn pointed to a shelf behind her, noticing that her cheeks had suddenly become hot. She hoped that he would put the heightened colour down to working in this stuffy room.

He crossed a bit too close and she was aware

of the power in his shoulders and how his body had felt against hers when she had helped him from the beach. And yet he carried the spinning whorls as delicately as if they had been precious glass.

After he had put the bag of whorls on the shelf, he turned back to her with an expectant expression. Belatedly she realised that she had been staring.

'Are you sure you're up to it? Going around the estate, I mean?' She winced as the words left her mouth. They made her sound far too breathless.

'My powers of recovery have always been remarkable. Kara…' He stopped. 'Others have commented on them.'

'Kara? That was the healer? Yes?' Her insides twisted. The woman he'd thought she was when he kissed her so passionately. Kissed her as if he'd meant it.

'I mentioned her to you?'

'The first day…' Alwynn gulped. She could hardly confess about the kiss she'd given him.

'Ah. I see. I wasn't myself.' He inclined his head. 'I apologise.'

For what? For kissing her? For not remembering? Alwynn glanced everywhere but at his face. Finally she cleared her throat to break the silence.

'Anyway, how do I know you won't collapse?' she asked and fixed him with a stare.

'I laid a new thatched roof yesterday without difficulty.' He wrinkled his nose. 'Even if I wasn't fully fit, I would say I was in order to prevent Gode from insisting on another poultice. The stench turns my stomach.'

'Gode knows what she is about. She might not be able to grow herbs as well as I can, but she knows their uses.'

'I will take your word for it.' He lowered his voice. 'And I am fresh out of adventure tales for your stepdaughter.'

'Merri needs to concentrate on improving her weaving and learning how to spin without breaking the thread. She knows enough tales for two lifetimes. She even believes the thirteen treasures of Britain exist, from Diwrnach the Giant's magic cauldron to Drynwyn the sword.'

'She swears she no longer needs Clydno Eiddyn's halter as she has the horse she most desires.'

Alwynn shook her head. 'You try very hard to keep children from being disappointed, but one day she will be. And it will be worse if you keep stuffing her head full of new tales.'

'Tales can sustain you when times are hard.'

'Tales can blind you to reality.'

He caught her elbow. 'Is that what happened to you? Why did you stop believing?'

'I grew up.' She pulled away from him. 'We can do a quick tour of the hall and I will introduce you to the servants. Not many needed now.' She gave an artless wave of her hand and hoped he wouldn't hear the pain in her voice. 'I lost the hall. The king decided that he would be better served by Lord Edwin controlling the *maenorship*. And the *maerdref* became his.'

'Why didn't your late husband ensure you were looked after? Or is it the custom in Northumbria not to look after widows?'

Alwynn opened her mouth to give a polite lie, but then she noticed his expression. 'There were debts,' she said. 'I didn't know how many until he died. But they are paid now. I am hopeful that Merri will have a decent dowry when the time comes. She is the closest thing to a child that I will ever have.'

'And all this is for Lady Merewynn's dowry?' He waved his hand towards the sacks of wool.

'It is early payment for the quarter rent on the various hides.' She gave a feeble laugh. 'Goodness knows what Merri said about you or how Oswald twisted it. But suddenly the farmers are paying their portion before time. And thus far, they refuse to take it back.'

'Or maybe they want to ensure that they stay in favour with a good landowner,' Valdar said quietly. 'Because they have seen what Lord Edwin can be like. I have been listening as well as telling tales to Merri. Gode knows what is happening in the area.'

Alwynn gave him a sharp look as she beat down the fierce sudden hope which sprang within her. Could the explanation for all the early rents be tenants expressing their relief that she intended on staying rather than their fear of Valdar's wrath? 'What do you mean?'

'Fear will only get you so far. Maybe they wanted a sign to prove you intended to stick around. You had not bothered to replace the steward, yet a steward is necessary to run an estate when the landowner is away or unable to collect the debts. In these dangerous times tenants look to men with swords for protection.'

Alwynn ran her hand through the nearest sack of wool. Valdar had a point. Certainly Edwin had not bothered staying. He and his men had left two mornings ago with banners fluttering in the wind and the sacks of wool had started arriving soon after that. 'Why would you say that?'

'They know nothing about me or my reputation.'

'Do you have a ruthless reputation?'

His face became shadowed and hardened to planes of granite. When he looked like that, Alwynn had to wonder how many battles he had seen. Who did he fight for? Who was Raumerike aligned with? 'If I do, would I share it with you?'

'You will not behave ruthlessly with my people! They are finally free of one oppressor.'

'Your late husband?'

'He disliked anyone crossing him,' she admitted.

A tiny smile tugged at his mouth. 'Are you so ready to believe the worst of me? Is it because of your husband?'

Alwynn hugged her arms about her waist. How to admit that she'd turned a blind eye for so many years? And that she'd kept giving excuses because she'd thought he loved his daughter and was doing his best for them as a family? It was only after Theodbald's death that she even realised what sort of cruel man he'd been. 'I know little of you, but I suspect that you are not afraid to use your sword.'

'Knowing how to use a sword doesn't make a man a brute.' He tapped his heart. 'What makes a man is within here. Without a code, all men become like the animals. A man must keep to his code or he risks losing everything.'

Alwynn wished she could take the pain from him. Whatever had happened to make him jump off that ship must have been something truly terrible. And she knew deep within her that he had not abandoned his friends.

'You are alone in the world?' she asked instead.

'I have nephews and a sister-in-law, who pokes her nose far too often into my business. However, she says that she runs it better than I do.'

'Do you have a large estate?'

A muscle jumped in his jaw. 'A reasonable size. My father ensured it. I do know how to run an estate, my lady.'

Alwynn stared at him. Merri's proclamation that he was an atheling was maybe not so far off the mark. 'You are a prince, then, in your country?'

She watched the shutters come down on his face. A tiny pang went in her heart. She much preferred his face when it showed warmth. Whatever his past was, he wanted to keep it from her. She concentrated on a spot behind his head. That was fine with her. She understood about secrets. There were some things about her past that she wanted to keep hidden.

'Nothing like that,' he said before she could make a meaningless comment about what needed to be done next. 'I farm, I trade and I serve my king when called on. I leave the politics to someone else.'

'If Raumerike's politics are anything like Northumbria's, you are wise.'

'I had my fingers burnt once,' he admitted with a shrug.

She released a breath. The moment of danger had vanished.

'Is that why you were on the voyage? Because of her? Because of the healer you knew?' The words spilled from her like a sore that she couldn't stop picking. This Kara person should make no difference to her, but she hated that the woman had some sort of hold over him, that in his mind he had been kissing that woman instead of her that first night. 'My apologies. You don't need to answer that. None of my business.'

He picked up a whorl and tossed it in the air before neatly catching it.

'Partly.' His voice was barely louder than a whisper but gathered strength as he went on. 'We needed new markets. Our traditional ones are being closed down. But I wanted to go. It was harder than I thought seeing her happiness and knowing that it had nothing to do with me.

I was happy for her. There was just an ache inside me which would not go away.'

'Did you find any new markets?' she asked when she trusted her voice.

'A very poor voyage, but the crew should return home and report my death. My sister-in-law knows what is to happen. There will be no reason for her to fear for her estates.'

'But once you return, they'll know you're alive.'

His face broke out into a heart-stopping smile which tugged at a place deep within her. She wished that there wasn't this attraction between them.

'Yes, they will. Everyone will.'

'That pleases you?'

His smile widened, but his eyes became remote. 'I will be able to find out if there was a gnashing or wailing at my funeral. Who sang the lament. Who fainted.'

'How like a man! Do you expect it?'

He looked at her, all humour vanished from his face as if it had never been. 'Who would weep for me?'

She put a hand on his shoulder and felt the hard muscles shift under her fingertips. 'Someone will. Someone always does if you have a good heart.'

He blinked twice. 'And you think I have one?'

'I'm sure you do.' Alwynn knew as the words tumbled from her throat, she spoke the truth. He did have a good heart and probably had not deserved whatever had caused him to separate from his crew.

'Thank you for believing in me, even though you are a healthy sceptic.'

'It is an instinct I have.' She gestured towards the door. 'Let's begin the tour of the hall so you can begin work properly now you have recovered.'

He bowed low. 'I'm grateful for the trust you put in me. I won't abuse it.'

'That is good to know.'

Valdar followed her out of the storeroom. He had thought the pull she exerted over him would go once he had healed and become strong again, but seeing her just now, he had wanted to take her into his arms. It was as if Kara had never existed. The great aching hole he had carried around for so long had vanished as if it had never been. He wanted to believe that the curse had indeed lost its power as his brother had claimed.

He listened with half an ear as they toured the estate and Alwynn pointed out various parts of the land and storehouses. It was obvious that Alwynn was trying hard. There were a couple of things he'd organise differently, but on the whole she was very capable. At last he could understand why she was reluctant to hire a steward.

'If you will follow me, I will show where I keep the ledgers.'

Alwynn's words jolted him back to the present and his own precarious situation. Ledgers. She expected him to be able to write and read. He had no problems with runes, but Northumbrians used an entirely different script.

By the time he caught up with her, she had gone into the small steward's room. It had a variety of inkstands and rolls of parchment strewn about. A bit of candle stood in one corner. Alwynn went over and opened the shutter, allowing the sunlight to filter in.

'We should start with the latest rolls, so you get an idea of how the records are kept. The method is quite straightforward. I am sure you will pick it up in next to no time.'

'I look forward to it.'

Her step faltered and she glanced back over her shoulder. A frown marred her smooth brow. She placed the roll of parchment down. A light faded from her eyes. 'Are the ledgers a problem?'

'Will you expect me to write? I can speak

Northumbrian, but it is not a language I have written before.'

He silently hoped that the Northumbrians kept records in a different language from the Franks, but he had a sneaking suspicion that they both used Latin—a language which he could read, but had trouble writing.

'Are you saying you can't write?'

'Can most warriors?'

She pressed her hands together. 'If you give me a verbal report every day, I can write it down. But the ledgers must be kept up to date.'

'Impressive. An educated woman is rare.'

'My mother had visions of grandeur for me. I was supposed to return our family to greatness since my older brother died before I was seven. It also helps to keep stewards honest.'

'In what way?' Valdar picked up the roll. Two different hands had made notations. He assumed Alwynn was responsible for the later entries. If so, she wrote with a fair hand.

'How do you think I discovered the discrepancy in the first place?' She rolled her eyes. 'My husband pretended that he knew how to figure and read, but he didn't know more than a few words. He was simply clever at asking and then accepting. Of course, he never allowed me to see the ledgers as I was a woman.'

'Then he was a fool.'

'Yes, in more ways than one. It is a pity that I didn't see it until it was far too late.' She took the parchment from him. 'A verbal report will do. Every evening. I will fill in the details. I will not have the king taking my lands using the excuse that my records are not properly kept.'

Valdar concentrated on breathing steadily and not taking her into his arms. Last night's dream had been full of anxiety about what would happen when she discovered he couldn't keep written records. And it seemed she had expected it.

'Will you teach me?' he asked before he lost his nerve. 'It will be a good thing to know.'

She blinked in surprise. 'If you can stand being taught by a woman.'

'If the woman was you, I'd consider it an honour.'

She tucked her chin into her chest but her being positively glowed. Silently Valdar hoped her late husband was suffering for what he'd done to her.

'We can begin tomorrow. After you give me your first report.'

'So…did you? Attain the grandeur that your mother longed for?' he asked to distract his thoughts. He had no business feeling possessive about this woman. He needed to think about what he owed other people. It was odd how in a few days they felt far less real than the woman who was standing in front of him.

'My mother died disappointed, but I think my father was pleased. He wanted the match. It suited his purposes for the estate and I was young.' A sad smile touched her lips.

Valdar realised that he wanted to take the sadness away. He wanted to make her eyes sparkle as they had a few heartbeats ago. He concentrated on the parchment and the promises he had made to his dead friends. The gods demanded he fulfil his duty. Until he had done that, he had no right to want the things a normal man would want. He had no right to hope that the curse had been lifted.

'These things can happen. More often than you think. Sometimes it works out.'

'I only found out after we married what my husband was truly like. He had bedded my friend and she was in thrall to him and desperate that her husband not discover the affair.' Her knuckles were white where she clenched the writing quill.

Giving in to impulse, he leant over and eased the quill from her fingers. 'I hope that is not your late husband's neck.'

A quick smile flickered across her face. 'It

was only after he died that I discovered the full truth. I'd had some misgivings, but I hadn't been aware of the full extent of the mismanagement. I had been living in a rose-tinted dream world, seeing only what I wanted to see and not enquiring too closely about the rest.'

'Maybe some day people will respect a woman for her brain, rather than looking towards a man with a strong arm.' Silently he swore that he would be there for her. Telling her the truth about his heritage would only complicate matters. She needed his skill. He could leave this estate viable and then he would have done something, paid back the life debt he owed her, but he knew he would still worry about her and he would never forget her. The realisation shocked him to the core.

'You are trying to make me feel better about the wool and the flour.'

'A bit,' he admitted with a shrug. Silently he thanked the gods that she hadn't guessed his feelings. 'You have to stop punishing yourself.'

'It is working.' This time her smile was like the pure sunlight coming out after a long spell of rain.

'Did Gode speak with you? When you visited the other day? Is that why you sent Merri instead?' he asked, wondering whether the old nurse had let slip anything about his true origins.

Gode had said very little to him after Alwynn had left and he dreaded facing the horror in her eyes when she did find out.

Her face went bright red and he knew she had been avoiding him. Something to do with Gode. 'You must pay no attention to my nurse. Everyone knows that she is moon-touched. Some days she is better than others, but she is liable to say things which have no meaning.'

He stepped forward. Had Gode already told Alwynn? Or had she spoken in riddles? He hated that the hope sprang in his breast. Maybe the gods were with him and he could enjoy some happiness. 'What did she say to you, Lady Alwynn?'

Her eyes flickered everywhere but on his face. 'I should be getting back to where the women are working. There are a thousand things which could go wrong.'

'Alwynn, what did Gode say to you?' He put out his hand. 'Surely you can trust me with that! If we are going to work together, we need to trust each other. If she has done something to upset you, let me know.'

Alwynn spun about on her heel, knowing her face flamed. The last thing she wanted to do was tell Valdar about the conversation with Gode and her proposition that she make him her lover. She mistimed her step and her arms circled several times in the air.

His hand came out and caught her about the middle before she fell. He hauled her against his strong body.

She forgot how to breathe, looking up at him. Her entire world seemed to come down to this instant. She wanted to go on staring at him and the curve of his lower lip, but she also knew it would be a bad idea. And how could she confess about Gode's suggestion? Particularly as it felt so right to be in his arms. 'I…I…'

'Hush.' He bent his head and his lips touched hers, gently but with firm intent.

The wild fire which had inhabited her being that first night had merely been banked, lying there glowing, waiting its chance. Her entire being fizzed and she knew she wanted more. Her body arched towards him.

She collided with his hard chest as his arms tightened about her, deepening the kiss still further. She sank into the warm, deep taste of him. Her memory of his mouth did not do it justice. This time she knew he was kissing *her*, not some ghost of a woman who had broken his heart.

His mouth trailed from her lips to the sensitive part of her neck and back again. A moan emerged. From her throat? From his? She didn't know which. But the sound was enough to give that tiny sane part of her freedom.

She stiffened and pulled away, making a show of straightening her dress.

What did she think she was doing? Kissing in this room of all places? Anyone could walk in on them.

'You are supposed to be my steward, not...'

'Not what?' He reached out a hand and trailed her cheek. 'Your lover? What would be the harm in that? If it is something we both want?'

His words flowed over her like honey.

She resisted the temptation to turn her lips into his gentle touch. Theodbald's touch had never been gentle, not even in the days when he had been courting her. Then she had been too young to understand anything. Her head had been turned by a warrior actually paying attention to her and she had never thought to question why.

'Don't touch me, please,' she whispered instead.

His hand fell to his side. 'Is there some reason? Tell me you feel this as I do. I dream about you.'

'A kiss. Nothing more.' Her mouth pulsed as she said the words.

'Look me in the eyes and say it is nothing.'

She lifted her chin and stared directly into his dark gaze. She wanted to drown in his eyes. It was worse now, knowing precisely how his mouth had moved against hers. But someone had to stop this madness.

All the vile abuse Theodbald had flung at her echoed around her brain. The last thing she wanted was for Valdar to see her the same way, to learn of her barrenness and her failures as a wife.

'I am looking and my answer remains the same.'

'Can you tell me why?'

'What you ask is impossible. I need you as my steward. I've no need of a lover, despite what Gode might have told you.'

He tilted his head to one side and his eyes became unfathomable. 'Is that what she spoke to you about?'

She blinked twice. 'Did she put you up to this? Ask you to be kind to me? Pity the poor lonely widow? It is the sort of thing she might do. Well, I don't need your pity or anyone else's! I can manage just fine on my own.'

A muscle jumped in his jaw. And she knew she had hit a raw nerve. His entire face changed. From lover to warrior in the space of a breath.

'I do my own courting,' he ground out. 'Always have done. I have never had any need to ask anyone for advice. And I've kissed women for many reasons, but never out of pity.'

'I'm sorry if I offended you.'

'You're a beautiful woman, Lady Alwynn. I refuse to lie about that.'

'Thank you for saying that, but I know I'm not.'

He watched her for a long heartbeat. 'Some day, my lady, you will tell me who hurt you and who made you afraid. Know that if it is within my power, I will keep you safe.'

She turned her face away from him. 'That day will never come. You may go now.'

He inclined his head. 'Forgive *me* if I acted inappropriately. I am your steward. I was given to understand you might be receptive...'

'From Gode?'

'I know little of your customs. Women in my country are free to act as they please provided they are not pledged to another.'

She closed her eyes. He was a stranger here. And she had acted wrongly.

'It isn't you. It is me. I should have confronted Gode and I didn't. I regret that she put any ideas into your head.' She gave a half-smile. 'My only need from you is for a steward who will help me run this estate.'

'Is that what you truly desire?'

Her heart beat rapidly and she was certain he must know the lie. But it was either that or risk everything she had worked so hard to protect for a few moments of passion with this stranger. 'Yes.'

She heard his footsteps as he left the room and released a long trembling breath. Her fingers touched her aching lips. She'd done the right thing sending him away.

Alwynn woke from her sleep with a dull ache thrumming in the apex of her thighs, making her long for a warm muscular body to curl up next to. Not just any body, only Valdar's.

Her brain clung to the final remnants of the dream. The raw, wild images in her mind, the memories of how Valdar touched her in her dream and where his lips had kissed her, shocked her. She'd woken to find her hands at the apex of her thighs and her undergown tangled about her body.

She gingerly touched her mouth. It tingled as if he had just kissed her.

She flopped back against the pillows with a

sigh. Dreams were just illusions. They had no basis in reality.

The reality was that Valdar would be leaving. He had a home across the sea. And her home was here. He wasn't a hero from some mythical tale, but a real person. And real people disappointed you. The only person she could count on was herself.

If she allowed her brain to become muddled with dreams, she'd lose everything.

Chapter Eight

The day had gone better than Valdar had hoped. He had worked harder than he'd worked since he'd been an unbearded boy trying to prove himself on his first voyage. To the casual observer, he was certain, it merely looked as if he were dedicated to his job, rather than trying to avoid Alwynn.

For the most part, Alwynn's tenants were pleased to see him. Several confessed they worried about Alwynn, being without a warrior and at the mercy of Lord Edwin. No one had a kind word for Edwin or indeed Alwynn's late husband, Lord Theodbald. He was more convinced than ever that her late husband had abused her in some fashion.

That she had come through the abuse and saved the estate as well as looking after her step-daughter only made her more desirable in his eyes. He found himself thinking about her and wondering how she was doing at odd moments during the day. Did she think about the kiss in the same way he did?

One of the older women had asked him outright if he had thought about marrying Lady Alwynn. He declined to answer. Staying here was not an option. Once they discovered who he was, they would all turn their backs on him, particularly Alwynn.

Valdar frowned. Right now, his main concern should be this farmer and the missing sheep. One of Alwynn's tenants had reported that his sheep had gone missing and he wondered if Cleofirth the Plough had had anything to do with it.

This farm had a different feel about it. Cleofirth the Plough was a gaunt man with eyes which never rested. But it was his wife who concerned Valdar more. She was pretty enough, but she sported a fresh bruise on her right cheek and moved as if she expected the next blow to land at any moment.

While he never hesitated in battle, he knew he would never strike a woman. It would be against his code. Warriors fought warriors. They did not make war on children or women. He knew some, like Girmir, disagreed with him but it was the way he'd been brought up.

'You won't mind if I look around just to reassure Owain. It may be that I can spy a few places where your security is a bit lax,' he said, spying the slight cringe the woman had given. He'd have a quiet word with Alwynn and Gode to see if his fears about Cleofirth's wife were justified. And if they were, he'd try to figure out a way to keep the farmer from using his fists against a helpless woman again.

The farmer made an insolent shrug. 'If you want to…I don't know what my lady could be thinking of…hiring a foreigner as a steward. She could have used the brother of Lord Edwin's steward. Now, there is a steward who understands.'

'What do you know of him?'

'There is no law against sharing a drink after finishing a hard day's work in the fields. He comes from around here, so he knows what's what. And I've been well pleased since my lady sold this farm to Lord Edwin.'

Valdar raised a brow. The man deserved to be pummelled for what he'd done to his wife. 'I want to inspect that barn. The one you wanted me to hurry past.'

Alarm showed in the woman's sunken eyes. 'Stewards don't usually inspect that barn. You told me that.'

'Lady Alwynn's new steward is checking the barn, my love,' the farmer said, giving a hearty chuckle. 'I won't have Owain blackening my good name in this village.'

The woman's cheeks flushed, revealing that she might have been pretty once. 'You said that no one was going to look at that barn. You weren't going to allow it.'

'You know what poor simple creatures women are. She hasn't been right…well…since she lost the bairn to be honest.' He gave a simpering smile. 'It is all right, pet, Lady Alwynn's steward needs to do this. He won't disturb anything. There ain't anything to harm. You run along and let the men handle this.'

Valdar wanted to wring his neck. And he silently vowed to make sure Alwynn knew about the wife's plight. In her herbs and potions, there might be something that could help the poor woman. But it could be that she was indeed touched by the gods.

He watched the woman's retreating back. Somehow he would find a way to help, if possible.

'The barn if you please.'

'Here you go.' The farmer swung the door open. 'For a steward, you are not very talkative.

I was going to suggest sharing a tankard of ale, but I presume you are in too much of a hurry.'

Valdar raised a brow. 'My lady would take a dim view of such behaviour.'

The farmer's face flushed. 'No harm meant.'

'No offence taken.'

The surprisingly small barn was empty except for the fresh hay piled up against the wall. Valdar walked outside and checked that his eyes had not deceived him. From the outside it appeared as if it should be much larger.

The farmer watched with a slight insolent grin.

'Do you only use this during the wintertime?' Valdar asked, keeping his face carefully neutral. He thought he could hear the faint baa of a sheep, but he couldn't be certain.

'The cows are out on the pasture in the summer. Sheep as well. It is how we do things around here.'

'And the straw? Any particular reason why it is piled against the back wall?'

'Best place for it.' The farmer rubbed his hands together. 'Now, if you have seen what you need to…'

Valdar walked over to the straw and a vague memory surfaced. His father used to tell a story about a man who had a series of trapdoors and secret hiding spaces in his storerooms. It made no sense to have the straw there. He tilted his head, listening, trying to catch the sound of baaing sheep again. Nothing but his instinct told him that there was more to this than the farmer wanted to share. 'What else is the barn used for?'

'Nothing in the summer. In the winter, I keep the animals in here. My lady knows all about the arrangement. I am one of her better farmers— or I was until she had to relinquish these lands to pay her debts. Lord Edwin approves as well.'

'I see. Then you won't mind me moving the straw. I want to be able to give a good accounting of myself to Owain and my lady.' Without waiting for an answer, Valdar walked over and began to move it away.

The farmer began complaining about how Lady Alwynn never questioned him and what a liar and braggart Owain was. Lazy and unreliable. Because he wasn't from around here, Valdar might not be aware of his neighbour's reputation. On and on.

The vague irritation Valdar had grew. He might not know Alwynn very well, but instinctively he knew she would not stand for a man using his fists on his wife. He concentrated his anger on moving the straw quickly.

In a few heartbeats, Valdar could see the

outline of a door hidden behind the straw. He stopped. The sound of shuffling feet and baaing could be clearly heard. 'And you say there is nothing behind here.'

The farmer's eyes widened. 'I could have sworn...'

'There are sheep behind that door.' Valdar drew his sword. 'Would you mind explaining who they belong to?'

'Wife!' He added a few other choice phrases, each filthier than the last. 'Where did these sheep come from? What have you been hiding from me?'

Valdar clung on to his temper by the slenderest of threads. It was not worth removing the man's head from his shoulders, a treatment he was sure the man richly deserved. He also couldn't touch a man who wasn't his lady's tenant.

The woman appeared in the doorway and sank to a low curtsy.

'I was asked to put the sheep there by my husband. I guess I did it wrong.' The woman visibly flinched at the farmer's tone. 'I... That is...we know nothing about it. We never do anything to harm my lady. It is all our sheep. I wanted to hide them from the Northmen.'

'The Northmen?'

'They are demons in human form who steal sheep and take them back to their homeland.' She glanced at her husband for confirmation. 'Everyone knows that. Now that Lord Edwin and his steward have gone to protect the king...'

'The Northmen travel across seas in boats. What need do they have of your sheep? Where would they put them on the boats?' The words burst from Valdar before he had time to consider.

'How would I know what they want them for!' she exclaimed. 'All's I know is that they take 'em.'

Valdar's jaw ached from holding back his temper. If he continued on, he would make enemies, not friends. Northmen stealing sheep? What a lie! And Alwynn needed to be here to see the woman and assess her injuries. She also might be able to get to the bottom of the mystery in a way he couldn't. This man and his wife had been her tenants until recently. She would know the whole story.

Valdar refused to consider that he'd missed Alwynn.

'Very well, we go to the hall and fetch my lady and see what she thinks of the sheep.'

The farmer puffed out his chest and flexed his knuckles. 'What are you accusing me of? Those are my sheep. I ain't going anywhere. You can't make me.'

Valdar drew his sword and held the point of it under the farmer's chin. 'Can you prove it? In my country we mark sheep to show which flock belongs to which farmer.'

'Aye, we do that here and all,' the woman said.

'Hush your mouth,' the man retorted and lifted his fist.

Valdar caught the man's wrist. 'No. Your wife has the right to speak her mind without fear.'

'Lady Alwynn shall hear of this high-handed treatment!' the man whispered. 'I promise you. You will be out on your ear for spreading lies about a respected member of the community.'

'We fetch her together. Owain as well. I presume he knows his sheep when he sees them.'

'My lady. This new steward of yours, he is impossible.' Cleofirth the Plough stormed into the hall, closely followed by Valdar.

Alwynn blinked in surprise to see one of her former tenants visibly upset. Valdar should not have been anywhere near that farm. This was her fault. She had deliberately not been getting involved in his day-to-day activities. She'd hoped that her blood would cool if she avoided him for a few days. 'What is the problem?'

'He behaves worse than any Northman.' Cleofirth threw his hands up in the air. 'Go on, ask him what he has done. I demand compensation for blackening my good name! Those are my sheep, not Owain's! There is a simple explanation.'

'Then why did you hide them behind a secret door in your barn?' Valdar shrugged, seemingly unconcerned, but his bulk filled the doorway. Her heart did a little leap to see him. 'It seems odd for a man to hide sheep in a room behind a pile of straw if they belong to him.'

'It were on account of the Northmen, my lady...'

'Sheep stealing isn't one of the crimes I have heard laid at Northmen's feet before.' A muscle jumped in Valdar's cheek. 'However, I am always willing to learn about these monsters from people who seem to know them so well.'

Alwynn put her sewing down as her maids began to gossip. There was no mistaking Valdar's sarcastic tone.

Her heart sank. She had given Valdar instructions to go slowly and now this. Sarcasm and accusations of sheep stealing. Cleofirth was one of the most prosperous farmers in the area and had a reputation second to none.

In one way, she had been sorry to sell that

particular hide of land. Although he was a good farmer, she had never liked his bluster nor been impressed by the rumours of his heavy fists on his hired hands. But she couldn't afford to alienate her neighbour's tenants, plus every time she spoke to Urien, his wife, she spoke of how hard her man worked and how pleased she was to have found him.

Urien had worked at the hall until her marriage and the couple seemed happy enough, despite Urien's repeated miscarriages and the loss of their baby girl last winter. The familiar hollow opened within Alwynn. She had not been able to find the words to comfort Urien. The last time they'd spoken, the woman had begun sobbing uncontrollably. And after that Alwynn had avoided her.

Cleofirth had assured her that, though his wife was fragile, they did not need any help.

'What is the precise problem?' she asked.

'This farmer believes that he can keep sheep hidden in a secret room behind piles of hay— sheep which most likely belong to one of your farmers—and claim them for his own,' Valdar answered, crossing his arms. His entire being glowered. 'I suggested that he might like to take his complaint directly to you, since he doesn't trust a foreigner to do his job properly.'

Alwynn held out her hands.

'What would you have me do? Lord Edwin would be the one who would normally handle this type of complaint.'

'I believe you should come out to the farm and see what is going on. Make up your own mind. We can all look at the markings on the sheep to see who they truly belong to.'

Alwynn tilted her head to one side, confused. 'Good idea.'

'This farmer objected although he believes you will back him.'

'Is this true, Cleofirth?' A hollow opened within Alwynn. She had been avoiding going out there ever since Urien had lost her baby girl. What could she, a barren woman, say to Urien, who had lost a much-longed-for child?

The man's ears went red. 'I may have been a bit hasty in my speech, my lady. No man likes a stranger to question his honour like this here steward is doing. You should have had a steward from around here, one who understands local ways.'

'My lady's choice of steward has nothing to do with the sheep that are hidden in the barn!' Valdar thundered. 'Will you allow me to look into that storeroom or not? See what else is hidden there?'

'I don't see the point,' Cleofirth said with a curl of his lip. 'My word should be good enough. They are my sheep. Like I said, you might not understand our marking system, being a foreigner and all. Here, my lady, you tell him I was a good tenant to your late husband. He never had any trouble from me. I paid what I owed on time.'

'Will you allow my lady to inspect your barn?' Valdar asked in a silken tone. 'You can have no objection to my lady viewing the sheep with her own eyes.'

'In the late lord's day, my word was good enough.' Cleofirth held out his hands and screwed up his eyes. 'My lady, why would I try to hide anything from you? Owain is always losing his sheep. You know that as well as me. Every year, he complains someone has stolen his sheep and that is why he needs more time to pay his rent. To have your new steward brand me as a sheep stealer is insulting.'

'But that still doesn't explain why those sheep were hidden and why you swore to me that all your sheep were out on the fields,' Valdar said, his accent becoming stronger with each word he spoke.

'Maybe your steward's grasp of our language isn't good. Him being foreign and all.'

A muscle flickered in Valdar's cheek. 'I understand well enough.'

Alwynn pasted on a placating smile. 'My steward has my full support. If he asks for a credible explanation for hidden sheep, then I see no reason for you not to give it.'

'He is a foreigner. He could be a Northman for all I know. Set to murder us all in our beds. A spy! He could be selling the information for gold.'

There was an inward take of breath and all eyes turned towards Valdar. With his height and flowing hair, she could see why he might be taken for a Northman. But being from this place called Raumerike didn't make him a Northman barbarian. She felt sure of it.

'Cleofirth! Remember to whom you are speaking. Are you questioning my judgement?'

'A thousand apologies, my lady.' Cleofirth wrung his hat between his hands. 'In your husband's day, proper stewards were hired. Not strangers from a strange land.'

Alwynn pressed her lips together and counted to ten. In her husband's day, the steward had been crooked, but she could sympathise with Cleofirth. Since the Northmen's attack, there was a natural wariness of strangers. She wanted her tenants to see her as a fair mistress, to respect her and her judgement. But they also had to know that her steward, despite being a foreigner, had her support and that they needed to obey him.

She glanced up at Valdar and had the strange suspicion that he had manipulated this so that she would have to go out. She wished she knew why he was doing this, but she had to trust him.

She stood and pressed her hands together. Silently she cursed the dream for putting ideas in her head. Valdar was not interested in her as a woman. 'Perhaps it would be best if I went to inspect the sheep. It is bound to be a simple misunderstanding. Then when Lord Edwin returns, a full account of the matter can be put before him with me as an expert witness. Surely you are not going to accuse me...'

Cleofirth gulped twice. 'No, my lady. I merely didn't want you to have to make an unnecessary journey. Urien tells me how hard you are working these days.'

Alwynn frowned. He made it seem as if she had seen Urien recently, but it had been months. 'It has been a long time since I saw your wife. How does she fare?'

'She is doing well. As you know, the loss of the bairn in the new year hit her hard.' Cleofirth's face crumpled slightly. 'Hit us both actually.'

Alwynn's heart squeezed. She should have gone to offer comfort to Urien, but she had not known what words to say, and besides, they were no longer her tenants. 'I hope she will visit my hall one of these days.'

'When she feels up to it. It is a struggle to get her to go to church, to be honest with you.'

'Then you should have allowed my new steward to investigate and determine whose sheep they are to get this matter over and done with. I would hardly want to have a dispute between my steward and someone as important as you, Cleofirth the Plough.'

Cleofirth gave a self-satisfied smile. 'I want no more than justice.'

Valdar met her gaze. It was obvious that he wanted her to go to the farm. She gave a mental sigh. She had hoped to hide in the hall and forget that the kiss had happened, but she would have to get this problem sorted. She would have to go out and spend some time alone with Valdar.

When they arrived at the farm, Cleofirth took them directly to the barn. Alwynn was surprised that Urien did not come out to greet her, but

Cleofirth had informed her that Urien was having one of her bad days and wanted to be alone.

Alwynn inwardly winced. The last thing she wanted to do was intrude and make Urien's suffering worse, particularly as Cleofirth appeared to be so concerned about her.

Valdar had seemed unsurprised by the announcement, but did remark about how he had enjoyed meeting Urien earlier. He gave Cleofirth a strange look.

'Are you going to tell me why you asked me here?' Alwynn said in an undertone. 'I doubt it was to see a hidden storeroom filled with sheep. You could have forced the issue if you thought they were indeed Owain's sheep.'

'And started a feud with your neighbour's tenant? I think not,' he answered quietly. 'This needs to be done with you. Cleofirth has to see you are in charge so he cannot deny what happened later to Lord Edwin. Plus, you need to see his wife.'

'What do you hope to find?'

'Honestly? I hope for nothing, but I suspect that there is more than meets the eye. If I am right, he should be thrown off this land for sheep stealing.'

'This had better be good. Cleofirth is well thought of and Lord Edwin will be displeased if

I accuse one of his tenants without proof. He is the king's instrument of the law in these parts.'

'If you will come over here, you will see the difficulty,' Valdar said in an undertone. He moved some of the straw which had hidden the small trapdoor. 'The barn is slightly too big on the outside for its size on the inside.'

She stared at it for a long moment, trying to recall if she had seen it, before turning back to Cleofirth. 'What do you say about this? Is there a secret room?'

The farmer had the grace to go beet-red. 'I'd forgotten it was there. It is quite a small storage space. My wife's uncle had used it to store turnips. Your steward is making a mountain out of a molehill. No doubt in time he will learn our ways.'

'Then it should be empty. And there is no reason not to show it to us. Valdar may be new here, but it is no excuse for you to refuse a reasonable request from my steward.' She gave both of them a look.

'I don't know how the sheep got there. Honest. But I am sure they will all bear my mark.'

'If you don't know how the sheep arrived there, how can you be sure that they belong to you?'

Valdar put his shoulder against the door and

it opened with a loud creak. 'You need to see this, Alwynn.'

The large storage area was full of sheep and sacks of wool. Alwynn's mouth dropped open. She recognised various notches in the ears which were not Cleofirth's mark.

'It would appear you have a problem, Cleofirth. The third sheep to the left sports Owain's notch, not yours.'

Cleofirth's mouth opened and closed. 'Owain's sheep must have wandered on to my land and got mixed up with mine. You know how careless he can be. I know my rights. I demand to see Lord Edwin. He is the law in these parts. Not this here foreign steward. Lord Edwin is my overlord now.'

Cleofirth the Plough was far more prosperous than she'd considered. Silently she kicked herself for not inspecting the farm more closely before selling the title to Lord Edwin. She knew Cleofirth had been good friends with her former steward. She clenched her fists, hating that she had been naive and ready to believe the best of everyone.

Cleofirth had had Urien plead a poor lambing season last year and all the while he'd been amassing this. If he had paid the proper amount due, she would never have had to sell the land.

Her stomach ached and she stumbled from the barn. She drew deep breaths of fresh clean air, hating that she had made another mistake.

'How long have you been keeping things back?' Valdar demanded. 'How much have you cheated? Where I come from, men have had been deprived of their lands for less.'

'I didn't want the Northmen discovering all my secrets,' Cleofirth began pleading. 'A man has to make preparations.' He gulped twice. 'That is…I knew nothing about the sheep. Urien…'

'Valdar is my steward, Cleofirth, not a raiding Northman. Urien does not farm here. You do,' Alwynn said in a measured tone, but her insides churned. 'Lord Edwin will hear of this. It will be up to him to administer the proper punishment.'

Cleofirth rubbed the back of his neck. 'Some of Owain's sheep might have become mixed with mine. During the storm, like. I haven't had time to sort them and then I heard your steward was poking his sharp nose in. I panicked. A man is allowed to make a mistake. But it were Urien who did it originally. I won't have my name blackened.'

'Shall we see about getting Owain's sheep returned to him?'

It made her blood boil that Cleofirth had used

her in this way. She concentrated on breathing steadily. Her mother had taught her many years ago that giving in to her temper solved nothing. It was important that she appeared calm and confident, even if she wanted to shake him. 'Why did you hide this behind the straw? Why did you say that you would be unable to make the full rent because of two poor years? How long has this sheep stealing been going on?'

Cleofirth adopted a face of injured innocence. 'It was an accident. My wife has already confessed. I panicked when I heard your new steward was coming looking for sheep and things. My wife will back me up.'

Valdar looked at her and slowly shook his head. She understood the unspoken message. 'Where is Urien? Is she even here?'

'She is in the house.' Cleofirth ran his hand through his thinning hair. 'Look, it is a simple misunderstanding. The room must have been here since before my time. I honestly thought it was just a few mouldy turnips not worth bothering with.'

'Lady Alwynn should question Urien without you being there. In the interests of justice.'

Alwynn caught Valdar's gaze. He wanted her to see Urien on her own. Alwynn's stomach knotted. How much had she allowed to go unnoticed?

'Somehow I doubt what you say, Cleofirth. You came to me accusing my new steward of being unjust, but it was you.'

He tugged at his collar. 'It will not happen again. I'd…I'd forgotten about the sheep being in there. An honest oversight.'

Alwynn turned towards her new steward. Valdar's face was implacable and his hand rested lightly on his sword. She was grateful that he was there and willing to back her up. 'Valdar, I would like a complete inspection of this farm. I want to know precisely what has been hidden. How many other sheep have accidentally made it into this fold. A full accounting will be given to Lord Edwin when he returns. Cleofirth, you go with him. I will see Urien. She is an old friend.'

'It would be my pleasure,' Valdar said.

'I have done right by her, even though she lost the bairn she'd been carrying. Third one since we married and then there was my little girl who died of the fever last winter,' Cleofirth called out. 'I swear that woman is cursed.'

Ice-cold fury entered Alwynn's soul. All the things they whispered about her.

'The child and your marriage to Urien was

one of the reasons why my husband gave you this farm, do you remember?'

The man flushed red, but refused to answer.

Alwynn walked quickly over to the farmhouse.

'Urien, I've come to see you,' she called out. 'After all this time…'

Urien stood beside the fire, stirring the pot. 'My lady. It was me who done wrong with the sheep. I feared the Northmen would come and take them. They have before, like. My man is trying to cover for me. I herded them wrong during the storm and what with one thing and the next, there hasn't been time. None of them died, like. I knows some of them is not ours, but promise me Cleofirth won't be punished for something I've done.'

Urien burst into tears.

Alwynn went over and put her arm about Urien's shoulders. The woman was far too thin. Urien shivered slightly and drew away from her. 'It will be sorted. I believe Owain simply wants his sheep back. He is not seeking to press charges. Neither am I. But the law must be upheld. It will be for Lord Edwin to decide when he returns.'

'That is good to know.'

'You should come outside with me. It has

been far too long since we sat and talked. I've missed that.'

'I have the supper to be seeing to, my lady.' Urien gave a quick curtsy. 'Begging your pardon and no offence intended, but my man likes a hot meal at the end of the day.'

She pointedly went back to stirring the stew pot and keeping her face from Alwynn's.

Alwynn crossed the small room and looked closely at Urien's face. The bruising was clear and it appeared at some point she had had other injuries. Alwynn swallowed hard, hating that the woman had not felt able to turn to her. 'Are you going to tell me who did this? Or do I have to guess?'

Tears filled the woman's eyes. 'It were my fault. It happened when I was milking the cows. I'm so ashamed about it. Right clumsy I am. Everyone will think...' She reached out and grabbed Alwynn's hand. 'He is a good man. He has been good to me. Most of the time. And I wanted to let you know that the bairns I lost, they were his...not as some said... I've never had another man.'

Alwynn's throat closed. She curled her fingers about Urien's. In her heart she wondered if Urien was telling the full truth about her injuries. 'If I had known about your face, I would have brought some salve.'

'I'll mend. I always do.'

'It is no trouble. I grow my herbs to be used, not to collect dust.'

Urien gave a tiny smile. 'Your concoctions are always welcome. But send someone else. You will be too busy at the hall. There is always so much to be done.'

Silently Alwynn promised to send Merri to visit in the morning. It was very possible Urien would say something to Merri as Merri could worm a secret out of a snail shell. 'If you ever need it, you know there is place for you at my hearth. No questions asked.'

The woman gave a tremulous smile. 'Begging your pardon, my lady, but you have enough troubles of your own without me adding to them.'

'Hush now.'

'Urien refuses to leave,' Alwynn said in an undertone when she rejoined Valdar in the farmyard. 'She wants to stay with her man. Goodness knows why, but she does.'

'Do you believe her story about taking the sheep because of the Northmen?' he asked.

'I don't know what to believe. She certainly seems to fear the Northmen. She could have done it. Owain just wants his sheep returned so he can pay his rent. Cleofirth does have Lord Edwin's ear. And if it was Urien, how can I demand a punishment? The poor woman is suffering. And if Lord Edwin decides against me, then he would be in his rights to demand compensation for one of his tenants being kept off his land all summer. We will make the king's tribute, but I don't want this.'

'She needs to get away from him.' He raised a brow and Alwynn knew precisely what he was thinking. There was no way that a woman could have moved all that straw on her own, particularly not a woman who seemed as slight and fragile as Urien. 'She needs to leave with us.'

'But I just explained…'

Valdar jerked his head towards where Cleofirth lounged, his face growing smugger by the breath. 'I suspect he will beat her tonight. Instead of sheep borrowing, we might find she has an "accident" and takes all the blame with her to her grave.'

'Possibly, but I can't force her. She is a free woman.'

'She can stay with Gode until this mess is sorted,' Valdar said. 'Sheep stealing is a crime and Lord Edwin is away. There should be a trial.

And since she has confessed, you take her to a safe place.'

She blinked up at him and a tiny smile tugged at her mouth. He understood her dilemma. 'Where will you sleep?'

'At the hall.' His face became grim. 'I've seen your retainers. You need protection, my lady, and my arm is strong.'

Something twisted within Alwynn. It had been far too long since anyone had offered protection without strings.

'Warriors like to be in a household where there is a chance of advancement. They left... after Theodbald died.'

Valdar put his hand under her elbow. The little touch did much to reassure her. 'Think about it as rescuing that woman from a beating or even from death.'

Alwynn nodded. They made a good team in a way that she and Theodbald never had. 'I agree.'

She walked over to Cleofirth, who lounged against a doorway, but straightened once Alwynn approached. 'We are just about finished here. Owain has claimed his sheep. He doesn't demand punishment or compensation.'

Cleofirth gave her a baleful look. 'I told you your steward was making a nonsense out of this.'

'However, Urien is coming with us.'

'Why?'

'You have accused her of sheep stealing and she has admitted hiding the sheep, including sheep which did not belong to this farm.'

'To keep them away from the Northmen,' Cleofirth said. 'Many fear the Northmen's raids!'

'Since when do Northmen steal sheep?' Valdar asked and there was no mistaking the underlying steel in his voice this time. 'They attack churches and take gold, but not livestock. Not even in countries which border their lands.'

'She will need to stay under my protection,' Alwynn said firmly. She had to admit that Valdar was right, now she thought of it—while Northmen did take gold and attack monasteries, she had never heard of them stealing livestock to take back up north.

A small voice inside her asked her how he knew such a thing. She ruthlessly silenced it. Where he came from, they probably had the same sorts of problems with the butchering Northmen. He'd said that he had lands back home—perhaps he had also experienced their brutal raids.

She lifted her chin and concentrated on Cleofirth. Now was not the time or place to be questioning Valdar. She knew who the culprit was. 'When Lord Edwin returns after the law-giving, then we can sort this mess out. He will not be pleased to learn of this. Tenants who commit crimes cannot go unpunished.'

Cleofirth gulped twice. It was clear that he wanted to object, but didn't dare. 'When Lord Edwin returns, it will be cleared up?'

'Yes.'

'It might do her good. She ain't been herself since…' His voice cracked. 'I've always tried to do right by her, but I won't be hanged for being a sheep stealer. It was Urien which done it. Not me. I would be willing to undergo a trial by ordeal to prove it as well.'

'Shall we go?'

As they went away from the farm with Urien carrying her small pile of belongings, Alwynn's heart clenched. Valdar had rescued Urien. It would be easy to fall for him, but it also would be the biggest mistake of her life.

She had to remember what Theodbald had called her. That she had no right to happiness. All her children had withered in her womb.

She had to stop believing that a hero would come and rescue her. Valdar was not a magical warrior sent to right wrongs. He was a man who stayed because he owed her a life debt and he would be leaving when the autumn winds arrived. The trouble was her heart was having a hard time believing it.

'You seem very thoughtful. Is there anything else that needs to be done?'

She rapidly composed her face. 'Owain thinks you are a hero. He doesn't know of many who would go against Cleofirth. He's been known to use his fists.'

'A strong sword arm normally beats a pair of heavy fists.' Valdar caught her chin between his fingers. 'And you have my arm.'

Chapter Nine

'Gode was happy to accept Urien. She thinks you will be better served with me closer now that I have healed,' Valdar said, appearing in the hall's garden, where Alwynn was busy tidying the plants. She had retreated there after they returned. Her place of sanctuary where few dared venture. She might only have established the garden after Theodbald's death, but already it had flourished.

The perfumed air hung heavy and she could almost taste the rain which would surely come.

The entire hall buzzed with talk about Cleofirth's comeuppance and Urien's rescue. There would be thunder before nightfall. The shadows were already long, stretching over the beds. Soon she'd have to go back into the hall and face the whispers and gossip.

A number of the women blamed Cleofirth,

but she blamed herself. She should have visited the farm and looked properly at the barns after her husband died. She had known Cleofirth and her former steward had been as thick as thieves. All she had done was to allow Lord Edwin to become stronger.

'Will she stay there?'

'She understands what is at stake. Gode has promised to look out for her. Gode will find an extra pair of hands useful.'

'What is that supposed to mean?'

'Your old nurse is slowing down,' he said finally.

'There is little I can do about that. She refuses to move in here and neither will she allow me to examine her. I will always be the pupil in her eyes.' Alwynn sighed. 'Cleofirth beats his wife, but it is not against the law.'

'It should be.' Valdar also sighed. 'Right now she wants to return to her home as soon as the misunderstanding is cleared up.'

There was nothing she could do to force Urien without demanding a trial and the inevitable punishment that would follow. She could tell that Valdar was not happy about the situation either.

'More reason to distrust Cleofirth,' Alwynn murmured. 'It is a far worse problem than I suspected. I blame myself. It was very easy to accept his word and I had no wish to intrude on Urien and her grief.'

'Once you know about a problem, it can be solved.' His face became hard. 'We will find a way of keeping her safe. She will be fine with Gode. Gode seems to have a way with injured creatures.'

'What would you suggest I do?' she asked, hugging her waist. 'Edwin will do very little. The sheep have been returned and Urien accepts the blame. I suspect Cleofirth will try to take Urien back and she insists that she wants to go. You saw how she clung to him when we left.'

'Give her a few days. She may speak out once she feels safe.'

Alwynn concentrated on the rosemary. 'I hated looking into her eyes. They are so dead now, so unlike the girl I knew before her marriage. Urien was so full of fun. If there was any mischief about, Urien was sure to be in the thick of it. She made us all laugh. I honestly thought she was happy. I hate myself for believing him. But she won't leave him.'

'A hard fist caused those bruises.'

'For now, she swears that a cow kicked a bucket into her face when she was doing the milking yesterday morning. Clumsy, but not un-heard of. And she swears that she put the animals there and then panicked when she heard you were searching for missing sheep.'

He raised a brow. 'Do you believe that?'

'Until she tells me otherwise, I have to give her the benefit of the doubt.' Alwynn concentrated on pulling up a weed, rather than meeting Valdar's eye. She could hardly confess about the rumours which had swelled about Urien before she left. 'She kept going on about what a wonderful husband he is and how good he is to her. She blames herself for not having any surviving children and she swears that they were all his.' Alwynn's voice trembled on the last word. 'I wish…I could make her stay with us, but the law of the land won't let me. She belongs to her husband. She swears that she doesn't want to become a nun.'

'Where I come from, women can divorce in the event of such behaviour.'

She tilted her head to one side and the tiny seed of doubt stirred again. What sort of Christian country allowed such a thing, except when a woman had a calling to join a religious order? The only pagan countries were across the sea to the north and he wasn't a demon in human form. Of course he was a Christian. Alwynn pushed the thought away.

'In Northumbria, things are different.'

'We will figure out a way to make sure she is safe. I will check the farm tomorrow. There has to be some evidence implicating him as the one behind the sheep stealing.'

'I had planned on sending Merri with some salve if Urien had still been there. She has sharp eyes and could have reported back. But we shouldn't go again. He might make things worse for her when she does return.' Alwynn blinked back tears. 'I feel dreadful. I should have noticed the barn size a year ago. I should have demanded to see her after I heard about her loss. The Urien I knew wouldn't turn away from people. She needed people.'

Valdar put a hand on her shoulder. The touch burnt through the layers of fabric. It took all of her will-power not to lean into him and draw strength from him. She wanted to believe that he didn't judge her.

She concentrated on a clump of lavender just behind him, rather than looking at him directly. If she stared into his eyes, she would do something completely wrong—like kiss him or throw her arms about his neck and seek the comfort of his body.

'The important thing is that you noticed now and are taking steps.' His velvety voice rolled over her. 'We will solve this before I leave.'

Alwynn stepped backwards and nearly stumbled on a tree root. Valdar's hands were there instantly to hold her up. The now-familiar tingle went through her, pulsating and insistent. But she kept thinking about the great hollow which had opened up within her. She found it difficult to believe how well matched they were, yet he was speaking of leaving. She knew he had a home and lands to return to and it was what she'd told him she wanted. It was the right thing, but she was tired of doing the right thing.

'My feet are steady now. Your going is still several months away.' She forced a smile. 'You promised.'

'And I will keep my promise.' He let go of her elbow, but stayed close to her. His eyes creased with concern. Every particle of her being was aware of him.

'Did your husband ever hit you, Alwynn?' he asked in a low voice. 'Is that why you think you should know the signs? Why do you consider you are to blame for this?'

She wrapped her arms about her aching middle.

'The way he hurt me doesn't leave physical scars,' she said before she could think. 'He wanted to force me into a convent so that he could marry again. Someone who could give him children. I refused to go. I've no calling for a religious life. And I stood to lose everything, my dowry and all my land. I couldn't abandon Merri to another woman. Losing one mother is hard enough. I love that girl as if she was my own.'

Valdar gently lifted her chin so that she met his dark gaze. 'What did he do?'

'Names don't draw blood. Words don't cause purple bruises.' She took a deep breath and forced a smile. 'It no longer matters as he is dead and unlamented.'

'But they hurt and they leave wounds inside you.' Valdar touched her arm. 'Trust me, my lady. I know when someone is hurt and I can guess who did it. You are worse than a nervous horse. Until you forgive yourself, you allow him to have power over you.'

She glanced up at his face and knew he'd guessed some of it. The words tumbled from her as she sought to explain. 'Theodbald blamed me for being barren. He called me all sorts of things. I desperately wanted children. Twice I thought maybe, and once I thought there was a quickening, a little flutter of movement, but I was proved wrong two days later when I lost the babe. Oh, how I wanted them. At first, all was sweetness, but as the months and years went by, he became more and more cutting until in the end he avoided my bed. There was a rumour he was going to force me into a convent, but he had an accident and died before it happened.'

'Did he have any other children? Besides Lady Merri?'

Alwynn frowned and turned her head away. She refused to listen to a tiny spark of hope. Could it have been Theodbald? 'Not that I know of. There was some talk about Urien right before the marriage, but today she said that she'd only ever been with her husband and I have to believe her.'

Alwynn stared at the thyme. She had encouraged the match between Urien and Cleofirth as she had been jealous that Urien might have a child, her husband's child. It had been wrong of her and Urien had been abused.

'I should never have allowed the match. There were rumours about his fists. He drinks far too much ale.'

'You thought she might be pregnant with your husband's child.'

'She swears not.'

He raised her chin and she found only sympathy. 'Then it might not have been your fault. Men as well as women can be barren. This is well known where I come from. Why it should be any different in Northumbria, I have no idea.

It takes two to make a child. And two to make a happy marriage bed.'

She gave in to impulse and laid her head against his chest and listened to the steady beat of his heart. Did it really matter that he was going in a few weeks? She needed the comfort of his arms now.

Overhead she could hear the distant coo of wood pigeons. The faintest of summer drizzles bathed her. He gently moved them under an oak's spreading branches.

For how long they stood there with her head against him, she could not say. His arms came about her waist and gathered her closer.

She glanced up and there was something in the depths of his eyes.

Her hand went around his neck and brushed back his hair from his face. Groaning, he lowered his mouth and claimed her fully.

This time she was more than ready to meet him and this powerful urge which grew inside her. She opened her lips and accepted him, drawing him fully in and rejoicing in the clean taste of him.

The nature of the kiss changed. It became far more urgent, calling to a dark place within which she had not known existed until his mouth touched hers. She moaned in pleasure as the heat blossomed inside her.

'Shall we stop? Shall we go back into the hall and sit amongst the others speaking of nothing of consequence, pretending we are strangers?' he murmured, pulling back slightly so she could see his passion-filled eyes.

Her heart expanded. He was giving her a choice. But she also knew if she refused him this time, there would be no going back. She knew then that she wanted to go forward. She needed more than a simple meeting of lips. She wanted his touch on her skin. She wanted to be made new. The last thing she wanted was for him to stop.

'Why should we? No one can see us here. We were strangers once, but not any longer.'

She touched the high planes of his face. His flesh was sun-warm and infinitely exciting. He nibbled her fingers, one by one.

'But your pledge? What of that?'

She gave a shaky laugh. 'My pledge of not kissing you seems feeble. Barely a day has gone by and I've broken it. Utterly and completely. I want more from you. Madness, I know, to hope, but there you have it.'

'Madness?' He kissed her palm. 'You are maddening, but it is not madness to want you.'

'You want me? I thought…'

'Everything you thought before was wrong. The world has been reborn for me. For you. Out here in this garden, it is only Alwynn and Valdar, no one else.'

'Truly?'

His eyes turned serious. 'You have nothing to fear from me. Ever. We go at your pace.'

'I know that.' As she said the words, she knew they were true. He might be a warrior, but there was an inner goodness and strength in him. 'I have never feared you.'

'My fair summer lady.' He pressed kisses against her cheeks and brow. Little nibbles that made her feel alive. She arched towards him, encountering his hardened arousal. He wanted her! All the poison Theodbald had whispered seemed to be drawn out of her with each new touch of his mouth. She had never imagined it could feel like this to be touched. So alive and on fire. She had been encased in ice and stone before.

Now she understood why poets spoke of love and maids whispered in corners with shy smiles and longing glances towards their lovers. But she didn't want to be just the recipient of his kisses and touches as she had been up until now. She wanted to participate. She wanted to make him burn.

'I want this to be different.' She cupped his face with her hands and returned the kiss. This time her tongue traced the outline of his mouth, demanding entrance. She tasted and explored.

'Different is good,' he growled.

'I've dreamt of you,' she confessed, ducking her head. 'Each night. The dreams grew.'

'Good dreams or bad?'

'Interesting and intriguing dreams.'

'Then you should see me.' He undid his cloak and pulled his tunic over his head. His skin gleamed golden in the late afternoon and was far better than any of her dreams.

Several silver scars decorated his torso, but they added to it rather than detracted. She ran her forefinger along one of them, tracing it from start to finish. The muscle was firm but pliant, making her want to explore. Always before she had wanted things to be over with as quickly as possible, but with this man she wanted to linger.

His nipples puckered. She rubbed her palms over them, marvelling how they felt and how the burgeoning heat deep within her increased.

His faint scent of pine and something uniquely him rose about her and held her within its intoxicating embrace.

Her breasts ached for his touch and the secret place deep within her burnt with an all-consuming fire. All her hard-won control seemed to be slipping through her fingers like water through a sieve. She drew a low breath and tried to bid the dizziness to go.

'Do I pass? Do I match your dreams?' he asked with a husky laugh.

She tried for a matter-of-fact tone of voice, something to help her regain her distance. 'You have healed very well. No scarring from the battering you took in the sea.'

'I wear my scars with pride. It means I've survived the battle.'

'Is everything a battle with you?'

He captured her hand and raised it to his lips. 'Most of my life, but it has made me cherish the good times. And you are one of the good times.'

Her heart fluttered and began whispering dreams. She tried to silence it. 'I am? I haven't done much.'

He smoothed her hair back from her forehead. 'I know who saved me from the sea. I, too, have dreams. One particularly vivid one of kissing you. Was it merely a dream? I wonder…'

Her cheeks grew hot. 'It was to keep you quiet!'

'I want you to always kiss me like that.' He undid her hair and ran it through his fingers. 'Silken night is the colour of your tresses. It shone in the fire's glow, just as it shines now. Beauty personified.'

A trembling started in her soul. He thought her beautiful. She wanted to believe him. She wanted to believe in the goodness of life again. That her life could be the way she had dreamt it. That the nightmare of the past few years was coming to end. She wanted to believe and it frightened her.

'Stay with me,' he murmured. 'Be with me.'

'I am here.'

He captured her chin with his fingers and held it so she could only look into his unfathomable eyes. 'Good.'

Giving in to instinct, she undid her cloak and allowed it to slip to the ground, joining his discarded clothes.

His hands roamed down her body, tracing her curves and causing her inner place to throb. A small moan escaped her lips. He stopped to cup her bottom, pulling her more firmly against him, allowing her to experience the hardness of him. It was exquisite torment which caused a thousand points of light to explode in her mind.

'May I see you? All of you?' he murmured against her neck.

The instant he said it, she thought of how her couplings with her late husband had always been furtive and in the dark and she knew that she wanted something entirely different. She didn't want to imagine him. She wanted to see every inch of him.

Unable to speak, she nodded. He tugged at her gown and slowly lifted it. He then took off her undergarments until she was naked. The warm breeze caressed her skin, making her nipples pucker to tiny points.

'I've never done this before.' She gestured with one hand. 'Any of it.'

'I'm honoured and flattered.' He ran a hand over her naked shoulder. The simple touch sent hundreds of fiery tingles coursing through her body. 'Let me show you how good it can be.'

Her knees trembled and he slowly laid her down on the nest of clothes. He loomed over her, golden and warm. All about her, she heard the soft patter of the rain and knew that they were cocooned in this little place.

His lips moved down her arm to the soft inside of her elbow. He lazily drew little circles with his tongue.

Her breasts grew heavy and her nipples became tightly furled. She arched upwards, wanting his mouth there rather than where it suckled.

He seemed to understand and trailed his glorious mouth to her breasts, where he lapped at the nipples. He took each one in turn into his mouth and suckled. Her body bucked upwards and heat seared through her, making her feel reborn.

His hands slipped down her body, tracing the hills and valleys of her flesh. Her skin seemed to be newly alive. Each touch made heat thrum through her. He moved between her thighs.

'May I?' he murmured against her belly. 'May I feast?'

Not knowing what to expect, she nodded.

He moved his mouth to the apex of her thighs. His tongue moistened her inner core and her world exploded in a haze of stars. Her body thrust upwards, seeking him, wanting him deeper within her. His tongue probed and teased, sinking inside her and undulating against her. The stars became blinding light.

Giving a great cry, she collapsed back against the nest of discarded clothes. Slowly the world righted itself. He loomed over her with a very male smile on his lips.

She blinked up at him, unable to believe what had just happened. Her entire body ached with a sweet longing. She buried her hands in his hair and drew his face close.

'Thank you,' she whispered.

He returned to her mouth and she tasted a

faint salty sweetness that had not been there
before.

'See how good you taste to me?' he murmured
against her ear. 'Why I wanted to feast on you?'

She tugged at the waistband of his trousers.
His arousal sprang free. Far larger than she
considered possible. She put out her hand and
wrapped it around him. Hot, silken and heavy.
Infinitely exciting.

'Will you allow me to feast?' She barely recognised her voice. 'To do to you what you did
to me?'

A moan came from the back of his throat.
'I can't. I want you. I need you too much. Next
time.'

He positioned himself between her thighs and
this time, he entered her. Her body welcomed
him in and she wrapped her legs about his to
pull him deeper inside.

They rocked together. Faster and faster, each
finding the rhythm from the other. Until the
waves crashed over her and a great shuddering
engulfed them both. For a second time in a matter of heartbeats, the sweet longing filled her.

She knew in that instant as she teetered on
the brink that she had never felt more alive or
more satisfied. He completed her in a way she
had never even dared to dream about. And she

knew that the tales people told were not all lies. Sometimes dreams did come true.

An insistent rain began to fall, cooling Valdar's fevered skin as he lay spent, breathing in the sweet scent of her. Never had anyone given him so much of themselves, so freely and without hesitation. She'd been one with him, matching him.

As he slowly returned to earth, Valdar raised himself up on his elbow and stared down at Alwynn. Her lashes made dark smudges against her rosy cheeks as her soft breath fanned his cheek.

He doubted he'd ever seen anyone as lovely. She had unstintingly given her all to him. He doubted if he had ever had such a responsive partner. They had seemed to move instinctively in time with each other and yet he knew he could spend a lifetime exploring her body and not tire of her. The depth of the feeling nearly overwhelmed him.

But there could be no lifetime for them. She couldn't be his for ever, no matter how much he might wish it. He didn't need any witch's curse to tell him that. He knew the facts. Sooner or later he'd have to tell her where Raumerike was and who he was.

He ran his hand along her flank and felt her soft skin ripple under his fingertips. He should have told her the truth about where he was from before this had happened. Gode had been right.

There was no way he could tell Alwynn now without losing her and right now he didn't want to lose her. He didn't want to see the fear and hatred in her eyes. He wanted the passion and the desire. He wanted to keep that closeness between them. He would tell her later, when he was leaving. It would make the parting easier.

He had not intended for this to happen, but it did not change anything. He had a summer and that was all. Because he knew that, because he was prepared for it, he would cheat the curse.

After he had gone, she would be on her own. She would have to face everyone, but at least she would be able to say that she had been fooled and that she hadn't betrayed anyone.

He hated being a coward, but he wanted to experience this paradise for a little while longer. Nearly drowning, being given a second chance by the gods had given him a new sense of purpose.

'We have the summer, Alwynn.'

She murmured in the back of her throat and snuggled closer, looping her arm about his neck.

He wanted her again. He could feel himself stirring already. He ran his hand down her thigh.

The huge great hollow, which had been such a part of his life ever since Kara had vanished, healed like new.

Somewhere he heard a shout and knew there were people about. He had no right to lie with her like this. No right at all. And yet she fitted so well in his arms.

With great reluctance, he rolled off her and stared up at the darkening sky. He had to keep her safe.

'We need to go, Alwynn.'

'Valdar?' she asked in a sleep-laced voice which promised much. 'Tell me it was more than a dream.'

'We should go back,' he murmured. 'Someone will come looking for us. The storm will break soon.'

'Do we have to go? We're dry under this tree.'

He dropped a kiss on her mouth. Arousal had turned it to the colour of ripe apples.

'This needs to be kept between us. I won't have people whispering about you. Come the autumn, I will be gone.' His heart tugged inside his chest. As he said the words, he wondered if they were more for him than her. Reassurance. He felt he had gone far too fast, too soon. What had happened between them transcended a physical act. He wondered if she realised that yet.

She raised herself up on one elbow. 'I made my choice. Discretion will be fine. And there will be no regrets. Life is far too short.'

'Good.' He traced the outline of her lips. 'You were beyond imagining, Alwynn. Better than any dream, because you were you.'

He silently winced. His tongue was worse than useless.

She reached for her clothes with the air of a thoroughly satisfied woman. There was something completely sensuous in the way she dressed. His fingers itched to unwrap her again.

'I'm not looking for for ever,' she said as she straightened her hair. 'There is no reason why anyone should know if we are discreet. No child will ever quicken in my womb.'

'You would have been a good mother. I see how you look after Merri and everyone on the estate.'

She gave a small shrug. 'I can't help caring about them. I owe them my life. I gave a promise when I married Theodbald to look after Merri and keep her safe.'

Her easy acceptance of the end made his heart ache worse. He wished he wasn't cursed. He wished he could give her his heart. He wished he didn't have a vow to honour his dead friends and return home to tell of Girmir's treachery. 'Then we shall enjoy the time we have. Who knows what tomorrow will bring?'

'I plan to.' Alwynn withdrew her hand. Her heart was so full that she thought it would burst. What had happened between them was beyond imagining. But it was just physical and not about making a life together.

Valdar would go when the leaves turned and the autumn winds began to blow. He had another life. She knew that. She could be coolly practical about it. Why shouldn't she experience a bit of happiness in the meantime? It wasn't as if she was going to have a child from their coupling. There would be no evidence.

'We will need to keep it a secret. If Lord Edwin discovers…' A faint shiver ran down her spine. 'He wants this estate and I can't allow him to have it. Already he has turned some of the old tenants off the land he acquired. I took in those whom I could…'

'Your secret is safe with me.' He touched her cheek. Featherlight tingles went through her. She wanted to sink into him again, but she kept her body still. 'Trust me. Please trust me.'

Alwynn's heart turned. Valdar had probably played this game a thousand times before. He

knew precisely what to do and the right words
to ensure all was well. She didn't have a clue,
but she knew she had to protect her heart. When
she was younger, she had given it too readily.

It shocked her that she was willing to play.
But how could she give him up? Gode had been
right. This summer she deserved a bit of happiness and joy.

'I will. And you're an excellent lover.'

A dimple flashed in his cheek and the warmth
smouldered in his eyes. 'I shall take that as a
compliment.'

'It was meant as one.' She stretched and tried
to be sophisticated about it. 'It is about us now.
The future has no meaning.'

His eyes grew storm-tossed. 'And the past?
There is something you should know…'

She put her fingers on his mouth. The last
thing she wanted to know was that there was a
woman waiting for him at home. That was the
true meaning of her dream last night. 'I live in
the present, not the past.'

A wariness vanished from his eyes. 'Agreed.
The here and now is all we speak of.'

'Shall we return before anyone starts looking for us? We will find other opportunities if
we are clever.'

He gave a crooked smile and her heart did

an odd little flip. Just looking at him made her feel as if she was special. 'My thoughts exactly.'

'I still intend to teach you to read and write. Then wherever you are in the world and you use that knowledge, you will think of me.'

'You're unforgettable, Alwynn.'

She matched her footsteps with his. Their shoulders were nearly touching. 'That will give us an excuse.'

'I have an added incentive.' He dropped a kiss on her forehead. 'I can now steal a kiss with impunity.'

'As long as that is all you intend…' She glanced over her shoulder.

His eyes grew serious. 'I live in hope for more. What happened just now was beyond all reckoning, Alwynn. Truly.'

Her heart turned and she wished that there wasn't going to be an ending, but she had to be realistic. Things like that only happened in bard's tales. In real life, one had to be practical and pragmatic. One had to face up to hard choices.

Valdar had another life somewhere, a life which she had no part of. Come autumn he would return there and she'd be left with her memories.

What was between them was physical. It

had to be. She could keep it that way. She had changed from the naive woman who ignored the facts, preferring only to see the beauty in the world.

She turned a deaf ear towards that little part of her which whispered *liar*.

'We fit well together but that is as far as it goes. When you depart, I will shed no tears. The here and now is our pledge.'

Something faded from his eyes. 'I expected no less.'

Chapter Ten

Valdar hurried through his tasks, trying to get things done as efficiently and in as short a time as possible.

However, everyone appeared to have heard about his altercation with Cleofirth and the recovery of the missing sheep and they all wanted a word. He was left in no doubt that Cleofirth was little liked. Several of the wives brought small gifts to welcome him.

The gifts touched him more than he thought possible. These people trusted him and seemed excited when he spoke about repairing roofs and mending walls. And yet he knew if they were aware of his heritage, they would turn their backs on him. But each time he fixed a wall or had a look at a plough, he knew he was making things easier for Alwynn after he left. He was giving her a chance.

'What is all this?' Alwynn asked, coming into the scriptorium and eyeing the cheese, bread and eggs that he'd been given this morning.

'Bounty from grateful tenants.' He shook his head. 'Where I come from, they expect far more from their overlord.'

A frown appeared between her arched brows. 'My husband preferred to forget that he had any duty except for drinking and hunting.'

And whoring, Valdar silently added. Several of the farmers' wives had whispered the rumours, particularly about Urien and why she had been married to Cleofirth with such haste.

It was also clear from their joining that Alwynn was new to physical pleasure.

'I simply want to leave this place better than when I arrived.'

Something tugged at his heart. He never became too close to the thralls who worked his land. So why did these people matter to him?

She set down her basket of flowers. 'You already have. I saw the work you did to the barns this morning. New stabling for Purebright. Merri is thrilled.'

'It was nothing. There had been a small hole in the thatch.'

He gave in to impulse and drew her into his arms. She smelt of summer flowers and sunshine. All things good. He lifted her chin and tasted her mouth.

She yielded for a long heartbeat, but then drew back, glancing over her shoulder. 'We must be circumspect.'

He closed the door with a decisive click. 'You mean like this?'

A laugh bubbled from her throat. 'That is one way of doing it.'

'Perhaps the only way.'

She leant her head against his shoulder. Her hand reached up and stroked his hair. He turned his face and kissed her palm. 'Now, about this reading and writing you plan on teaching me. I want to learn.'

Her eyes danced and he knew he'd stay with her until the last possible moment. 'Is that why you are here?'

'Why else? I plan to be an attentive pupil.'

A week later, the garden hummed with bees in the hot summer sun.

For once, the rain had held off and the flowers bloomed. Alwynn concentrated on pulling the weeds while she hummed a new tune, trying to work out what she'd sing for Valdar after supper. It turned out that he could play the harp after a fashion and his voice complemented hers.

Everything about him complemented her. She'd never known anyone as easy to be with. They could sit together and the silences were not awkward. She kept telling her heart that miracles didn't happen, but in her heart she kept hoping. Somehow, they'd find a way to be together.

She rocked back on her heels. 'No.'

The lavender had flowered. Early. She would have to collect it to dry, but it always seemed to herald the start of the late-summer flowers. Early summer was behind her.

The swifts' chicks had hatched from their nests. Soon they would be off to their winter home. They were amongst the last birds to arrive and the first to leave, according to her late father.

She should have known that it was too good to last. The blooming lavender was a sign of that. Time was moving on. They were going to have to end. Valdar was going to have to return to his past.

Out of habit, she picked a sprig. Normally she loved the scent.

Whom was she kidding? She wanted to slow down time and make each day last a lifetime. She wasn't ready for it to end and she knew she had lied that first day they made love.

When he went, she might not weep in front

of him, but she would weep into her pillow for many nights.

The here and now. She had to stop thinking about the bleak future.

'You are a sight worth waiting for.' Valdar's voice rolled over her. 'I have searched for you in three different places, my elusive lady. I had almost given up, but then I heard the most wondrous sound, like a stream playing on the rocks, and I knew it was you, singing in the garden. What was the song? I have never heard it before.'

She put her hand to her throat. She had been singing. Her heart leapt. 'Something I made up.'

'You must sing it for me properly so I can truly appreciate it.'

Her heart did a little jump. When she had been younger, she used to dream of her husband returning and being pleased to find her in the garden. Theodbald had never sought her out. He had never wanted to hear her songs. But she'd stopped singing when he'd gone. Of all the things he had taken from her, it was the one thing she resented the most. But now her voice had returned. She had started singing because of Valdar. 'When it is perfect.'

'You look perfect to me. Any song you choose to sing will be perfect.' He came over and put his arms about her waist, pulling her against his hard body. His mouth covered hers for a long and soul-satisfying kiss.

She allowed herself a moment of pleasure before escaping. 'Someone might see us. Merri— she can't keep a secret.'

He looked over his shoulder. 'Nobody is here and I have been thinking about this all day. It made Owain's complaints about the sheep enclosures more bearable. They are fixed for now, but the gate on the left-hand one will need to be replaced next spring.'

'You thought of me while you were supposed to be seeing to the sheep enclosures? What sort of steward are you?'

'The very best sort.' He put his hand about her waist and drew her into the circle of his arm. 'You will be pleasantly surprised by how good the harvest will be. The fine weather is bringing everything on. And I come to find you like this in the garden. My day is complete.'

'You are very full of yourself.'

He ran his hand down her back, cupping her bottom. 'I'd rather be full of you like I was yesterday and the day before. What new place will you have us go to? Some day I would like to spend an entire night wrapped around you.'

Her cheeks burnt, but her heart nearly burst with its dreams. 'Valdar!'

'You react beautifully to teasing.' He paused. 'I stopped by to check on Urien on the pretext of being worried about scabies and Cleofirth's sheep. To ask her if she had seen any sign of it.'

Alwynn rested her head against his chest. The problem with Urien remained no nearer a solution. Despite going out to see her several times at Gode's, the woman always defended her husband and spoke about returning to him once Lord Edwin returned and her name was cleared. She still insisted that it was the Northmen and Cleofirth would find the proof.

'How is she?'

'Jumps at every noise. And her hands are never still.'

'The woman I knew was never like that.'

'Give her time.'

Alwynn closed her eyes. Time, something she had too little of. 'Thank you. Have you been back to Cleofirth's as well?'

'I believe Cleofirth is aware of our suspicions. But I am not sure he is in a hurry to get his wife back. Owain told me that he has his eye on a wench from the tavern. He has been drinking heavily.'

Alwynn gulped hard. The news Cleofirth had another woman saddened rather than surprised her. 'Gode needs to be aware of it. She might let the news slip and it isn't what Urien needs.'

His eyes narrowed. 'Is that right?'

'No secret is safe with Gode.' Alwynn waved a hand. 'Ever. Sooner or later she tells. She has always been this way.'

Valdar put his hands on her shoulders and his face turned grave. 'Hopefully the situation will be sorted before…'

'Before the summer ends,' she finished saying for him. 'It will be soon. The lavender has started flowering.'

His brow knitted and he tilted his head to one side. 'Is that important?'

'The dried flowers help to keep the bedding sweet in the winter. I didn't realise time had moved on so quickly. I want each day to last for ever.'

He cupped her cheek and the simple touch sent a spear of warmth through her. 'So do I, but it seems the more I hold on, the quicker time goes.'

She raised herself up on her tiptoes and brushed his lips. 'We are doing what we can.'

He put his arms about her waist and deepened the kiss. Her entire body reacted. He was a drug that she could not get enough of. He had become necessary to her well-being. He was the best man she'd ever met.

A small cry shocked her back to her senses.

She turned her head to see Merri running off. They had been so careful. And now this. Her body ached where he had touched her. His lips were against her ear, suckling and murmuring.

'Merri!' She pushed against Valdar, freed herself from his seductive spell.

At his questioning glance, she explained, 'Merri saw us. Together. Just now. She will tell everyone because it will only fuel the fantasy she has. She likes to believe you're a prince and will marry me. If she tells…'

He caught her arm. Concern was etched on his face. 'Do you want me to fetch her? It will give you some time to compose yourself. Merri will understand why things need to be kept quiet.'

'No, I will go and speak to her.' She shook her head. It amazed her that he wanted to do something like that for her. He made her feel cherished. 'I should have been more careful. This is why we should never have…'

He lifted her chin so she looked in his wonderfully expressive eyes. 'I'm not ready to give you up, Alwynn.'

'You don't know how tempting that is, but I must tell her that…that we are friends. Yes, friends.' She held out her hands. 'Shall we speak no more of it? Let us be friends. We made an agreement. I mean to keep to it.'

He inclined his head. His eyes hardened to stone. 'Forget I asked. Of course we keep to the agreement. Have I suggested otherwise? I simply wanted you to know that you had options. You're not alone.'

'You mustn't worry about me.'

'I'll always worry. Wherever I am.'

Her heart clenched. She had hurt him, but it was the right thing to do. And she knew she could never go back to their old agreement. She needed his touch too much. 'I will find a way, Valdar. Merri will have to learn to hold her tongue around the others.'

Valdar watched her walk away. He crushed the lavender between his fingers. He wanted Alwynn in his bed and by his side. He wanted to know what she was thinking, to protect her, to cherish her. But he had no rights. He knew why the gods had given him this second chance and what they expected him to do. This was but a fleeting period in his life, though he would remember it for the rest of his days.

As if she could read his thoughts, she turned back. 'You do think I am doing the right thing?'

'Seeing Merri on her own? Of course.' He

snapped his fingers. 'Easier on the both of us. You will have to deal with her when I go in any case. I'll keep out of the way. I want to take another look at the sheep enclosures on the home farm. Just let me know how you put it.'

'I understand completely.' She walked away from him and there was nothing he could do to bring her back.

Alwynn discovered Merri in the stables.

The girl was sitting hunched up next to Purebright, her head resting on her knees.

'Merri?' she said, holding out her hand.

The girl raised her head. Instead of tears, her eyes danced. 'I saw you. Kissing Valdar. You never kissed my father like that. Ever. You looked so happy. You've even started singing again. You don't know how I've longed for it. Of all the things my father caused, that was the worst.'

'Your father had little to do with it.' Alwynn gave a careful shrug. She refused to have Merri thinking any more bad thoughts about her father. 'It was more that I didn't have time to think, let alone sing. With Valdar here, I've more time.'

'You're singing because you're happy. Some day Valdar and you will marry. He is a prince in disguise and all your dreams will come true.'

Alwynn shook her head. 'You must stop speaking nonsense. It shouldn't have happened. Think about what Father Freodwald would have said.'

'But it did! And Father Freodwald isn't here. He is stuffing his fat face at Lord Edwin's.' She clapped her hands. 'Are you going to marry Valdar? Has he asked you? I know he wants to. I can see it in his eyes. They follow you whenever you are near. He has made you beautiful, Stepmother. He'll stay if you ask him.'

Alwynn shook her head. Here she thought they had been so careful. Probably everyone had noticed. She had to hope that no one truly knew how far things had gone. 'He has another life, a life which has nothing to do with either of us.'

Merri's face became mutinous. 'He kissed you. It has to count for something. It will be just like a bard's tale. Only better because it is really real. Like you giving me Purebright.'

Alwynn's heart squeezed. The last thing she wanted was to destroy Merri's innocence. There would be time enough for her to learn about men. She leant down and patted Merri's hand. The girl's slender fingers curled around hers. 'Men are like that. And let's keep the tales where they belong—for after supper. In real life, sometimes we have to make hard choices and there isn't a happy ending.'

'Let him know how you feel!' Merri jumped up and began to pace about the stable. 'We need a warrior here. Someone else could look after his lands. Someone *is* looking after them now. If he had died out on the sea, they would have had to look after them for ever. He has no need to return there to his past. He should think about his future.'

'If only it was that simple…' Alwynn hated how her heart leapt. She had thought that she could keep her heart out of it, but she knew she hadn't. Secretly she had been hoping that a solution would present itself, but asking Valdar to stay wasn't one of them. His past was also his future. He needed to go back. He might not have a wife or children, but he had a family who loved him. 'Think about the people he left behind. How sad they would be. It is better not to get too attached. He will go.'

Merri's face took on a stubborn cast. 'If he asked, would you go from here? Would you sail off to his great estate? Would you leave us all?'

Alwynn held out her hands. There was little point in explaining that it had been all she could think of for a few days until she'd looked at Merri's latest attempt at tablet weaving and had known it didn't matter if he asked or not. Her answer would be the same. 'What? Leave you? How could you think that? My life is here.'

As she said the words, she knew they were true. She had a responsibility to the people who lived here and she took that responsibility seriously.

'Is it because of me you won't go? Some day you might wish you had.'

When Merri turned her face away, Alwynn went and sat beside her. She gathered Merri's small hands within her own. 'I promised you when you were a little girl and missing your mother. Remember? I'll see you safely married and settled on your own estate. I love you as surely as I would love my own child, if I'd been granted such a blessing.'

Somehow that steady ache to hold her own child had grown less in the past few days. Theodbald was wrong. She wasn't something less than a woman simply because she hadn't borne a child.

Merri tilted her head to one side. 'I think you have done more than just kiss him.'

Alwynn pretended to be very interested in the arrangement of Purebright's straw. The pony let out a snort as if he agreed with Merri.

'Well?' Merri asked. 'Are you going to tell

me? What did Valdar do to get you to sing again?'

'I refuse to answer that. It is none of your business. You shouldn't know such things. You are far too young.'

Merri laughed. 'I hardly live in a convent. I know what passes between a man and a woman. It was hard not to, stepping over the bodies after one of my father's feasts.'

Alwynn pressed her hands together as guilt flooded through her. She had always thought that Merri was safely tucked in bed. She should have listened to Gode that Merri's nurse was skittish and rather more inclined to spend the night with one of the grooms than look after her charge properly. 'I wanted to spare you that.'

'I am an early riser. And Mildreth was always missing on the morning after a feast day.'

'You should have told me.'

'And spoil my fun? Mildreth allowed me lots of freedom, unlike Gode, who would have been on me like a hound on a blood trail.' Merri tucked her hair into her couvre-chef, making the cloth tilt worse than ever. 'Besides, knowing about it is not the same as trying it myself.'

Alwynn turned around. Merri looked so grown-up, standing there with her jaw jutting out and her head back. She was growing up so quickly. 'Young lady!'

'You look far less careworn and your eyes sparkle. I have even heard you laugh. I can't remember the last time you did that.'

'There has been too little laughter recently.'

'You deserve some happiness after all the hard work you put in to save this estate. I asked Gode about it a few days ago. She agreed with me. When you are happy, you are less cross with life.'

Alwynn pinched the bridge of her nose. She had been trying so hard. 'How long have you known?'

Merri waved an airy hand. 'Since we brought him from the beach… What about if you have a baby? My father has been dead for far too long to claim it is his.'

'Merri!'

'Stepmother. I've heard Gode gossiping about such things with Mildreth.' She gave a smile which was pure Merri—half-innocence and half-rogue, but all things lovable. 'You needn't worry. I won't give this secret away. If it comes to it, we will figure out a way to silence the priests and gossipmongers.'

Alwynn put a hand on her flat abdomen.

Merri made it sound easy. But there was no good even considering such a thing.

'Why did you go into the garden? You normally find another place to be.' She nudged Merri in the ribs. 'Too afraid of being made to weed.'

Merri wrinkled her nose. 'I hate weeding. Mucking out after Purebright is much better. He shows his appreciation. Plants never do anything except curl their toes and die for me.'

Purebright gave a little whoosh of breath.

'You weren't spying on me?'

'Spying is something that people like Oswald do.' Merri jumped up. 'Oswald said that he saw a second Northman ship in an inlet. Or maybe it is the same ship except its mast isn't broken.'

An ice-cold shiver went down Alwynn's spine. She had convinced herself that Merri's story was just a made-up tale. But a Northman ship appearing at the same time as Valdar? Could he be...? Her mind immediately rejected the idea. Valdar was nothing like a Northman. He was kind and considerate and he rebuilt things. Nothing like a Northman. The memory of his fevered words scratched her mind. She hurriedly closed that door. She might have been blind about Theodbald's faults but Valdar was a different man. He was trustworthy and honourable.

Doubting was the surest way to distrust, as her mother used to say, and Alwynn knew she could rely on Valdar.

'How can Oswald be sure it is the same ship?' she asked more sharply than she intended. 'Ships often look the same. It could be from any country.'

Merri leant forward and lowered her voice. 'It has the same dragon prow. Oswald knows these things.'

Alwynn rubbed her temples and tried to keep the niggling pain at bay. 'Merri, if there were Northmen in this area, I would know about it. We all would know about it. Churches would be burning.'

Merri's face fell and she played with her belt. 'I thought Valdar would want to know. That is all.'

Alwynn's stomach knotted. For once, she hoped Oswald was wrong. 'Oswald likes to tell stories. He enjoys teasing you and scaring you.'

Merri was silent for a long while. 'He does like to scare me.'

'There, you see.' Alwynn hated the trembling in her heart. She hated that for even one heartbeat she had wondered if Valdar had been connected to this mysterious ship. How could she doubt him like that?

'Oswald said that grain has gone missing from his father's gristmill. And several farmers have had sheep missing.'

'The mysteries of Oswald's missing grain and Owain's missing sheep have been solved.' Alwynn firmed her mouth.

Merri's brow furled. 'I think Oswald is telling tales. Maybe his father wants to save the fine flour for Lord Edwin's lady like he was doing before. He wants to make sure that he and his family have good relations with all their neighbours. Oswald thinks Valdar should stay and teach him about swords. That was my idea—the sword bit.'

'I think you are right about the gristmill. But we both know Valdar has another life and that he will return to it once the harvest is in.' Alwynn leant forward and kissed Merri on the forehead. 'I will have Valdar look into this. If Oswy is going to start giving us problems, we need to know. It needs to be solved one way or the other before…before the summer ends.'

'I wish Valdar would stay. What does he have waiting for him at home? He doesn't have a wife. I asked him about it.'

Alwynn stood and shook her skirts. She hated that Merri echoed her innermost thoughts. But she could hardly beg him to stay. They had made an agreement. She was trying to grab hold of the precious days, but the harder she tried, the more they slipped away.

'Right, you and I are going to see Oswald,' she said to steer the conversation away from Valdar. The winter was going to be hard enough to get through once he was gone without her thinking about it every heartbeat. She had to live for the now. 'I want to hear his story from his own mouth.'

'Why not wait for Valdar?' Merri stuck her chin in the air. 'I promised Oswald that Valdar would come to see him. About the swords.'

'Ah, now the truth comes out.'

Merri covered her mouth with both her hands. 'Can you blame me? Everything is better when he is around.'

'Since when did I hide behind a man? I want to understand what is going on at the gristmill.'

Alwynn paced the scriptorium. After returning from Oswy's gristmill she had tried to find him, but Valdar had gone off to one of the outlying farms and she'd had no choice but to wait. Oswy's wife had questioned her closely. It seemed a number of women felt she should marry Valdar and that he was precisely what this neighbourhood needed—a warrior who wasn't afraid to get his hands dirty repairing buildings and walls. Her attempts to explain why he had to leave after the harvest sounded feeble, so she'd made her excuses and left.

'You appear lost in concentration.' Valdar's voice rolled over her. 'Is Merri fine with your explanation? I expected you to find me when I returned from Owain's. But when you didn't, I presumed you and Merri needed time… And now I find you holed up in this room, writing.'

Valdar's face was creased with concern, but relaxed slightly when he saw her. Her heart did a little jump. His being there seemed to help. He was rebuilding the estate, not destroying it. He wasn't going to betray her.

She put the parchment roll down. 'Merri approves, I think. She says that Gode knows about us. The whole hall probably knows. I have been such a fool to think we could keep it a secret. All the talk is about when we will marry.'

He laced his fingers between hers. 'As long as no one has confronted you, it is only gossip.'

'Inevitable, I suppose.'

'Yes, because you are a beautiful widow. People will always talk whether or not anything passed between us. Without proof, though, it is just talk.'

Her being glowed. He thought her beautiful.

'You are right. Once you depart in the autumn, then it will die down. Everything will go back to how it was.'

He made no move to take her in his arms, but simply stood stiffly at her side. 'I hope you're right.'

She hated how her heart sank. He spoke so casually of leaving and to her it was like a big black day looming on the horizon. Silently she vowed that she would never tell him how she dreaded the day and never try to hold him.

He had another life and, once the life debt was paid, he would go back to it.

'You asked to see me as soon as I returned from my rounds. What is it?' He laughed. 'Has someone complained about my high-handedness? Small things done now will prevent larger problems come the winter.'

'Oswy has complained about missing sacks of grain again. He thinks a gang of outlaws are operating in the area. Oswald swears it is the Northmen, the same Northmen he saw in the bay about the time I discovered you.'

All the colour seemed to drain from Valdar's cheeks.

'What's the matter?'

Valdar waved her hand away and concentrated on breathing deeply. He had to have heard wrong. There would be no Viken raiders here. There wasn't a large monastery or town with lots of gold to attract them.

'The Northmen? What Northmen did he see?' His voice sounded strangled to his ears. He swallowed hard and tried again. 'Why did you keep this tale from me?'

'It was some tall tale that Oswald told Merri. He saw a dragon ship on the day after we found you. It had a broken mast.'

'Did he?' Every sinew in Valdar's body tightened. Impossible. Girmir and his crew would be back in Raumerike now, living off the tales of their adventure. Everyone would think him dead. There was no way on this earth that Girmir remained in Northumbria. 'Why did no one tell me?'

'Because it was just a tale. Merri went and looked. There was no ship.'

Sweat poured down his back and he felt as if he had run a long way.

Words bubbled inside him. He wanted to explain and to order precautions to be taken, but he couldn't get anything out. Acting rashly would accomplish nothing. Once he knew the truth, then he would know what to do. Whatever he did, he would keep Alwynn safe. Alwynn meant more to him than he thought possible. The knowledge caused his breath to stop.

'If it was just a tale, why is it important?' he asked carefully.

'Oswald told Merri the ship had returned and now has a fixed mast. He says that it is about to start raiding. It is why they lost sacks of grain at the gristmill.'

'How did he know it was the same ship?'

'He claims it has the same dragon prow. A snarling beast of a prow. Some sort of fantastical bear combined with a serpent.'

Valdar's heart raced. The description matched Girmir's boat. The memory of how proud Horik had been of that carved figurehead swamped him. He had worked on the expression until he declared that it would frighten all the monsters from the sea. Horik had chosen a bear to represent his father, who had been a notorious berserker who had died in the East.

But if Oswald could describe it, it meant Girmir was here. Had he returned to unleash a storm of havoc as he'd promised?

Valdar counted the days. There would not have been enough time for him to return to Raumerike, refit a boat and make the return voyage. If Girmir was here, then he had only the same crew. Valdar's jaw tightened. This was why the gods had saved him. They had washed him up on this shore in order to avenge Horik's murder. It might be his only chance. Once he returned to Raumerike, Girmir would ensure his version of the tale became the accepted one.

But if he could destroy Girmir, he might be able to return to his old life. It was odd that in many ways his old life held no attraction. It did not have Alwynn in it. Valdar closed his eyes and reminded himself of the curse, of the pain of losing Kara.

'He wants to know what we are going to do about it,' Alwynn said. Her slender fingers tightened about an ink quill. She might make light of it, but the tale had clearly unnerved her. 'I mean, it is far too fantastical. If Northmen were here, they would attack the church. Or maybe the hall, not a small gristmill. They'd burn everything to the ground.'

He wanted to reach out and tell her that he'd protect her from all foes. He would battle until his dying breath to keep her and hers safe. He knew he had never felt this way about anyone before and it frightened him. They could have no future.

'When did this happen? All was at peace when I visited the gristmill yesterday. The wheel will need replacing before next spring, but it can wait.'

'Last night, apparently. Someone broke into his grain store. Oswald swore the Northmen were driven off by the dogs' barking.'

Valdar went completely cold. His mind raced. He had to have heard her wrong. Northmen did not raid gristmills and take sacks of grain. But hungry men could. And there were other desperate men besides men from the North. 'It sounds like outlaws.'

'Or merely an excuse to get you out there with your sword. Apparently Merri promised—'

'Wait! Where did Oswald see this ship?'

'Merri knows.' She broke the quill and put her hand to her head. 'I'm sorry, you are right. Just outlaws. It brought back memories from last summer. We lived in such fear. I'd hoped that St Cuthbert's storm had finished them. For ever. They are truly the scum of the earth. Demons in human form.'

'Because they attacked a church and stole gold.'

'Yes, and butchered people who had done them no harm.' Alwynn put the broken bits of the quill down with trembling hands. He wanted to take her into his arms and kiss her until the only thing she knew was passion. He hated that his countrymen had caused these shadows in her eyes. 'My second cousin died during that fight. I'd hoped that it would be the end of it. And then this. A plague on all Northmen.'

'Even the ones who played no part?'

'They're all guilty.'

Valdar stared up at the ceiling. Even if he wanted to explain about his fears, he didn't dare now. The instant she found out about his heritage, she'd turn against him and he wanted a few more weeks with her. Surely the gods could grant that?

'I don't see any burning houses,' he said, quietly coming to put his arms about her. 'All seems at peace. As you say, Oswald likes to tell tall tales.'

She rested her face against his chest for a few heartbeats. And with each heartbeat, the time seemed to be slipping from him. 'My point precisely. If it were a raid, we'd know. There would be burning from here to Bamburgh.'

'Oswy has done this before, remember?'

'I know, I know.' She moved away from him and began pacing. 'It just feels like there is something wrong. He has no reason to fake anything now. Why did Oswald give such detail?'

'To impress Merri? I gather he likes her.'

Alwynn gave him a sharp glance. 'I hope for a better husband than that for Merri.'

'We need to pay Oswy a visit. Together. I want to show Oswy that we are as one on this and that we do take it seriously. I had bothered with him before as he had made a point of delivering the missing flour here, but that may have been a mistake.'

'I've already been out. He showed me the broken lock. A thief did break in.'

'You went without me?'

'You were away. I had to go.' She put her hand on her hip. 'I can look after myself. I will have to do it once you are gone.'

Valdar watched the delicate curve of her neck. His stomach revolted at the thought of Alwynn ever meeting Girmir. The bastard would take great pleasure in torturing her, particularly if he knew Valdar cared about her.

All his muscles tensed, ready to do battle against his enemy. He had to find the men first. Before Girmir discovered that he had not drowned, before he learnt these people were important to him and burnt this place to the ground.

'I want to see this inlet where Oswald claimed to see the ship.'

'You won't find anything there. Trust me.'

'Humour me.'

Right now, Raumerike seemed like a distant prospect. He wished he could be more honest with Alwynn, but he wanted to grab the little chance of happiness he had. He could be the brave warrior she thought he was. He wanted to be that man for the rest of his life. But he also wanted her to love him—but how could she if there were secrets between them?

He caught a tendril of her silken hair and ran it through his fingers. Sighing, she leant back against him and closed her eyes. Her head was warm against his chest and she felt so right in his arms.

'What are you expecting to find?'

'I've no idea,' he said against her hair. 'But I will get to the bottom of the mystery. It's my job to look after you and your estate. I will do that to the best of my ability while I am here. You don't need to stand alone. Whatever is there, we cope. Together.'

She gave a tremulous smile and pulled away from him. She smoothed her gown and straightened her hair. 'Thank you. It has been a long time since I've leant on anyone. I hate the thought of clinging. I hate needing anyone.'

He watched her with a lump in his throat. He wanted this moment to last for ever.

'Sometimes it is good to feel that someone else is there supporting you.' He put his arm about her shoulders and pulled her against him. 'I'm here.'

Chapter Eleven

The sheltered cove where Oswald supposedly spotted the Northman ship was peaceful and utterly devoid of humans except for Alwynn and Valdar. A few gulls skimmed the water.

As they came around the corner and the entirety of the cove was laid at their feet, Alwynn drew in her breath. She'd forgotten how beautiful it looked with the sunlight playing on the water.

If she shaded her eyes, she could make out settlements along the coast over twenty miles away. There was something commanding about the hilltop. The only sounds were the lapping water and the gulls playing on the surf.

'A good hiding place,' Valdar remarked once they were down on the sand. 'The anchorage looks right and there is an advantage to being able to see if anyone is coming.'

A shiver went down Alwynn's back. Had

Northmen camped here? It was so peaceful. She didn't want to imagine a band of murderers here.

'You see, no one is here.' She wrapped her arms about her middle. 'Another of Oswald's stories. He is a boy who wants things to be exciting and when they are not, he makes things up. He wanted to see you and ask about how you use a sword.'

She waited for Valdar to laugh with her. He was singularly quiet. She fancied that the colour had faded from his cheeks.

'There is no ship here now,' he said. He kicked some charred wood that she'd overlooked. 'But someone has camped here recently and tried to cover it up.'

Alwynn bent down. The wood was completely soaked. 'There is no telling when the fire happened. But we haven't had much rain for days. It could have been weeks ago. Before you ever arrived. People do travel along the shore—shepherds, tinkers and the like.'

He weighed the piece of charred wood in his hand before tossing it into the water. The small plop echoed around the inlet and several gulls rose up into the air, screaming at being disturbed. 'Possibly.'

'You sound cautious. I'm sure it was just a story that Oswald told.' She impatiently tucked her hair behind her ear. 'I know what it is like to want your life to be more exciting. I used to tell stories, too. I wanted to believe they were true. But I stopped and Oswald will have to do the same.'

His dark gaze seemed to pierce her soul. 'You said the lock had been forced. Why would Oswald or his father force the lock? What could they hope to gain?'

'I don't know, but I can't imagine Northmen doing that. They would be likely to break the door down and then burn the mill for good measure.' She forced a laugh. 'Everyone knows that about Northmen. No manners whatsoever!'

Valdar remained solemn. 'You have a low opinion of the men from the North.'

'When have they ever shown that they are civilised?' She crossed her arms. 'You have to admit, Valdar, breaking a lock is what an outlaw would do, not a raider.'

'Are all Northmen raiders? All of them? What if they are not? What if some are like you or me? People trying to lead good lives.'

'I wonder if Oswald forced the door to make his story about missing grain more plausible.' Alwynn concentrated on the waves in the harbour rather than trying to fathom Valdar's mood. Sometimes it was easier to change the subject.

After Lindisfarne, everyone knew how North-men behaved. There was no point arguing about it. 'Oswy seemed ashamed that you offered to guard the mill.'

'I would have been happy to keep watch.'

'He saw that as an affront to his manhood.' A bubble of laughter rose within her as she thought about how Oswy had reacted like a wet cockerel, spluttering and stuttering at the mere mention of Valdar standing guard.

Her eye caught Valdar's and a laugh burst from him. 'I never thought a man could strut as well as a cockerel, but Oswy certainly can.'

'I know precisely what you mean.' His fingers reached for hers and curled about them. And the awkwardness vanished as if it had never been.

She curled her fingers tighter and thought how wonderful it was to be with someone who understood.

'If I was going to build a hall, this is where I would build it,' he said, pointing to the head-land overlooking the cove as they made one last circuit of the bay.

'It has been a long time since I have been out here,' Alwynn admitted. 'I used to love it as a child. My father would bring me here sometimes if we had been visiting farms. His parents had a hall near here, but he had wanted something grander and more imposing.' She stopped and tilted her head to one side. 'Why would you build a hall here?'

'Ease of access to the sea. It gives a commanding view. It is important to see who might be coming calling.' He put his arm about her waist. 'But what do I know? My hall is far away from here. And not close to the sea.'

'Where is it?'

'On a wide river, one of the best rivers in all of Raumerike. It stands in a sheltered glade. On summer mornings, when I was a boy, I used to stand outside and watch the eagles circle overhead. I loved watching those eagles.'

'This is the first time you have really spoken of your home.'

'Where I grew up,' he corrected. 'Sometimes it feels a very long time ago and very far away.'

She put her arms about his waist, pleased that she had decided to go with him. It was even better that it had been a wild goose chase, but she had enjoyed being alone with him. She raised herself up on her toes and brushed his lips.

'I will bear your advice in mind if I ever decide to move the hall,' she said against his mouth. 'Which of my tenant builders would you recommend to design this new hall?'

He tightened his arms about her waist. His kiss had a promise of something more.

'Your current hall's location is far from the best. It would be hard to defend.'

'Other than the Northmen, who would attack us? We have no riches.'

'I still worry.'

Her heart soared at the words. He felt something for her. He had not said it in words, but if he worried about her… Her heart started dreaming futures that it had no business to.

'We should return.'

He caught her hand and brought it to his lips. The gentleness of his touch made her knees wobble. 'Not yet.'

'Why?'

He tightened his grip on her and pulled her against his arousal, leaving her in no doubt of what he wanted. She tilted her pelvis slightly so they were closer. His reaction was instant.

Alwynn inwardly smiled. She had power over this man. Her failures were in the past and had everything to do with her late husband. Out here, with Valdar's arms about her, she knew she had truly begun to believe she was a desirable woman. And some day she might have children. Right here, and now, she believed that good things might still come to her.

'I want to finish what we started in the garden,' he said in a husky rasp. 'Do you have any objection? Out here, there will be no one to interrupt or prevent us. No missing sheep to locate and no weaving to untangle.'

Instantly a heated spring coursed through her veins. Over the past few days, every time things started to become interesting, something had happened. 'You are jealous.'

His cheeks reddened slightly. 'Of anything that takes you away from me, yes, I am.'

'Why do you think I so readily agreed to your suggestion to come with you?'

He pretended to consider her statement. 'You were eager to find the Northmen?'

'It had to be a tall tale.' She smoothed his dark blond hair from his face. 'However, I am flattered that you were willing to fight for me.'

'I would always fight for you.'

Alwynn caught his face between her hands. The intensity of his look made her knees weak. She wished she knew more about what drove this warrior of hers, but it was better to keep it in the here and now. Not to wonder about the past or dream about tomorrow. 'It is comforting to know that. But I sincerely hope you never have to fight.'

He started to speak, but she put two fingers

over his mouth. 'Hush. I'll hear no more about it. We are at peace.'

His hands undid her cloak and it fell to the ground. She reached and rapidly took off his tunic. His skin was warm in the late-afternoon sun.

She playfully gave him a gentle shove. 'I want you on the ground.'

He lifted a brow. 'My lady is very insistent.'

'Time for me to see if I can play you like you play me.'

The dimple at the corner of his mouth increased. 'I would be honoured.'

She ran her mouth along his body. She took care to caress each dent and scar. It was the body of a warrior and there was not an ounce of fat on him.

At his chest, she allowed her tongue to play on his nipples. He groaned and his body bucked upwards.

She quickly undid his trousers and his erection sprang free. She took him in her hand and held his steely silkiness.

Another time, she would have marvelled at her boldness, but with Valdar, she simply wanted to taste. She bent her head and ran her tongue round and round his tip. A sense of power filled her. She was doing this to him.

He groaned as his arousal grew. 'Please.'

The whispered word echoed about the grove.

She lifted her head and saw his passion-lid-ded eyes. 'Please what? You don't want me to stop, do you?'

He shook his head, his body thrashing about on the ground. The giant warrior brought to the edge of madness by her.

'Please, I need you. Ride me. Ride me hard.'

She quickly manoeuvred her body so she was astride him. The tip of him touched her inner core. She slowly impaled herself on him, spreading her thighs so he fitted comfortably in her, and then she began to ride him. Her gown spilled over the both of them.

His hands reached and teased her breasts over the cloth. The roughness of the linen rasped against her tightly furled nipples, sending fresh waves of pleasure throughout her. As each wave crested, another began, taking her along and increasing her sensation.

When she thought she could stand it no more, he teetered over the edge, drawing her into his shuddering climax.

She lay against his chest spent, listening to the sound of his heart thudding.

His arms came about her and held her tight.

'I never thought that was possible,' she confessed, drawing circles on his bare chest. Her entire body ached with a sweet languor.

He gave a playful tap on her rear end. 'What, making love out in the open?'

'Being this happy and content.' Sure of her appeal, she stretched upwards like a cat. 'I want to slow down time.'

He loosened his arms and she felt him withdraw slightly from her. 'That is something that neither of us can do.'

She rapidly stood. 'I…I didn't mean—I wasn't asking you to stay. I just want this to continue. The here and now. Autumn can wait.'

He reached for his tunic. Something made him go completely still.

'Is everything all right?' she asked, pleased she had not revealed her growing love for him. There would be time enough to think about that when he had gone.

'Nothing.' Valdar placed a rock in the leather pouch which he tied to his belt.

'It doesn't look like nothing to me.'

'A stone. A memento of today, in a way. I hope you don't consider me a fool.'

Her heart filled and she blinked away sudden tears. 'Oh.'

'Shall we go back? The sun is starting to go down. They will be lighting the torches soon.'

Valdar kept his voice steady as though he was speaking to one of his horses. Inside he felt sick.

It wasn't just any stone, but the sunstone he had given the boy before he had jumped from the ship. It bothered him that the lad's name escaped him. Girmir and his company had definitely been here. The big question was where were they now? He hoped the boy lived, but the presence of the stone and its placement made him think. Without a navigator who could read the sunstone, no wonder they hadn't returned to Raumerike.

He doubted that he'd find a body. Girmir and his henchmen would not be inclined to leave such clues.

One more injustice to avenge.

He thought he'd done enough to save the lad's life. And now this unwelcome discovery.

He had to find them before they found him and before they wrecked this land. Or harmed Alwynn.

Valdar stared out at the still waters. Once he had dealt with Girmir, he would have done as the gods and his honour demanded. He wouldn't have to return home. He could live out his life here with Alwynn. His heart thudded. It amazed him how much he wanted to stay. His past had faded into insignificance. What mattered was keeping Alwynn safe.

This was why the Norns had spared him. He hadn't understood that until this very instant. Not just revenge, or to go back to his old miserable existence, but a chance at a new life with Alwynn and her people. They needed him in a way that his people back in Raumerike didn't. And he refused to allow Girmir to destroy this newfound hope.

'You look very fierce.' Alwynn linked her arm with his. 'There is nothing here to be concerned about. Perhaps you are right, it would be a good place to build a hall.'

The simple touch did much to soothe his soul. He wanted to dream dreams of great halls and worthy sons. He wanted to take her in his arms and whisper words of love. 'It is where I would build mine.'

Her eyes shone and for a single heartbeat, she was a vision of extreme loveliness. He wondered that he had ever considered he might be able to leave her. If he did, he might as well tear out his heart and bury it.

'Won't your family miss you?'

'My family?'

'The people who are waiting for you. The healer...'

'She has her own husband, a child and another on the way. No one will miss me. Not for more than a few weeks.'

'I'll miss you when you go.'

The words rose again in his throat, but he choked them back down. The last thing he wanted to see was the hurt in her eyes when she discovered what he'd been connected with. But if he found Girmir and destroyed him, he could make it right. All this could be his, if he could keep his secret.

'We should return. I would hate to think what new problem someone will want sorted. There is enough work to keep me busy to the new year.'

As he'd hoped, her face instantly became a wreath of smiles. 'It is wonderful to have someone else to help. I hadn't realised how overwhelmed I've been. I have been drowning in all that needed to be done.'

'I am doing my best, my lady. I aim to please you.'

Her merry laugh rang out, startling some wood pigeons. He resolutely turned from the cove. He would protect her for the rest of his life. He had to.

Alwynn put her hands in the centre of her back and stretched. Picking the lavender made it ache.

Her dress clung to her back. The heat had increased over the past few days since she and Valdar had gone out to the cove and had discovered the truth—that Oswald had been lying to gain attention. There was a thunderstorm brewing and it couldn't come quickly enough for her liking.

Ever since they had returned from the cove, Valdar had seemed distant and preoccupied. He had even allowed her to win at their nightly game of King's table. Twice.

'My lady!' Gode came running up.

Alwynn brushed her hands off on her apron. 'If you need more of any herb, it will have to wait.'

'Urien has run away, my lady. I turned my back for an instant and she was gone.'

Alwynn's heart thudded. 'You promised to look after her.'

Gode's withered cheeks reddened. 'I may have dozed off a little. I think she put some valerian in my drink.'

'Gode!' Alwynn put her hands on her hips. 'At least give me some credit. Urien knows nothing about herbs.'

She stared at the woman hard. Gode waved her hands in mock surrender.

'All right, all right,' she muttered. 'I tend to fall asleep in the afternoon these days. But I thought Urien was quiet, like. I didn't think she would go anywhere. That she understood why she needed to remain with me. She had taken to sitting in the garden, not doing much, just staring. I only nodded off for a brief instant and then when I went to fetch her, she had gone. Vanished, like.'

'You think she has returned to her husband.'

'That no-good blight on humanity?' Gode narrowed her eyes, considering. 'Yes, I do.'

'Why would she do that? She was safe.'

'I heard he'd taken up with another woman. He needs someone to fetch and carry for him. And the pig-keeper's widow isn't too picky about her men. Then there was this message he sent, something about him solving everything. I told her not to go and to trust in you.'

Alwynn pressed her lips together. Gode being Gode had no doubt imparted that information about the pig-keeper's widow. Accidentally, perhaps. Or from a desire to convince Urien not to return to Cleofirth, but now it seemed it had had the opposite effect.

'As bad as he is, Urien wants to keep him.'

'Aye, I reckon so.'

'We shall have to go and fetch her back. I won't have my authority undermined.'

'Do you want to go on your own?'

'Cleofirth won't harm me.' Alwynn glanced over her shoulder. 'Valdar is busy at the grist-mill. It will be late before he is finished. He has been back late every day this week.'

Every day since they had made love on the bluff. Alwynn frowned and tried to push the thought away. She had thought then that they were closer than ever, but he seemed to be pulling away from her. She could feel the days slipping through her fingers but she didn't dare bring up the prospect of his staying. They had made a bargain.

'Will Lady Merewynn go with you?' Gode asked, giving a slight cough.

'I can cope,' Alwynn said. 'Why the sudden concern? I was the one who rescued this estate! Me, on my own. I have faced tenants before and I will face them on my own again when…later this autumn.'

'Yes, my lady. I thought you could use a lit-tle company.' Gode placed a hand on Alwynn's sleeve. 'Lady Merri is capable of more than you think. And I, too, can be of assistance. Some-times you do not need to go it alone. Sometimes you should accept help.'

Alwynn opened her mouth to refuse, but thought better of it. Gode was right. Going alone was not the answer. She wished Valdar could come, too, but there was no time to wait for him. If she needed him, she could always send for him. Merri had strong legs for running. 'It will do Merri good to come with me and learn how to deal with tenants. She has been spending far too much time with that pony.'

Gode crossed her arms. 'If you think you are getting rid of me that easily, my lady, you have another think coming. I was wrong to fall asleep. I mean to make amends. I am coming with you.'

'At the first hint of any trouble, you are to return here. I will not risk losing you, Gode.'

The old lady's eyes filled with tears. 'We all have to go some time, my lady.'

'Is there something you are not telling me, Gode?'

Gode adopted a guileless expression. 'Have I ever kept a secret from you, my lady?'

Once she had found Urien, she would question Gode closer. Gode was hiding something from her, something important. 'You had better not.'

Valdar crouched down on the top of the ridge, watching the inlet. Girmir and his crew would be back. He could feel it in his bones. The place was perfect for beaching a long boat. That Girmir had used it before gave him hope. Girmir was a creature of habit. He had sacrificed the lad here. He would return here. He had to hope that it happened before they attacked and destroyed any more property.

'And you are sure you saw the dragon ship here?' he asked Oswald, who sat on a nearby rock, copying Valdar's every move.

Since his trip to the cove, he found Oswald had become his shadow. First secretly following him about and then more openly. Valdar found little jobs for him to do in exchange for his teaching him how to use a sword. There was a hunger in the lad to be a warrior. Valdar silently promised that he would make sure he reached his goal. Precisely how he would accomplish this, he wasn't sure.

The boy nodded. 'Why does no one believe me?'

'It helps when you have a reputation for telling the truth. Once it is lost, it takes time to recover, but it can be done. I have seen it happen many times. You need to show everyone that you are a man of honour. Eventually they will believe because you believe. Or so my father once told me.'

Valdar realised with a start that he could apply the same logic here, if he found Girmir and dispatched him. Alwynn would never have to know.

Oswald's eyes shone. 'You once told tall tales?'

'I was a boy like you. Far from here, but I, too, wanted things to be exciting. Then I learnt that hard work can have its own rewards.'

'When I grow up I want to be a warrior. I want to fight in battles and gain glory. I don't want to have to grind corn.'

'There is more to life than glory. Men need to eat.'

'You can say that because you live somewhere else, not this backwater of a place.'

'Where I live is not so very different from this place. The people are the same. They want to live their lives without being molested.'

'And where is that?'

Something stuck in Valdar's throat. His lie was one of omission. And every day it seemed to get bigger. It didn't help that Raumerike felt like a dream. Northumbria was far more real. He cared about its people. One person. More than he thought possible. And if she discovered the truth, any feelings she had for him would turn to dust. 'A long way from here. Across the sea.'

'Have you ever battled the Northmen?'

He gave a laugh and ruffled the boy's hair, but his insides clenched. Lately he had told so many half-truths. And his heritage didn't matter. It was how he lived his life now. 'When the occasion demanded it.'

'And you survived?'

'They are men like any other.'

Oswald frowned. 'I thought the raid on Lindisfarne was the first time anyone had heard of the barbarians from the North. And I know all the names of the men who fought during St Cuthbert's storm. Yours was not amongst them.'

'Maybe here, but where I come from, no. We had heard of them.' Valdar looked out at the shimmering sea. 'Describe precisely what you saw the other day. I need to know every single detail. How many men do you think you saw? Can you describe any of them?'

Oswald began to recite his story again. Valdar listened intently. Somewhere in the boy's retelling would be the clue he needed to prevent a massacre.

The boy broke off his monologue and pointed. 'Tell me you see it.'

'See what?'

He pointed towards the horizon. 'A sail.'

Valdar tightened his grip on his sword. He

could see something which might be a sail, but it was far too early to tell. 'Good lad. You have excellent eyes. What shape is it?'

'What do we do now? Meet them at the shore?'

'We wait. We watch. We see what sort of sail it is. It might not be a Northman's sail at all. Running off to tell everyone can just lead to people thinking you don't speak the truth. Wait until you know for certain.'

Beside him, the boy quivered with a combination of excitement and fear. Valdar knew the same nervous anticipation ran through his veins. Like Oswald, he wanted it to be a Northman. He wanted it to be Girmir.

He could do this. He could vanquish Girmir and there would be no reason for anyone to know the truth of his origins.

He could lead a new life with Alwynn, one where he would build a hall on this bluff, have many strong sons and lead a life as a pillar of the community. The gods had granted him a second chance and he intended to grab it.

'It's not a Northman's sail,' Oswald cried out and collapsed back down to the ground. 'It is just a Northumbrian fishing boat. They would have really laughed at me if I had gone running to the village.'

'Some day it will be, Oswald.' Valdar gripped his sword. 'And we will be ready.'

'Why did I have to come out here?' Merri kicked a stone and sent it skittering into a mud pool. 'Looking after Purebright takes time, you know.'

'We need to find Urien. I don't like this any better than you do,' Alwynn explained for the fifth time.

'Valdar could have done it.' Merri became mutinous. 'It is too hot.'

'He has other duties.' Alwynn concentrated on the road. The heat shimmered off the rough stones.

'Do you think Lord Edwin will be back soon? Oswald says…'

Alwynn stopped in the middle of the road. Oswald again. 'I have no idea and neither does Oswald. His tale-telling has become out of control. He has everyone running about like headless chickens.'

'Are you angry with me?'

Alwynn winced. She had given vent to her frustration over Valdar and the heat. 'No, sweetling, just tired. The heat makes me cross.'

'It makes everyone cross.' Merri sniffed. 'I can smell burning.'

'What sort of burning?'

Merri pointed. 'There is smoke. It is coming from Cleofirth's farm. I know it is. It is the only farm over that way.'

Alwynn's mouth went dry.

'Raiders?' Merri whispered.

'Don't be ridiculous, Merri. Everyone has Northmen on the brain,' Gode said. 'It will be Urien. She will have found her husband in bed with that tramp from the village and her mind will have snapped.'

'Whatever it is, they need our help.' Alwynn began to run.

'Why you are going this way? We should go back to the gristmill and get Valdar,' Merri said. 'I bet he is good at fighting fires.'

Alwynn stopped. Everyone seemed to have forgotten who had saved this estate in the first place. 'Let's get a bit closer. If we need to, you can go. You know the short way.'

They crept closer. From a small crest above the farm, they could see the barn and the house were ablaze. It was far worse than she had thought. Could Gode have been right? Was Urien capable of such a deed?

A woman's scream tore the stillness.

Alwynn put a hand on Merri's shoulder, preventing her from going closer. 'Go and fetch Valdar now. Tell him to bring his sword.'

'What is going on?'

'I don't know, but you were right. Valdar needs to be here. We need his help.'

'What are you going to do?'

'I'm not sure.' Alwynn bit her lip. Had all this happened because she took Urien away? But she couldn't have left her here, not with the bruising to her face and her admission of guilt. 'Go now! Once Valdar is here, we can decide, but I can't do this on my own. I need his sword arm.'

Just as she had hoped, Merri ran without looking back. Alwynn breathed a little easier. Whatever was going on here, Merri was out of it and safe.

'Valdar will arrive soon.'

'It depends on whether or not you can count on his help,' Gode muttered.

'What do you mean by that? Valdar is not an enemy.' Alwynn knew her cheeks burnt bright red. She had to hope Gode didn't know that he had made love to her. 'He is my steward.'

'He is also one of them.'

'One of whom?'

'One of the Northmen raiders!' The words burst from Gode.

Alwynn's stomach churned. Of course that was nonsense. Gode had been the one to cause this by falling asleep. 'Impossible. You are wrong. It is wicked of you to say such a thing. You could cost Valdar his life. He is a stranger, yes, but not all strangers are Northmen.'

'He and I made a bargain. He'd keep my secret. I'd keep his.' Gode crossed her arms. 'I never thought he'd do this. We have been harbouring a viper in our midst, my lady, a viper.'

Alwynn didn't believe Gode. He couldn't be a Northman. He was from Raumerike, somewhere in the Frankish lands. He had a Frankish sword and he'd looked properly horrified about the Lindisfarne raid. True, she'd never seen him go to church, but that didn't mean anything. Work on the estate had kept him busy. And anyway, her father had stopped going after her brother died. And Northmen carried double axes, not Frankish swords.

But then there were the tiny insistent doubts, the things she should have questioned. How did he know what Northmen did or how they raided? Who had he prayed to in his fever? Even now, her mind shied away. He was unlike any Northman she had ever heard of. Had she been taken in again? Had she trusted the wrong person?

'Is this true, Gode? Tell me, please tell me the truth.'

Gode hung her head. 'Yes, my lady. I didn't want to worry you and he was only one man. Plus, he seemed like a good man.'

'I don't have time for this now. Believe me, Gode, when I say—Valdar is no Northman.' As she said the words, Alwynn prayed she was right. 'He would have told me if he was. But he has done so much good here. Everyone says so.'

'He is a Northman. I'm telling the truth.'

'And what secret did he keep for you in return?'

Gode looked down and paused before taking a deep breath. 'I'm ill, my lady. I'm dying. The monks have confirmed it. I didn't want to worry you when you had so many things to take care of.'

Alwynn's heart knocked against her chest. It would explain Gode's slight yellowish colour and why she had been moving so slowly. She kicked herself for not questioning Gode more closely.

'Gode, no! This can't be happening. We'll talk about this later. Right now, I have a farm to save. And some outlaws to catch.'

'As you say, my lady…'

'And I am not going to do anything. I am just

going to watch and make an assessment of the situation.'

Alwynn crept closer with Gode following hot on her heels. The fire had taken hold. But no one seemed to be fighting it. An eerie silence hung over the yard.

'Urien! This is not the way!'

The echo ran about a silent farmyard, mocking her.

'My lady,' Gode whispered. 'There is something about this place that I don't like. We should go. Come back with men. You can do nothing about this fire by yourself.'

Then she saw them, off to the right and nearly out of the farmyard. The raiders. Northmen. She could no longer tell herself it was outlaws. The men were dressed in a motley gear and speaking a foreign tongue. Her heart knocked. Since when did outlaws speak in a foreign tongue? Or brandish double axes?

She wiped her hands against her gown. Valdar was from the North. Of course he was. The ship with the broken mast. It made sense. He had known what was hidden in that cove and he had distracted her. She had silenced every single doubt because she'd believed in him, in a person who didn't exist. This raiding, this was his reality.

She'd been such a fool.

Steadily she began to back away, hoping against hope that in the confusion no one had seen her.

A crunch of footsteps behind her made her pause.

'Valdar,' she whispered. 'Please let it be you.'

Chapter Twelve

'This way, Oswald! A slicing motion.' Valdar showed the boy how to make the correct movement with his sword for the third time. After the incident with the fishing boat, Valdar was keeping half an eye on the cove. Girmir would return here, he was sure of it. It was the perfect spot for conducting raids. When he did, Valdar would be ready for him and his murderous crew.

That boy, Eirik—why now could he remember his name?—would never have given up the sunstone readily. Valdar's blood ran cold to think about what must have happened to him. All he knew was that he had to prevent Girmir and his gang of mutineers from harming anyone else.

'A sword is not a pitchfork. Do not attempt to prod people with it. Now you try it. Slowly and carefully.'

'Valdar! Valdar! There is trouble at Cleofirth

the Plough's farm.' Lady Merri entered the glade at a run. 'Come quickly. There is a fire.'

Oswald dropped the sword with a loud clang. 'Can't you see Valdar is teaching me to be a warrior?' he proclaimed.

'Oswald, son of Oswy, so help me...' Merri drew back her fist.

'You will never become a fine lady if you go around punching warriors.'

'Hush, Oswald. A warrior always listens to a fair lady in distress.'

'Cleofirth the Plough's farm is on fire.'

'Where is Lady Alwynn?'

'She has gone there with Gode. Urien escaped and now the farmhouse is ablaze.' Tears ran down Merri's face. 'I am so worried. I should be there. I should be helping. But my stepmother sent me here.'

'Lady Alwynn is sensible. Return to the hall with Oswald. He can protect you.'

Both looked aghast at the prospect.

'It is what needs doing.' Valdar glared at them both. 'Oswald, you protect Lady Merewynn. It is what a warrior would do—protect a fair maiden. And, Merewynn, you stay out of harm's way. Behave like a lady.'

'Fighting fires is easy,' Merri said with her bottom lip poking out. 'I can throw water on a fire. There was one Oswald made two weeks ago which blazed out of control until I threw a bucket of water on it.' She paused. 'You won't tell my stepmother, will you? She doesn't approve of such things.'

'If you stay with Oswald, I will keep my lips sealed,' Valdar said with a smile.

'Shall I raise the alarm with my father?' Oswald asked. 'He and the other villagers will want to help. Lady Merewynn could stay with my mother.'

'Yes, that is a good idea. We will need many hands to deal with a fire.'

Valdar set off at a run. Silently he prayed that Alwynn had not done anything stupid. Fire was nothing to play around with. The thought of her being there alone, battling the blaze, made his legs move faster.

He ran quicker than he thought possible and soon reached Cleofirth's farm. The fire blazed out of control. Slaughtered animal carcasses littered the ground. The pit of his stomach tightened. There was only one person who would have done this. He prayed to any god who might be listening that Alwynn had fled.

He spotted the body of an old woman nestled in the hollow of a tree and knew his prayers would be unanswered. He gently shook her shoulder. 'Gode? Are you alive?'

She opened her eyes. 'You were right, Northman. I should have told her sooner about the pains in my stomach. My race is nearly run.'

'Where is Alwynn? Has she gone into the farmhouse?'

'Other Northmen. Not like you. Rotten to the core those lot. I waited for you. I hid.' Each word was said with a laboured breath. 'Find her. Keep her safe.'

'I'm here now and I will. I promise.'

Valdar tried to hold his fears at bay. The stakes were far greater than any battle he'd encountered before and the only way to win was to keep a cool head.

He knew in that instant that destroying Girmir and his men was as much about protecting his future with Alwynn as it was about honouring his past.

'Alwynn!' he called. 'Alwynn, where are you?'

For three heartbeats there was no answer, then he heard her scream off to his right. But it was the sound of the other voice which sent a chill down his spine.

Girmir. A deep calm filled Valdar. He felt the peace. It happened every time before a battle.

And this fight would be the most important of his life. The knowledge rocked him.

Valdar drew his sword and rushed forward. The tableau was spread out in front of him. Girmir had slung Alwynn over his shoulder. The other mutinous members of the *felag* were loaded down with dead sheep, sacks of grain and a barrel of ale. He looked in vain to see if any of them might support him.

'Not a very good haul!' he called. 'Is this what I sacrificed myself for?'

'Valdar?' Alwynn squeaked.

'Put the woman down and leave this place!' he thundered.

Girmir and the remainder of the *felag* went pale. Several backed up. Shock and consternation filled their faces.

'A shade from the past!' someone shouted. 'The gods have sent a warning.'

'Why should we worry? He wasn't any problem before. He won't be any problem now,' shouted another.

'You have no idea what sort of problem I can be,' Valdar said through clenched teeth.

Girmir frowned. 'Flesh and blood, I reckon.'

'Put the woman down and walk away.' Valdar advanced steadily. The first task, the only task, was to get Alwynn free. 'And I may yet let you live.'

Girmir took a step forward, but stumbled slightly on a tree root.

'Does she belong to you, Lack-Sword? She tastes good.' Girmir licked Alwynn's cheek. Alwynn spat in his face and struggled against Girmir.

'That one is a wildcat.' Girmir wiped the spittle from his face. 'I plan on enjoying her. Maybe I will let you watch. Show you how a real man does it.'

The world became tinged red. He felt his self-control slip. He forced a breath into his burning lungs. Girmir wanted him unbalanced to gain an advantage.

'Let her go. Now. Unharmed. And you may yet save your crew,' he ground out.

'Why?' Girmir looked him up and down with a sneer on his evil visage. 'There are more of us than you. You will be cut down before you reach me. And I will slit her throat.'

Alwynn twisted and brought her knees up, connecting with Girmir's middle. Valdar wanted to tear him limb from limb for daring to touch his woman. 'Let me down. Unhand me.'

'Do as she asks.'

'Or what?'

'I challenge you. Warrior against warrior.'

'You will challenge me?'

Valdar inwardly smiled. Girmir always did have a big head. Now he had a plan—he simply had to fight Girmir.

'The gods favour me, Girmir. They always have. You know that. My swim in the sea proved it.'

'Your survival angers them. I will have no dealings with a person who has turned his back on our gods!'

'Why do you always seek to find a way to get out of every challenge? You can't slit my throat like you did with Horik. Nor can you poison my drink like you did with Sirgurd. Turned his bowels to water, wasn't that your boast?'

As he'd hoped, the remainder of the *felag* stopped. No one came to Girmir's assistance. Several murmured amongst themselves. They knew the rumours as well as he did. Valdar kept his gaze trained on Girmir.

'That was never proved!' Girmir shouted. 'The gods punished Sirgurd for speaking against me. And everyone killed Horik. Everyone put his sword into his belly. And those who didn't, they fought me and lost.'

'Didn't you tell them how you defeated Sirgurd, Girmir? The tricks you played?'

'I didn't put anything into his drink. Is it my fault that dust blinded him?' Utter silence greeted his coarse laugh.

Girmir glanced to his left and right. The men had started to back away.

'Valdar has the right to challenge you,' one of the men said. 'He is one of the *felag*.'

'You have brought us nothing but ill luck, Girmir Storm Crow. The gods favour Valdar. They have kept him alive.'

'Fools, it is because he didn't die that our mast broke.'

'You blamed that on my cousin,' someone grumbled. 'You slit his throat. And all that happened was that we were washed up back here without food. And not enough men to row. And our navigator is lost. All because of your bad temper.'

'Your answer, Girmir,' Valdar said. 'Will you fight? Or will you be cast out of the *felag* as a coward?'

Girmir dumped Alwynn on the ground. 'No man calls me a coward and lives.'

Silently Valdar prayed that she'd remain sensible and stay still. She curled up in a ball, but before she did, she gave him a look that cut him to the core.

Valdar clung on to his self-control. The only

way he could win was not to lose his temper. His father had hammered that lesson into him. Defend and wait for the opportunity to strike.

'Shall we fight? For the right to lead the *felag*? You against me with no other man involved.'

'Only members of the *felag* can fight for that.'

'I'm still a member—the gods chose to save me and the outcome of our fight lies in their hands.' Valdar advanced, swinging his sword in his right hand, savouring the feel of it. It was good to be fighting again, instead of running. He would avenge deaths, but more important he would keep Alwynn safe. After he was finished no one would attack this section of the Northumbrian coast for generations. 'They realised I had unfinished business. Now, will you fight or be branded as a coward for ever?'

Girmir glanced to his right and left. The men were still backed away from him. It was then Valdar knew he had a chance.

'I will fight.' Girmir drew his sword and tossed it between his hands. 'It will be my great pleasure to carve your liver out of your hide and then I will have your woman, Nerison. Slowly and without mercy.'

Valdar raised his chin and stared at him. 'The gods will decide what happens. They always do.'

The men made a circle about them. He could

hear the betting that always accompanied a challenge like this.

'Shall we agree the rules?' Valdar asked. 'It is customary—'

'Your challenge. My rules.' Giving a great shout, Girmir rushed forward, circling an axe in one hand and a sword in the other.

Valdar was ready for the charge. He'd seen the manoeuvre in his youth. At the last breath, he pivoted and Girmir plunged into the circle of warriors.

Girmir wiped the sweat from his face. 'I bet you think you are amusing.'

'I'm not the one who just ran past my opponent without landing a blow.'

Someone tossed Valdar a shield. 'You will need this. I'm betting on you to bring us home.'

He crouched ready for the next onslaught. Girmir charged forward.

Valdar's sword met Girmir's with a great clang as he raised his shield to deflect the axe. Rather than backing off, Girmir pressed forward.

The ferocity of the attack would have knocked a less fit man off his feet, but Valdar instantly adjusted his stance and regained his balance.

Girmir's reputation as a successful fighter might be well earned, but the man had no stamina. He resorted to cheap tricks before the fight had properly begun.

Valdar knew if he could keep up the defence, he would find an opening and would be able to defeat him. It was how his father had taught him to fight—with caution and patience, weighing up his opportunities and waiting until the perfect opening came along.

Valdar risked a glance at Alwynn. She hadn't moved. If Girmir had harmed one hair on her head... And then he saw it—the bruise to her right cheek.

Tossing aside years of caution, he drove forward, meeting each of the blows that Girmir thought to rain on him with a cut or thrust of his own. Girmir's eyes widened as he was forced on the back foot, forced to defend rather than to attack. It was obvious what he'd expected—the old cautious Valdar, the warrior who always defended.

Valdar gave an inward smile. That Valdar had drowned in the storm.

He brought his shield down on Girmir's axe hand and the weapon fell to the ground. Valdar kicked it away.

Round and round they went. He felt the searing heat of a knife hit his forearm and knew his luck was running out. The power in his arm was going and it was only a matter of time before Girmir landed another lucky blow.

Giving in to instinct, Valdar stabbed forward and down, and connected with Girmir's side.

'Where is the boy, Girmir? Where is your navigator?'

'The lad's disappeared. He was bad luck. Probably got by a boar or a wolf afore I found him. We was searching for him when we came across this here farm. The farmer should have let us take what we wanted. Wouldn't have been no trouble that way.'

Valdar clenched his jaw. There would be time to grieve for Eirik later. All the boy had wanted was to take part in a trading voyage. He had honestly thought the boy's skill at navigation would have protected him. One day when he could, he'd sing a lament for the lad.

'You deserve to rot in the ice of hell, Girmir.'

'No, you do, Valdar.' Girmir brought his blade down, missing Valdar's shoulder by a hair's breadth. 'You are too slow, Valdar Nerison. You are cautious. You are a practical man who never sticks his neck out. It is why men like me will always win in the end. Fortune favours the brave.'

Valdar felt the familiar doubts assail him.

A tiny sound from Alwynn shocked him back to reality. He redoubled his efforts and ignored the pain in his arm. He had this one chance. He had to do it for Alwynn and for her people.

'Fortune favours me today!' He lunged forward with all his might and felt the sword sink deep. Girmir gave an odd gurgle and fell backwards. 'Your rule of this *felag* has ended. For ever!'

Alwynn watched the fight with horrified eyes. Valdar, the man she'd given her body to, was one of them, one of the despised Northmen. He was speaking their language and the men seemed to know him. They called to him by name.

But deep down in her heart she'd always known it. Ever since that first night when they'd spoken in the darkness, but she hadn't wanted to admit it.

She'd made excuses and fabricated another life for him. Another land far away, across a different sea. She'd ruthlessly silenced all her doubts. So much for saying goodbye to the naive woman who blithely trusted her husband. Only she was worse than ever. She hated herself for not facing the truth earlier. She'd lied to everyone, but most of all she'd lied to herself because she lusted after Valdar and she'd known what he was.

The only things the Northmen brought were death and destruction. Looking around the burning farm strewn with slaughtered animals and dead bodies, clearly Valdar was no exception. Death and destruction indeed. He had lied about everything. He was a brutal raider, a murderer. He was not the principled man he'd claimed to be. He'd lied to her and she'd believed him because she had wanted to. He'd utterly betrayed her. She cursed that, even now, a part of her hoped that there had been some ghastly mistake, that he'd been their prisoner or slave, that somehow he wasn't a Northman.

She'd watched the battle from behind her hands and been glad that he'd killed the foul-breathed Northman who had held her captive. That one would have raped her in the blink of an eye. She had seen what he'd done at the farm. Urien barely alive and Cleofirth cut down.

She had rejoiced when she saw the sword sink deep into the brute's stomach. What did that make her? She retched slightly, despising herself. Inadvertently she had become the lowest of the low—a Northman's lover. Had Valdar known they were here all this time? Every inch of her skin crawled with shame.

'It's over,' Valdar gasped out, clutching his arm. 'You're safe, Alwynn.'

She took a step backwards, avoiding his hand. Valdar was one of them. All her dreams about a life together, a life with a kind and gentle man who loved her and would die for her, was an insubstantial fairy tale. The reality was the slaughter in the farmhouse. Valdar had… 'No! I can never be safe when you are here.'

The other Northmen started to move closer, more menacing than before. Whatever they said caused Valdar to go white. He moved in front of her. 'I will protect you, Alwynn, to my dying breath.'

Alwynn gulped. The odds were not good on either of them surviving.

'What is going on?' Oswy thundered behind her. 'We heard there was…'

She turned and saw a host of villagers armed with little more than pitchforks and shovels, but loaded with determination. Oswy brandished an axe.

'The Northmen!' she cried. 'They've attacked Cleofirth's farmhouse!'

The men looked to Valdar for confirmation that they should attack these peasants, then when one turned and started running, the rest took off after him. Only Valdar remained, standing resolute before the villagers, his bloodied sword half-raised.

'After them,' he cried. 'They would kill us all.'

The villagers needed no more urging and swarmed past, intent on righting a wrong.

Alwynn's legs refused to hold her up and she sank to the ground. She covered her eyes and laid her face against the soft moss. She'd been such a fool and her heart shattered into a thousand pieces.

She never knew how long she knelt there, but gradually she became aware of the utter silence. Where there had been a great rushing sound, now there was only stillness. An eerie sort of stillness.

'Alwynn?' she heard Valdar call in the stillness. 'Are you hurt? Did Girmir do anything to you? Did anyone hurt you?'

With furious fingers, she brushed the moisture from her cheeks. 'I'm fine.' *Except my heart is breaking.*

'You've nothing to fear. It has been a complete rout. Girmir can't hurt you any more, sweetling. None of them can.'

'Was that his name? Girmir?' she asked. She rose and kept her shoulders back. There was no way that Valdar would ever know her heart wept for him and the man she had thought he was. Her whole body seemed numb and she moved slowly as if she was moving in a dream.

'Aye, that was his name.' He crouched down beside her. 'He was one of the worst sort. The men who survived were mutineers and traitors. You must not think that all my countrymen are like that. Most are honest and law-abiding farmers.'

Honest and law-abiding? The words seemed hollow. 'You have a different notion of honesty, I think.'

'He and his gang are destroyed, thanks to you.'

'I didn't do anything.' She pressed her hands together to stop them trembling. 'Nothing at all.'

'You gave me my courage back. I could fight for you in a way that I could not fight for my dead comrades.' He came beside her and she saw weariness etched on the lines of his face. 'When I thought I was beaten, I turned my head and saw you. Fresh strength flowed through me and I defeated him. You saved my life. Again.'

Her heart ached anew, but she told herself sternly that those were just words. Valdar possessed a silver tongue. It could not distract her from what he was—a Northman who had come to wage war on an innocent people.

'I'm fine. There are other people…'

'They can wait.'

She glanced over and saw his ghostly pallor.

All her resolutions fled. Blood seeped from his arm. His blood. He had fought for her. The only reason why she was alive was because of him. She closed her eyes. One Northman was different from the rest. How could she judge him when he had saved her life?

There was no way she could betray him to the king, but also there was no way he could remain here. All her earlier dreams tasted like dust in her mouth.

She reached into the herb bag that she always carried and withdrew a little moss. The act made her feel better. She knew how to heal, even if her heart was bleeding.

She scrambled over to him and put his head on her lap. She stroked his forehead 'You are injured. Keep quiet now. Let me handle everything.'

He nodded. 'We will do this as you say. But know that I would never hurt you or allow anyone to hurt you. I would give my life for you. Gladly.'

'Oswy!' she called, trying to concentrate on the wound rather than his words. His flesh swam in front of her eyes. She blinked several times and tasted the salt of tears as they dripped down the back of her throat. Her heart wanted to believe him, but how could she? 'Fetch me some water. Valdar is hurt. I should be able to save him, but I will need herbs.'

'My lady?' The big miller tilted his head to one side. 'What is going on here? What has happened to Valdar?'

'Valdar fought the Northman's leader and won. If he hadn't done that, I shudder to think what could have happened.' Her voice sounded high and tight to her ears. Silently she prayed Oswy would not ask how the fight came about. She was through with lying. 'But he hurt his arm. I want to see if the blade went deep or simply glanced off.'

Oswy gave a huge smile. 'I will get the water for our local hero. Did you see the way he cut down that brute of a Northman?'

He trotted off faster than she'd seen him move for many years.

'Why did you fight him?' she asked. 'What did you hope to gain?'

Valdar sat up, cradling his arm. 'I fought to save you. The only way I could do that was to challenge Girmir. I'd hoped that would be enough to stop them all, but the others were too far gone. They called me a traitor because of you. I have no remorse about their fate.'

'I will take your word for that. I know what he and his men did in that farmhouse.'

He gave a faint nod and raised a hand to touch her, but she backed away. 'The villagers will be talking about how they routed the Northmen for ever. It took all my doing to persuade them not to go into their fishing boats and travel northwards.'

Her heart knocked against her chest. She had to hope that no one else had guessed about his true allegiance. Not while the blood was running high. He would be killed without question if any of the villagers suspected the truth.

'Were they your friends? Girmir and his men?'

Slowly he shook his head. 'You know the answer to that. I did not bring them here and I did not betray you.'

Alwynn bit her lip. She had trusted him and he wasn't the person he'd seemed to be at all. And yet he had saved her life. He had confronted that horrible barbarian and beaten him. He had stood between her and the other men, prepared to battle. Her stomach revolted.

What had Valdar's true purpose here been? Did she even want to know? He had used her, but then he'd saved her life. She owed him something for that. Her head pained her so dreadfully that it was hard to think straight. 'I don't know you, Valdar. I thought I did, but you are a different person entirely. I've no idea what sort of man you are.'

He reached out and put her hand against his chest. Under her palm she felt the steady thump of his heart. 'Do you feel that? My heart is true, Alwynn. Always. It beats for you and you alone.'

Her hand rested against his chest. She could feel its rise and fall with every breath he took. Her heart desperately wanted to believe, but she knew she couldn't.

Her trust had been shattered. With Theodbald, she'd had the excuse of being young and a wife. There was no excuse with Valdar. She'd lusted after him and that had blinded her to his faults. She hadn't listened to any of her doubts and she'd never questioned.

Thinking back, she suspected that Gode had tried to tell her that first day she visited the hut, but she hadn't wanted to listen. She could have asked him about the words he'd called out in his sleep. She could have questioned him about how he knew so much about the habits of Northmen raiders. If she had…they could have been prepared. The farmhouse had burnt because she'd been too cowardly to ask basic questions. She put her hand to her aching head. The guilt threatened to overwhelm her.

'Alwynn?' he asked, uncertainty creeping into his voice. 'Are you listening to me?'

She withdrew her hand. If she wanted to keep her wits about her, she had to keep from touching him.

'Why were you here if not to rob and murder? You are a long way from your homeland, Valdar. You came for a purpose. From the looks of Girmir and his men you didn't come to make friends.'

'You ought to believe me when I say that wasn't it at all.'

'Why? You lied to me. In the worst way.'

'I merely let you believe what you wanted to. If it was a lie, it was a lie of omission. I couldn't take the risk of telling you the truth. I thought once you knew me, you'd understand the sort of man I was.' He made a helpless gesture which reminded her of her late husband when he was caught in a lie. 'This thing between you and me, it wasn't supposed to occur. But it did and it has been the best thing ever to happen to me.'

This morning, his words would have set her heart fluttering. Now she realised they had no more meaning than a bard's tale.

'I never asked you to. It was all about a quick roll in the hay. Something to satisfy an itch.' Even as the words poured out of her, she knew they weren't true. It had been much more than that to her. It was why her heart felt as if it was in a thousand pieces. 'We have finished now. You and I.'

He caught her wrist and held her with a firm but gentle grasp.

She twisted her hand. 'Let me go.'

'Never cheapen yourself that way again!'

His face went white and he swayed slightly. Instant remorse filled her soul. He might not be the man she thought he was, but he had saved her life and it had nearly cost him his own. It could still cost him his life. She needed to get him away from here. Soon all the village and the countryside would know he was a Northman.

'Sit down. You are hurt. Let me examine you. All this can wait until later.'

'I will heal. I've done so in the past without difficulty.'

She rolled her eyes. 'Please.'

'What are you going to do? What can you do? The cut is clean. It is not bleeding overly much.'

The pallor of his cheeks told a different story. She pressed some more moss in the cut on his arm and wrapped seaweed about it. The cut on his chest looked superficial.

'I'm going to try to save your life. Then we

will be quits, but we will never go back to what we had.'

'I love you, Alwynn.'

'I doubt you even know the meaning of the words.' She turned on her heel and walked away. 'You knew what you were and how this was going to end. You never risked your heart.'

She stood looking over the smouldering remains for a long time. Violent shivers came over her as she thought about what had almost happened and she knew sleep would evade her for many weeks to come. She wanted to be so busy doing things she did not have time to think. She also knew that she never wanted to believe in anyone or anything again.

'Stepmother! Stepmother!' Merri rushed up to her. 'Our Valdar was the hero. Everyone says so...well, everyone but Urien and she is not in her right mind.'

'What is Urien saying?'

'That he brought this terrible misfortune on all of us. That he was in league with those men.' Merri's face crumpled. 'If that was true, we'd all be dead. We would never have survived. And why would they attack this farmhouse? There are more treasures in the church and the hall.

Valdar knew that. He stopped them from destroying everything.'

Alwynn put a hand on Merri's shoulder. Merri was real flesh and blood. She should be thinking about her not mourning something which could never come to pass. Valdar was a totally different man from the idol she had built up. But Merri was right. Because Valdar was here, these men had been stopped. They would not harm anyone else. Her insides felt as if they had been ripped to shreds.

'I'm very grateful to Valdar. He saved my life,' she said around a lump in her throat. Saved her life and broke her heart all at the same time.

'Shall they take him back to the hall?'

'Valdar says he won't go. One of the monks has re-wrapped his arm and his chest with seaweed.' Merri's eyes sparkled. 'He said that you did a good job, but were probably distracted because the one on the arm wasn't tight enough.'

Alwynn clasped her hands together so tightly the knuckles stood out. Monks had arrived. Who else? She peered at the scene and saw that the place swarmed with villagers. It was only a matter of time before they discovered Valdar was truly a Northman and then… Her mind shied away from the picture.

'I didn't realise that any had come,' she said

in a toneless voice. 'I'm not myself. I don't think I have been myself for the entire summer.'

'But you have started singing again. Please say you will still sing. No matter what.'

Alwynn stroked Merri's hair. The hair was soft as silk against her fingers. She shuddered to think what those depraved monsters would have done if they had got their paws on this sweet girl.

Lust. It was little wonder that the priests warned against it.

'You should keep your head covered,' she said when Merri gave her a questioning glance. 'You are growing up. I won't have people saying that you are allowed to run wild. I want you to make a good match.'

Merri gave a weak laugh and leant back against her. 'Same old stepmother. You never change. Always worrying.'

Her heart thumped in her chest. It surprised her that it was still beating. It felt as if there was a huge hole where it had once been. Merri might think she had not changed, but she knew she was not the same woman she'd been before Valdar had appeared.

Her fist clenched. She needed to get back to that woman who knew what she wanted from life and was content in her garden. She wanted the old certainties to return. She had to make them return.

She pressed her lips against Merri's hair. 'It's my job to worry about you, sweetling.' Her entire body was numb and it seemed as if she was moving in a dream, a waking nightmare. She watched the villagers' faces. None tried to hide their joy at the rout of the Northmen. Several sang Valdar's praises and openly wondered if he could be enticed to stay.

With each new adulation of Valdar, her stomach tightened. She wanted to scream that he wasn't the hero he seemed. But if she did that, he'd be torn apart before her eyes. And she knew her heart could not bear that.

She had betrayed so many people in her headlong lust for Valdar. It was her fault and only she could make it right.

She stared at the pile of bodies and knew what she had to do. It was what she should have done days ago when Valdar first appeared. Going against the rules had not made her stronger. It had endangered everyone she cared about. And she had to do it right this time.

'I need a rider! I need to send a message to the king.'

Chapter Thirteen

Valdar lay in Gode's hut, alone. Alwynn's words about not risking his heart circled around and around his brain. He could have explained about the curse, but what was the point? He had already lost her.

He had inwardly wept to see the pointless carnage. There had been nothing at that farm to interest Girmir. He had simply wanted to destroy. He did not believe for a heartbeat Girmir's story about searching for the missing lad. Girmir had probably murdered Eirik Thorenson in the woods.

Somewhere there was a boat and the bounty from the voyage, assuming it had not all been lost during the storm. By rights it belonged to him, but he didn't want it.

He sincerely wished he had found them before they'd done this to people he cared about. Nor-

thumbrians were not weak or simple-minded.
They were a good strong people and he'd been
proud to call some of them friends. He might
not have risked his heart, but he had taken them
to his heart, particularly Alwynn, all the same.

'Why didn't I die earlier?' he muttered. 'It
would have made things much simpler.'

But even as he said the words, he knew they
were a lie. He wanted to live because he wanted
to see Alwynn again. Even an Alwynn who
hated him for his heritage. He wanted her to
see beyond that to the man inside.

A noise made him turn his head. Alwynn was
silhouetted in the fading light.

'Merri said that you wanted to see me.'

'You need to know the truth, Alwynn. So you
can judge me fairly. You need to understand what
brought me here.'

'Everyone thinks you are a hero. Even Gode.
Well, everyone except Urien, who appears to be
out of her head. The monks think she is touched
by demons. She has even accused them of being
Northmen.' She plucked at the skirt of her gown
and spoke to the ground. 'I can't bring myself to
tell them differently. Not yet. They need to believe in heroes.'

He winced at the words. Everything was
wrong between them. He wanted to go back

to how it was before. And that was impossible. Girmir's raid stood between them. She now saw him as one of them, rather than as he was, as he wanted to be for her—a good and honourable man.

'You should never have gone to that farm on your own.'

'You should have told me of the very real possibility of Northmen and I wouldn't have ventured from the hall.'

He ran a hand through his hair. Each word cut into his heart. 'I wanted to protect you. I thought I could find them before anyone else, before they did any damage. I didn't want to alarm you.'

'They are right, you know,' she continued as if she hadn't heard him. 'You did save me in the end. I should never have gone there. I thought it was Urien or a couple of vagabonds. I thought Northmen raiders were a tale of Oswald's. Only you knew differently.'

'I told you not to leave the hall.'

She rolled her eyes. 'After Theodbald died, I swore that I'd only believe in real things. Things I could touch and see. And yet I fell for your lie. I kept offering myself excuses, explaining away every doubt that came into my mind. What a gullible fool you must have thought me.'

'Never that. You did what you thought was

right.' He put out his hand and captured her fingers. This time she did not pull away.

The small gesture did much to steady his nerves. There had to be a way of making Alwynn see why he'd kept his heritage a secret.

'You need to know why I am here.'

'You already told me. You jumped off a ship in a storm. No doubt you thought you would save lives. Ever the bold hero.'

Valdar shook his head. 'You need to know I was a coward who did nothing. I joined the *felag* because I couldn't stand to see the woman I thought I loved pregnant with another man's child, her beloved husband's child. The *felag* was supposed to find new markets, but every market was closed to us because of the Lindisfarne raid. And those people who would trade with us offered far less than they should have. You might hate the Viken for the raids, but I hate them for it as well. Our two countries have been at war for years and now we were being made to pay for something they did.'

'Is this supposed to make me feel sorry for you? It doesn't surprise me that you loved a woman who couldn't love you back.'

Valdar rapidly explained about Horik, the mutiny and its aftermath. How he'd known that they would kill him and how he hated that he'd failed his friend. How he'd changed the stones and taken the boy's place. How he thought the ship had continued towards home without him and how he'd planned to go back and denounce them after he'd fulfilled his obligation to her.

Despite everything, he could see Alwynn listening. Silently he pleaded with her to believe. He had never felt so naked and vulnerable before a woman. He was utterly defenceless against her and she could kill all his desires with a glance.

When he finished his recital, she was quiet.

'Well?' he asked into the silence.

'Girmir killed the boy you sought to save?'

'Apparently. Girmir went mad after the mast broke in the storm. He'd thought that the gods should have been appeased by offering them my death. Then he slaughtered the last of the decent men. From what I could gather, once they reached the shore, the lad ran off into the woods to escape Girmir. Only Girmir returned. I spoke the truth when I said that no Northman stole sheep. It doesn't make any sense why they would. Maybe one if they were starving, but not a whole flock. Someone else is blaming the Northmen for stealing sheep.'

'How convenient.' Her mouth twisted. 'We came here to plunder and possibly rape, but not to steal sheep.'

Valdar collapsed back against the bedding. The memory of her eyes would haunt him. The time had come to explain. He no longer risked losing her. With each breath she slipped further away and he hadn't realised how much he needed her. 'Believe what you like, but I'm a warrior and make war on warriors who threaten my home and my family. I am also a merchant who knows the value of trade. I came in search of gold and new markets for my goods. My lands produce amber, soapstone and fur. I am proud to be from Raumerike. It is a good land filled with good people. I may have failed my friend when he was murdered, but you made me believe that I could be a worthy man again.'

'Those men came to kill, not to trade.' A violent shiver went down her back and she ran her hands up and down her arms. 'He was going to…going to…'

He wanted to grab his sword and run Girmir through again. The sheer violence of his reaction astonished him. He concentrated on the way the light hit her hair.

'We came to trade, but then there was a mutiny. Every land has its share of bad men, even this one. I should have seen the signs in Girmir earlier. I should have held the watch like Horik wanted me to, instead of switching with one of the other men because I was exhausted from squinting into the sun and navigating. But Girmir could also be quite amusing, charming, convincing. It was easier to laugh and turn a blind eye. For my shame I never expected him to go as far as he did.'

'But he actually meant it.'

'Once it started, there was little I could do. At first, I thought one of the other men would defeat him. Horik had two close kin sailing with us. But Girmir had arranged for their deaths.'

At her incredulous look, he added, 'They needed me alive to navigate. They took my sword and knives. But despite Girmir's promises, I knew I would never step foot on the shore of my home again. He would have slit my throat as soon as we spied the shores of Raumerike.'

'How did you get away?'

Valdar put a hand over his eyes. 'When I thought Girmir was about to sacrifice the boy, I rigged the draw so I was chosen. The boy kept my bonds loose and I was able to wriggle free and swim. That lad saved my life and Girmir killed him. I should have taken him with me. I could have kept him alive.'

'You barely survived—a young lad would have had no chance. But the storm washed you ashore where I discovered you. Where I was all too willing to believe your lies.'

Each word cut into his soul. He knew he deserved them and more for what he'd inadvertently done to her. He wanted to get his Alwynn back, the woman who believed in him and cherished him. This summer had shown him how precious a good woman was. And he could feel her slipping away from him with every breath he took.

Valdar reached out to her. 'You were and are the most beautiful creature I have ever seen. I thought you were a Valkyrie when I first saw you. A shield maiden of Odin. But you are better than that. You are flesh and blood. The time we have had together…'

Alwynn put two fingers against his mouth, stopping him before he said something that they'd both regret. She should never have come. It would have been easier if she hadn't. But just to hear the possibility of those words sent her heart soaring and she hated that her feelings for him still had life.

But she also knew someone had to tell him what she had done and why. What he faced. She had just not expected it to be so difficult.

'That is over between us. That was then and this is now.' She pressed her hands together and tried not to remember how soft and yielding his lips were against her hand. 'What passed between us should never have happened. It must never happen again.'

'I love you, Alwynn. I've been lying here, racking my brains, trying to figure out a way we can be together.' He caught her hands in his good one. 'Tell me that you can see beyond my past. That you can see the real me. Tell me that you want me to be that man for always.'

She hated that her heart leapt anew and screamed *yes*. She dampened it down. He had used her before and now he was attempting to use her again. She withdrew her hands.

'You want me to abandon my home and go north with you to an uncertain future.'

'I have land. A great estate. My sister-in-law would welcome you.'

'And the woman you thought you loved?' She hated that the beginnings of tears pricked her eyes. 'Valdar, you don't know what love is. You knew what would happen once I found out. You didn't risk your heart at all. You've no idea about love and honesty.'

He closed his eyes. 'It might be tricky at the start, but I'm confident my jaarl would reach the right decision.'

'One which favours you.'

'We could find a life there. But if he decides against me, we can find somewhere else. There will be a place that we can be together. I've a strong arm and am not afraid to work hard, but we belong together.'

She stared at him.

That she actually was prepared to think about it frightened her. She was supposed to hate him. She had come here to tell him how much she hated him. And now her heart was screaming that she should say that she would go to the ends of the earth on little more than a promise. That she should accept this man who had lied to her.

'When did you know the Northmen were here?' Her voice broke as she stumbled to get the last few words out. 'The truth.'

'Once I learnt of Oswald's story about seeing the boat for the second time, I figured out that they had to be around,' he admitted. 'Girmir is no navigator. He would never have been able to get home and raise another *felag* in that short amount of time. And it could be no other boat because of the figurehead.'

'So you knew.'

'The gods had truly given me a chance to start over, or so I thought. I could fulfil my obligation to Horik's shade, kill Girmir, and everything would be fine. I wanted to find them and

confront them before they did any more harm.'
He raised up on an elbow and his eyes became
lit with a fire. 'Then I could concentrate on the
life I wanted to lead with you, the one we both
dreamt about.'

'And you never thought to warn me or my
people?' She held out her hands. 'Didn't you
think we deserved to know the monsters who
prowled in the dark? Or were we to be bait for
them?'

'I was scared of losing you,' he admitted.
'What we had together…'

'…was a lie,' she finished for him. 'From the
very beginning to the end. It was built on an
untruth. And you have lost me. Or rather, you
never really had me to begin with. You should
have told me who you were.'

'I told you I was from Raumerike. There
are many lands to the north filled with different kinds of people. We are not all raiders and
pirates. I am a farmer and a merchant. I use my
sword to defend, not to steal.' His eyes flashed.
'And you speak of me keeping my heart safe,
but what about you, my lady? I may not be the
perfect prince you thought I was, but I am still
the man who fought for you, who risked his life
for you.'

The room swam in front of her eyes. She

wanted to go back to before she had ever met him. Or for this to be a nightmare. When she woke, she wanted to discover that he was whom she had thought he was—a warrior from a foreign country, but not a Northman, not one of those barbarians.

'Impossible,' she whispered. 'What you ask is impossible.'

Moving more swiftly than she thought possible, Valdar reached out and pulled her into his arms. She tumbled down against his chest and lay there, breathing in his heady scent.

Her heart gave a lurch and the insidious warm curl started in her nether regions. This was where she belonged: in his arms, in the arms of the man who had risked his life for her.

'Valdar…' She pushed against his chest and attempted to maintain her sanity. 'This mustn't happen. It is not why I came here. Let me go.'

'Hush now. We've talked enough. More than enough.'

He rolled her over. His lips sought hers. At the faintest touch, her mouth parted and drank from him. The banked heat which his touch ignited flared through her, burning its way through the ice surrounding her heart. All the horrible pawing from the other Northman vanished under the tender onslaught of his kiss.

She buried her hands in his hair and gave herself up to that kiss, drawing strength and solace from its healing touch.

She wanted, no, needed this man.

In his arms she felt alive instead of numb. It was as if his touch was burning away all the horribleness and destruction that the day had brought, leaving her clean and made new. Here it seemed anything was possible.

A moan escaped her throat as he buried his face in her neck.

His hand slid under her gown and up her thigh, making patterns against her skin. She squirmed next to him and the heat grew ever more intense.

His fingers played in the apex of her thighs, circling around and around her sensitive inner core.

'Valdar.' The word was half-plea and half-promise.

He froze. 'If you want to stop...'

And she knew if he stopped, she'd never experience this again. She wanted it desperately. She wanted the healing balm of his touch. 'Not that. Anything but that.'

His hands lifted her gown and exposed her burning flesh to the air. Her body bucked upwards, seeking him and her final release.

He drove deep and she wrapped her legs about him, wanting him there, inside her, filling her up and making her alive. They rocked in tandem. Each movement drove him deeper within her.

At that moment she wasn't sure if she loved him or hated him. All she knew was that she needed him desperately and that this would be her last chance to experience this heaven on earth.

She allowed her body to tell him things that she would never dare utter in words.

Then all too soon the shuddering overtook her as he gave a great cry and lay spent against her. She put her arms about him and held him within her, trying to make the moment last as long as possible.

Much later Valdar held her in his arms and watched her softly breathing. His woman, in a way no other woman had belonged to him. He thought he'd loved her before, but now he loved her with his entirety. He could understand why Ash had sought out Kara and why she had chosen him when he had returned after all that time. It had not been about the child, but about her heart and the man who called out to her soul.

Alwynn had been correct when she accused him of holding part of himself back. Now that the shadow of his lie no longer clung to him, he could see that. And he knew that he could love her properly.

He hoped he'd done enough.

He hoped he'd shown how much he cared for her. With Alwynn, he wanted no part of his life or his body hidden. How could anyone be cursed if they loved with their whole heart? Even if it was for far too short a time. His brother had been right—the only curse was not loving enough.

'Love me,' he whispered. 'Love me for a little while.'

She murmured in her sleep and he fancied it was a *yes*.

'I will watch over you. Always.'

Alwynn woke in the semi-darkness, struggling to remember where she was. And then it all came flooding back.

She touched his shoulder, marvelling at how warm his skin was. And at how much this man still meant to her. She ran a hand down his back and encountered the bandage.

Her reasons for being there came flooding back. She was shocked that she'd forgotten even for a breath. She pushed against his chest and he rolled off her.

'This has to stop. This has to have been the last time. No more, Valdar, no more.'

He gathered her face between his hands. 'We are good together, Alwynn. You and I. We belong together. Wherever that together is.'

Her heart lurched. 'Impossible. And this was nothing but the meeting of two bodies. Don't try to change things.'

His eyes darkened. 'Never call what we just shared nothing. For me, it was something important. It is the centre of my life.'

'You must understand. It can't be. There are laws here against Northmen. All Northmen.'

'But do you care for me?'

'How I feel doesn't matter.' The huge hollow opened in her stomach. In his arms, she wanted to believe again in his goodness. 'Your life is in danger. It is what I came to tell you. You must go. We can't be together.'

'There will be a way,' he whispered against her lips. 'We belong together. You must believe that. I will find a way. I will always find a way.'

She attempted to wriggle away from him. 'We need to speak sensibly and I can't do that if we are like this.'

He ran a finger down her face and a flame of desire shot through her. 'I will be good. I promise. But I need you here where I can touch you.'

Her heart lurched. He knew how to play her body like a harp. Even now, despite everything they had shared, he was still trying to manipulate the situation. It pained her that he could.

'Valdar. No.'

He released her with a sigh.

She moved away from him and straightened her gown. Once she had it arranged correctly, she turned around.

'I've sent word to the king. He had to be informed that Northmen attacked us. I can't hide what happened. I can't pretend that it was outlaws or whatever else you might want to call them. The whole truth will emerge and the king will order your death.'

His mouth became a thin line. 'I understand. What else could you do?'

'When Lord Edwin returns, I mean to tell him the truth about what happened and the part I inadvertently played. I'm through with half-truths and lies.'

Valdar shook his head. 'That would be foolish. It would put you into danger. Say nothing.'

She pulled her shoulders back. 'It is the right thing to do.'

'What is the penalty for knowingly helping a Northman?'

'Forfeiture of the estate and, in extreme cases, death,' she said in a defiant voice.

'You are innocent. You thought I was from somewhere else.'

'Did I?' She pushed her hair back from her forehead. She had been so eager to believe he was anything but a Northman. But she had had doubts and she had refused to listen to them, allowing lust to blind her. She was guilty. 'Lord Edwin had issued an order. Any stranger from the sea was to be killed. I went against that order to save your life.'

'Rescuing a lone man? What harm could I have done? I was washed up on your shore in a storm. So what if I was born in a foreign land, in a country you had never heard of and one whose people held no grudge against you? What did I do except escape from a certain death? How are you responsible for Girmir's actions? How am I?'

'I don't know.' She wrapped her arms about her waist. 'Once I did, but since I've known you, many things have changed.'

'What if I had been a Frankish prince?' he continued on, relentless in his attack. 'Would your king risk war with the Franks simply because some nobleman declared all strangers must die?'

'I'm not sure what you are saying.'

'Rescuing me was the right thing. And my country is not at war with yours, even though it lies to the north. You should not be punished for saving me.'

She studied the knots in the table, rather than turning back to him. She had turned it over and over in her mind and she didn't have an answer. 'But my tenants deserve a better protector than me.'

He put his arms about her waist and rested his chin on her shoulder. 'The person who serves them best is you. You saved them from the Northmen.'

'Lord Edwin will think otherwise.'

'It depends on what the king says, not Lord Edwin.'

'But you understand why we can never be alone again.' She plucked at her gown. Everyone would be sure to guess where she had been and what she had been doing. 'It is important. From now on, what happened today is a barrier between us.'

He hung his head. 'I would defend you to my dying breath.'

'Our people are enemies, Valdar. Enemies.'

'Are we enemies, Alwynn?'

'We are certainly not friends.'

'Lovers.'

'That is in the past.'

He went over to her, magnificent in his nakedness. 'It will never be over between us as long as I have breath in my body.'

He raised her chin so she was forced to stare into his deep gaze. 'Tell me now, sweetling. Tell me that there can be nothing between us.'

'There can't be.' She broke her chin away. 'Trying to force me won't make it any better.'

'Then what was today? A sweet goodbye?'

'Autumn is coming. We both have other lives.' The words tasted bitter in her mouth. The foulest of lies, but if she was going to save his life, he had to feel free.

She pressed her palm to his cheek and knew every touch would live in her memory. One day when she was old, she would get her memories out and lay them along in a pile. It was the best she could hope for.

'Where will you go?' he asked softly.

'A convent will take me.' She tried for a smile. 'Hopefully they will let me work in the garden. I like to feel the sun on my face.'

'And Merri?' he asked softly. 'Are you going to condemn her as well?'

'I know what I am fighting for! I can't lose everything.'

'Why are you so afraid?'

'Fear has nothing to do with it.' She left the hut and went straight for Gode's garden.

Already the garden seemed a lost and lonely place. Recent rain had battered the flowers and they were now mud splattered and overgrown.

Alwynn wrapped her arms about her middle and allowed the tears to flow down her cheeks.

She heard Valdar call her name.

'Leave me be. If that is the last thing you do, leave me be.'

He came slowly into the garden. His cheeks were pale, but his eyes were resolute. Her heart turned over. Love for him surged through her. 'Alwynn, I will go, but first you must tell me one thing—do you love me?'

Alwynn regarded the planes of his beloved face. Once she'd have been tempted to lie and protect herself. But now she had to tell him and then maybe he'd understand why he had to go. She could not have his death weighing on her conscience.

'Yes, Valdar, I do love you, but that doesn't change a thing. I know what the reality is. And my future has no place for you.'

He crossed over to her and drew her into his arms. 'Hush. It changes everything.'

She put a hand on his cheek. 'If you love me,

you'd leave. I can live knowing you are alive and well somewhere, that you look up at the same stars at night.'

He placed his hands on her shoulders. 'What are you saying? Having just found you, how could I do that?'

She gave a soft laugh. 'You will never lose me, Valdar. You are imprinted on my heart. As long as you are still breathing on this earth, I will be content. I have the memories, you see. Before, I had no idea of what it was like to be cherished and now I know. We might not have tomorrow, but we had yesterday and that is something.'

'Alwynn…' He enfolded his arms about her. 'What am I going to do about you?'

She laid her cheek against his chest, listening to the steady beat of his heart. She knew it would be the last time she would be able to do it. Then she looked up into his face and memorised it. The memory would have to sustain her through a lifetime.

'If you care even a little bit about me, Valdar, you will do this one thing. You will go and save your life. You will forget you ever knew me.'

Chapter Fourteen

'Are you truly leaving? Giving up?' Merri's voice rang out. 'Valdar, I know you are in the hut.'

Valdar finished buckling on his sword. It had been more than a day and Alwynn had not returned. She loved him, but she had said goodbye. He'd stayed, hoping that she might change her mind. But she had not.

Somehow he had to make sure that she knew he'd come to her aid, no matter what. The ache inside him was far more than it had ever been. And he knew what he'd shared with Alwynn was a once-in-a-lifetime love. There would be no other woman for him, no one could measure up.

'Little point in me staying, Lady Merri,' he said, coming out into the warm autumn sunshine. 'Your stepmother has plans which don't include me. And my plans don't include her.'

'My stepmother feels guilty that the Northmen attack happened. From where I sit, she has nothing to feel guilty about.' Merri's face took on an earnest expression. 'It is not as if she encouraged it, and you saved the village. You saved everyone. I don't see how you can be a Northman. You build things up, you don't burn them down. It is a man's actions that count, not what gods he worships.'

'You have a way with words, Little One, but others will see it in another way.' He looked over her shoulder towards the trees which hid Alwynn's hall from view. 'When you are older you will understand.'

'My stepmother says that as well. I'm getting older and I still don't understand.'

'If I had an answer to that…I'd rule the world.'

'Is she going to lose everything?' Merri asked.

'I've no idea,' Valdar replied honestly.

Merri considered his words. 'I wouldn't mind losing everything. It frightened me the first time, but now I figure that perhaps I was born under an unlucky star.'

Valdar ruffled her hair. 'You've been lucky for me.'

'There isn't a guard, you know,' Merri whispered. 'Alwynn told me that this morning. Every-

one still thinks you are a brave hero and wounded
to the point of death. A blood infection.'

'What?' He stared at Merri. Alwynn had done
more than enough.

'My stepmother hasn't told anyone about
your…your heritage. She wants you safe and
away from here.'

'How do you know?'

Merri rolled her eyes. 'She wears your ring
on a chain about her neck. I saw it gleaming this
morning. And twice she has looked out to see if
the smoke still rises from the cottage.'

Valdar hated that his heart leapt. 'If she needs
to, she can send for me. She can send word north
and ask for Valdar Nerison of Raumerike.'

'You are going, then? You are not going to
fight for her?'

Valdar stared at the young girl. 'I can fight
everyone but your stepmother. I can't fight her.
She holds my heart.'

'You had better take Purebright. He's not
much of a horse for a warrior, but he is stead-
fast and true.'

'He is your pony.'

'That's why I want you to have him. So you
will have something to remember us by.'

Valdar nodded, unable to speak. He regarded
Merri for a long time. He wondered if he should

tell her what he had planned. He put his hands on her shoulders.

'You tell her that as long as she wears that ring, she will never be alone. Can you do that for me?'

Merri nodded.

'Good girl.'

'You're not really going to go.'

'I love her. Once I know she will survive, I will heed her wish.'

'If you marry my stepmother, will that make you my father?'

'You are getting ahead of yourself.'

'A girl has to have dreams.'

'A warrior as well.'

Once he knew Alwynn was going to keep her lands and her life, he'd leave. But right now, he had to make sure she didn't need his help. And the best way to do that was to make her think he had gone.

He used to long for someone to remember him, to tell his life story, but now he knew love was about far more. And he knew he'd love Alwynn with his dying breath and that it was not a curse, but a privilege. He could at last understand why Kara had waited. For Alwynn, he could wait for ten times seven years.

* * *

'Stepmother!' Merri came running up to Alwynn where she sat, pretending to tablet weave. 'Stepmother! Why did you do it?'

'Do what?' Alwynn put down the shuttle and concentrated on her stepdaughter.

'Send Valdar away.'

Alwynn let out a breath. Her entire being felt encased in ice. The world grew a little darker. She put her hand on her stomach.

Earlier, her insides had clenched and she knew her monthly time had come as well. She wished she wasn't barren. It would have been good to have a child, Valdar's child. She hadn't dared even hope and now all he would ever be was a memory. She pushed the thought from her brain. Some unknown dream child was of much less importance than Valdar's safety.

She concentrated on the weaving and knew her threads were hopelessly muddled. 'So he has gone before the king arrives. Good.'

'I wanted him to take Purebright, but he refused.'

'He knew how much Purebright loves you. Purebright would be unhappy to leave you.'

Merri's eyes shimmered. 'I wanted him to stay. Everything was better when he was here.

Things actually worked. I could stop being nervous and you were happy. I know you were.'

'We survived before Valdar. I dare say we will survive after. Wherever it is, we will be together.' Alwynn refused to think about her forthcoming confrontation with Lord Edwin and the king. There was no need for Merri to know what she had planned. Merri would be better off. Everyone would be. The only trouble was that right now her insides were torn to shreds.

'How do you do it, Stepmother? How can you be so serene? Don't you care?'

'I care, Merri, but I have to think of the land and my people.'

'I told Valdar you wore his ring and he still didn't stay. He said that as long as you wore it, you would never be alone. Honestly I don't understand adults.' Merri screwed up her nose. 'Will you wear it on your hand, rather than secretly under your clothes?'

Alwynn pulled the ring from out of her gown and slipped it on her finger. Somehow it felt right. 'For a little while.'

Merri smiled up at her. 'I wish things had worked out with Valdar. I kept hoping he'd find a reason to stay.'

'I'm pleased he found a reason to go.'

* * *

Alwynn went over to Gode's pallet where she lay in the small hall. Every time Alwynn had come in since the Northmen's attack, the old woman had her eyes firmly shut and had turned her face to the wall.

'You are breathing too steadily to be asleep,' she said quietly. 'You can't avoid me for ever.'

Gode opened one eye. 'Maybe I don't want to talk. Maybe I want silence. Helps with the healing, according to the monks.'

'You were born talking, Gode. You will be talking with your last breath. Why did you keep it a secret?'

'Should have told you before now, I guess,' the old woman admitted with a grimace, raising herself up on one elbow. 'But you had enough to do.'

Alwynn crouched down. 'Merri told me—Valdar's gone. He took the opportunity and left.'

'Are you happy about that?'

Alwynn patted Gode's hand. How could she begin to explain that she doubted if she'd ever be truly happy again, but at least she knew what it was like to be loved and to love in return. Before Valdar arrived in her life, she hadn't understood what true happiness was. 'I'd rather think him free and safe. If he'd stayed, there was every possibility that he'd have been killed.'

'He is not like those others. A good man. One of the best.' Gode coughed. 'He saved all of us. Killing someone for saving others sounds pretty harsh. I should never have told you who he was. I should have kept my mouth shut. I should have known that he'd keep his word and leave.'

'You know the law as well as I do.'

'Is it the king's law? Or one of Lord Edwin's orders?' Gode tapped her nose. 'Have you thought about that? Valdar never attacked any of us. He never threatened…'

Alwynn blinked. Might there have been a way to keep Valdar here? Had she sent him away for nothing? She twisted the ring on her finger. 'It is far too late to think about such things, Gode.'

'Only too late when you are dead, my lady.'

'Lady Alwynn.'

Lord Edwin's nasal tones told Alwynn that her time of grace had finished. Silently she gave thanks that Valdar had done as she asked. She schooled her features and prepared for battle.

'Lord Edwin, you returned far more quickly than I had considered possible.'

Lord Edwin's boots were mud splattered and his cloak damp. Alwynn's eyes widened. She had never seen him this unkempt. Had she been wrong? Did he actually care about the people who lived here? Or was something else going on?

Lord Edwin removed his riding gloves. 'Once I heard the news, I wasted no time. I rode as swiftly as possible. I only stopped to change horses. Where are the Northmen's bodies? Are you certain they are indeed Northmen? You must be certain on this point.'

'They were Northmen. Beyond a shadow of a doubt.' Alwynn tilted her head to one side. 'They have been buried in a pit. You may ask the monks about them. I believe they collected their badges to show to the king if he requires it.'

Edwin whistled. 'And they attacked one of my farms. Why?'

'They wanted food, I presume.'

'It doesn't matter what they wanted. It matters that they were here and my tenants foiled the attack.'

'All the villagers combined. Your tenants and mine.'

Lord Edwin's eyes narrowed. 'My tenants performed heroics with pitchforks. That is what the king wants to hear.'

'But…'

'The king will be arriving soon. He expects a feast. A celebration. He wants to reward the man who saved Northumbria from a terrible invasion.'

'I am sure you are more than capable of providing one.'

'Except…' Edwin tapped his fingers together. 'Except they all say it was your steward.'

'My message said nothing about my steward.'

'It didn't have to. The messenger was very clear on who the hero was.'

Alwynn struggled to take a breath. 'Then the king knows about my steward?'

'The king would very much like to meet your steward, as would I.' Lord Edwin snapped his fingers. 'Summon him.'

'Impossible. He has left.'

'Left?' Edwin arched a brow. 'After such a triumph?'

'We had an agreement. He had promised to return home by summer's end.' Silently Alwynn prayed that Valdar had gone and had not remained hidden somewhere.

'And his name?'

'His name?' Alwynn pasted a smile on. Her hands shook so she clasped them together. 'His name is unimportant.'

'Surely you know his name. What did you call him?'

She looked him directly in the eye. Edwin

was trying to intimidate her. A sudden cold but calm feeling swept through her. She raised her head and met Lord Edwin's gaze directly. 'Valdar, the son of Neri.'

Lord Edwin blinked rapidly. 'Those are not Northumbrian names.'

'I never said he was Northumbrian.' Alwynn inclined her head. 'Perhaps if you had stayed in the area, you wouldn't have to hear about this from your neighbours.'

She picked up a dropped spinning whorl. Valdar's ring glinted in the sunlight. Alwynn silently groaned. She should have taken it off, but it was her last link with him and she couldn't bear it.

'He is a Northman, your steward. That's what my farmer's wife says. And I, for one, believe her. I will make sure the king knows you have been consorting with the enemy. How long have you been a Northman's lover?'

Alwynn stood completely still. It had been too much to hope for that Edwin would overlook the ring. But she knew she wore it with pride. Pride in the man who had left it for her and pride in the love she bore for him. 'You may tell the king what you like. I know the truth about Valdar and how he saved this village while you went off to further your fortune at court. I know because I was there.'

'I will find him, Lady Alwynn, and when I do, I will make sure he is drawn and quartered like all Northmen deserve to be and then I will see you executed.'

'You had best seek the king's permission, then. After all, you don't want to do anything which will damage your reputation.'

Edwin stepped back. 'You've become unbecomingly bold, Lady Alwynn.'

'Your threats do not frighten me.'

'They should.'

Alwynn took great care with her court dress. After today, everything would change. Today she would give an accounting of her deeds and the king could decide. Where once Lord Edwin's words would have frightened her, now she was fiercely determined to have her say.

She kept tight hold of Merri's hand. Merri chafed under the unaccustomed formality of the court dress, but on the whole was well behaved.

'How much longer?' Merri whispered.

'There are certain to be others before us,' Alwynn replied. She steeled herself, waiting for the right opportunity to bow before the king and throw herself on his mercy.

She was the one at fault and it was only right that she should bear the blame. But she had the satisfaction of knowing that Valdar remained free. She hoped he was far to the north now, in Pictland, looking for a boat which would take him back home.

'And now to why we are here—Lord Edwin's routing of the Northmen.'

Alwynn's mouth dropped open. Edwin had claimed the victory for himself? He hadn't even been there. What sort of game was he playing now? Was he counting on her being so frightened of her own skin that she wouldn't say anything?

'Stepmother!' Merri pulled at her gown.

'Hush, Merri!'

'The Northmen's bodies have been disposed of, but Lord Edwin has the badges.'

Lord Edwin came forward and made a low bow. 'As you can see, my liege...this is how I deal with Northmen who dare set foot on my land.'

'Liar!' Merri cried. 'He is nothing but a gigantic liar. Lord Edwin was not here. He was off at court and his steward was with him. He left us unprotected.'

The entire court went silent.

'Who is this that speaks?'

'Lady Merewynn, my stepdaughter, sire,' Alwynn answered. 'And she is correct. Lord Edwin was away. It was one of his farms which was attacked, but it was my steward who fought off the attack.'

'Where is this mysterious steward of yours?' Lord Edwin said with a sneer. 'I have heard tell he is a Northman himself. Where precisely did he come from? And where has he gone now?'

'He came from the sea.' Alwynn held out her hands. She had to make the crowd understand. 'But what of it? Have we so lost our way that we condemn every stranger to death? That we act before we find out who they are? What sort of men they are? If this is what my country has become, I want no part of it. Actions like these protect no one and they harm us all. Without my steward, more lives would have been lost. Valdar Nerison was the sort of man to be proud of. He did nothing but good on the estate. And he was not afraid to fight. He fought for us, knowing if we discovered where he came from, we would kill him. I ask you, how is that right?'

Alwynn looked around at the increasingly hostile faces and knew she was truly alone.

'Where is he now?'

'Now?' Alwynn gulped. 'He has gone. His time here had ended and so he left.'

'Which proves his guilt,' Lord Edwin said.

'It proves he had somewhere else to go. Another life beyond Northumbria,' Alwynn retorted. 'My word against yours, Lord Edwin. It will be up to the king to decide.'

Edwin's sneer increased. 'Not quite. We have a witness. Bring forth the prisoner.'

Alwynn steeled her features. She'd hoped and prayed so hard that Valdar had escaped.

When a badly beaten young man was dragged in, she blinked in surprise. Was this Valdar's missing boy? The one he had sought to save by jumping into the sea? The one who had escaped and whom Girmir had been hunting when he attacked the farmhouse? The one whom Valdar thought murdered?

'Who is this?' King Athelfred asked.

'My proof.' Lord Edwin bowed. 'Cleofirth the Plough caught him and sent him to me for safe-keeping. He wanted his wife cleared of sheep stealing, a crime the Northman steward had accused her of.'

'If he was in your custody, then he took no part in the raid on the farmhouse,' Alwynn said. Her heart pounded in her ears. The boy could identify Valdar, but he was also innocent of the attack. 'He can know nothing of it if he was imprisoned in your hall, Lord Edwin.'

Lord Edwin's face fell, but he recovered. 'What does it matter? He tried to take some grain. The law is quite clear on what to do with thieves.'

The boy hugged his arms about his stomach and pleaded in a foreign tongue that none present could understand. Alwynn stood upright. With each word she uttered, her confidence grew. 'If we seek to prove we are better than the Northmen, then we must obey the laws. Men are innocent until proven guilty. Not because of their birth, but because of their actions.'

The entire court seemed to be shocked into silence.

Lord Edwin clapped his hands. 'A very pretty speech, but meaningless.'

'Your name, boy!'

The boy seemed to understand a little. 'Eirik, son of Thoren.'

'Was this Valdar, son of Neri, part of your raiding party?'

'Valdar, son of Neri, died in the storm which broke the mast. He volunteered to die to save us all, but particularly me.' The boy closed his eyes and continued in broken and heavily accented Northumbrian. 'I want to go home. I was supposed to be a merchant. I had furs to trade.

My mother waits for me. I've a field I want to plough, cows to milk.'

'Did you come to raid this country?' Alwynn asked, holding her hands out.

Slowly the boy shook his head. Then his eyes widened. 'You are wearing Valdar's ring. How did you get that?'

'It was given to me by its rightful owner.'

A smile flickered across the boy's face. 'Then my mother was right. The Norns decide the time of your death, not men. There is hope for me.'

'I will help you if I can,' Alwynn said in a low voice.

'I rest my case,' Lord Edwin said. 'The Lady Alwynn has been consorting with the enemy and deserves to die and have all her lands confiscated. She seeks to help this Northman. How many other laws will she break?'

Edwin's steward grasped her arm and dragged her over to where the boy was confined.

'Unhand me!' Alwynn said as she twisted against the steward's tight hold.

'Tell us where Valdar Nerison is,' Lord Edwin sneered.

'I am here!' Valdar thundered from the back of the crowd. 'Lady Alwynn is innocent of any wrongdoing!'

'And you are?' the king asked as all eyes of the court turned towards where Valdar stood.

Inside Alwynn died a little. Her eyes drank Valdar in, but she also knew that he was walking into a death trap. There was no way he would get out of here alive.

'Valdar Nerison.' He came forward with his head held high and his shoulders bristling. His sword gleamed at his side. 'I am a man from the North, but not a raider or a pirate. The men who were killed at the farm were outlaws. In my country as well as yours. They started the voyage as merchants and became pirates, bent on murder. They acted without the consent of their countrymen and outside of the laws of their land.'

The king leant forward. 'And what is your connection to them?'

'I was part of the original fellowship, but we parted ways when I jumped off the ship in a raging storm.'

'He saved me,' the lad cried. 'I got the black stone, but he exchanged it.'

Valdar gave him a dark look. The boy hung his head. Alwynn patted his hand and whispered that it was fine.

'When in Northumbria, I concealed my identity and persuaded Lady Alwynn to hire me. I

then fought and defeated the leader of the outlaws, but not unfortunately before he destroyed
Cleofirth's farm.'

'You defeated him in single combat?' the king
asked, tilting his head to one side.

'Yes, and I will happily defend that honour by
defeating anyone who challenges my version.'
Valdar gave Lord Edwin a hard look.

Edwin shrank back. 'Who defeated the Northmen is not in dispute. The entire village has been
celebrating it. But the fact remains that he is a
Northman.'

'It strikes me that if this stranger had not been
here, the entire village and all the harvest would
have been destroyed, particularly as you were at
court, Lord Edwin.' The king turned towards
Alwynn. 'Why did you rescue this stranger?'

'Because he was in need,' Alwynn said. 'Lord
Edwin had ordered that any stranger who appeared from the sea be killed. I thought it was
wrong to kill a man until we knew if he was
friend or foe.'

As she spoke, her voice strengthened. They
might not like what she had to say, but she was
determined to say it. 'Before I knew Valdar, I
thought like most people in this room that Northmen were all demons in human form and that
no one born in the North could have a drop of

compassion in his body. I was wrong. Northmen are like us. Some good, some bad and most
just doing their best for their families. Not every
Northman raids. In the same way that not every
Northumbrian is an outlaw. It is time we stopped
judging people on where they were born and
started judging them on their actions.'

'And what did you decide with this man?' the
king asked into the shocked silence.

'Valdar Nerison is a good man. He was a
friend to all Northumbrians. He has never given
me reason to doubt it either. He is the one who
saved us. Lord Edwin only managed to capture
a boy, but not stop the men who burnt down the
farm.'

There was a round of laughter at her remarks.

'I bet he looted churches in the past!' Lord
Edwin cried.

'Do you have proof?' Alwynn asked. 'In
Northumbria, we demand proof.'

'Answer my cousin, Lord Edwin,' the king
thundered. 'Where is your proof?'

Lord Edwin's cheeks flushed under the king's
intense gaze. 'I have none.'

Valdar laid a bag at the king's feet. Gold and
silver coins spilled from it, along with a twisted
gold torc. But there were no crosses or looted
treasures from a church.

'This is the bounty from my trading venture,' he proclaimed. 'I went and discovered the ship the outlaws had hidden. It should be used to ransom the lad and the rest can be claimed by you as bounty as the ship was on your lands.'

Lord Edwin looked as if he had swallowed a sour plum.

'And what should I do with booty?' the king asked. 'Give it to your countrymen when they next come calling?'

'The Viken who raided Lindisfarne are not my countrymen any more than they are yours. My people have fought many battles against them.'

'And have you won those battles?'

'An uneasy truce exists, but I know how to make places safe from men such as the Viken. I have spent my life doing it.' Valdar stood proud. 'You need someone who knows how to make your land safe.'

The entire court gasped as the king eagerly leant forward. 'If I allow this boy to go, will you enter my service? Will you help to make this country safe?'

'Give me the hand of Lady Alwynn and I will consider your request.'

The king turned a livid red. 'You dare ask for my cousin's hand. Do you covet her lands as well?'

'I have estates in my own country, but I have grown to love yours. Let me serve you. Let me show you that I am worthy.' Valdar's voice was a soothing balm. 'And if I prove worthy, then maybe you will see fit to give me the greatest prize of all—the Lady Alwynn.'

'And what does Lady Alwynn say?'

Alwynn stared at Valdar. He was willing to do that for her? Give up his country and his land? Protect Northumbria against the Northmen? All for her?

One look at him and she knew. He would. He was not some figment of her imagination, but gloriously real. He might not be perfect, but he was all she wanted. It didn't matter where he was born or what he'd done in the past, what mattered was what they did together in the future.

'Your Majesty,' Lord Edwin said, pushing forward, 'I must protest. This man is a Northman. He is a pagan of the worst sort.'

'This warrior cut the Northmen down. We have the testimony from the villagers.' Alwynn glanced over her shoulder and saw Oswy. 'Oswy the gristmiller was there. Ask him to speak the truth if you will not believe my version.'

There was a pregnant pause while Lord Edwin glared at Oswy.

'Aye. I will vouch for him,' Oswy said, glancing at his son. 'He fixed my roof as well as killing them there pirates. I don't care where he is from if he is willing to fight for us. And we do need help.'

Others joined in, saying what Valdar had done for them as Edwin looked more and more sour until it appeared he had swallowed an entire basket of plums.

The king reached down and picked up the pouch. He weighed it in his hand. 'I accept the ransom. Release the boy. I will not spill your blood today, lad, but if you ever raise your hand against my country, I will not hesitate. Do you understand?'

'Yes, sir, I do.'

'And Lady Alwynn's life?' Valdar said. 'She did nothing except save mine.'

'Her life is not in danger. It never has been from me. I would never issue such a law.' The king stared hard at Edwin. 'It is instructive to see how people truly behave in the face of danger, though. You have done me a great service. I am willing to count you as my friend and a warrior pledged to me. I take it that you would be willing to join the Northumbrian nobility.'

'I would be honoured.'

The king held up his hand. 'However, my cousin must make up her own mind as to her future. Will you have a husband, my lady, or will you continue to rule your estate as you see fit?'

'May I speak to Valdar on my own?'

The king smiled. 'Naturally.'

The small storeroom smelt of dried herbs and old straw. Alwynn was acutely aware of Valdar. She wanted to touch him to make sure that he was real, not some fevered imagining.

'What do you think you are doing?' she asked as soon as he shut the door.

'Attempting to keep you from throwing away your life?' he said with a low laugh. 'You might consider thanking me.'

Alwynn struggled for a breath. 'You heard the king—my life was not in danger. But yours is. If you fail to enter the king's service, he will have you killed. I thought you had left. That you were safe. Now this.'

'I don't have a life without you. How can I live without my heart?'

The words she had been about to say died on her lips. 'What?'

'I meant to do as you requested. I wanted to leave, but I couldn't. Not with you in danger. I wanted to share your fate.' He ran his hand through his hair. 'My father used to say the men in my family were cursed—we were destined to love more than the women and our hearts would be broken. I was determined that would never happen to me. I used it as an excuse but my father was wrong. It wasn't a curse, but a privilege—to love someone with all your heart and your soul. You are necessary to my existence, Alwynn, and you were worth waiting for. And the only thing I want after spending a summer with you is to have you for a lifetime. Without you, I might as well be dead.'

Necessary to his existence? A small shiver ran down her back. She knew she had to tell him the truth. He was the man she wanted. And she wanted him with her.

'I lied to you the other day. I don't want you to go. I want you here beside me. I love you. I only gave you up because I wanted to know you would be alive. It was a living death for me as well.'

He gathered her hands between his. 'Then you are willing to be my wife?'

'You mean to take the king's service?' she asked, unable to take it all in.

'I have come to love this country because of one woman. You made me see that I am needed here. Where I am from, I am not needed.'

'And what will happen about your estate?'

'It can be sold to my sister-in-law.' He gave a

half-smile. 'She already thinks she runs it better than any man alive.'

They both laughed. Alwynn relaxed against
him. 'You know I may never give you children.'

'We have each other and we have the child of
our heart—Merri.' He captured her hand and
moved the ring she wore to her fourth finger.
'Will you marry me, Lady Alwynn? Will you be
my bride in the church and in the green wood?
Will you stay with me for ever as my love?'

'With all my heart, I will,' she answered.

'Shall we go and tell the king?'

* * * * *

MILLS & BOON®

The Thirty List

At thirty, Rachel has slid down every ladder she has ever climbed. Jobless, broke and ditched by her husband, she has to move in with grumpy Patrick and his four-year-old son.

Patrick is also getting divorced, so to cheer themselves up the two decide to draw up bucket lists. Soon they are learning to tango, abseiling, trying stand-up comedy and more. But, as she gets closer to Patrick, Rachel wonders if their relationship is too good to be true…

Order yours today at
www.millsandboon.co.uk/Thethirtylist

MILLS & BOON®

The Chatsfield Collection!

MILLS & BOON®

Why not subscribe?
Never miss a title and save money too!

Here's what's available to you if you join the
exclusive **Mills & Boon Book Club** today:

- ✦ *Titles up to a month ahead of the shops*
- ✦ *Amazing discounts*
- ✦ *Free P&P*
- ✦ *Earn Bonus Book points that can be redeemed against other titles and gifts*
- ✦ *Choose from monthly or pre-paid plans*

Still want more?
Well, if you join today we'll even give you
50% OFF your first parcel!

So visit **www.millsandboon.co.uk/subs**
or call Customer Relations on 020 8288 2888
to be a part of this exclusive Book Club!

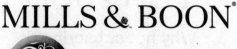

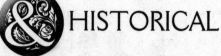

AWAKEN THE ROMANCE OF THE PAST

A sneak peek at next month's titles...

In stores from 3rd July 2015:

- **A Rose for Major Flint** – Louise Allen
- **The Duke's Daring Debutante** – Ann Lethbridge
- **Lord Laughraine's Summer Promise** – Elizabeth Beacon
- **Warrior of Ice** – Michelle Willingham
- **A Wager for the Widow** – Elisabeth Hobbes
- **Running Wolf** – Jenna Kernan

Available at WHSmith, Tesco, Asda, Eason, Amazon and Apple

Just can't wait?
Buy our books online a month before they hit the shops!
visit www.millsandboon.co.uk

These books are also available in eBook format!